PARAGON
RISING

CURSE OF THE PHOENIX

BOOK TWO

Also by Dorothy Dreyer

Phoenix Descending (Curse of the Phoenix Book 1)

THE EMPIRE OF THE LOTUS SERIES

Crimson Mage

Copper Mage

Golden Mage

Emerald Mage

Sapphire Mage

Amethyst Mage

Diamond Mage

From Black Spot Books

Black Mariah: Hanau, Germany

From Rosewind Books

Christmas in Silverwood

with Jenna Lee

Cauldron of Ash

DOROTHY DREYER

PARAGON RISING

CURSE OF THE PHOENIX

BOOK TWO

Paragon Rising

Copyright © 2017 Dorothy Dreyer

Edited by Cheree Castellanos

Cover design by Deranged Doctor Design

World map by Sora Sanders

Design framework created by Freepik

Original Work Published October 2018 by Snowy Wings Publishing

Hardcover Published July 2021

ISBN: 978-1-952667-34-3

First book in the series:

PHOENIX DESCENDING

CURSE OF THE PHOENIX

BOOK ONE

Solo Medalist Winner of the

2018 NEW APPLE SUMMER EBOOK
AWARD FOR EXCELLENCE IN
INDEPENDENT PUBLISHING

in the

Young Adult Fantasy

category

For Kindness
For Compassion
For Decency and Rectitude

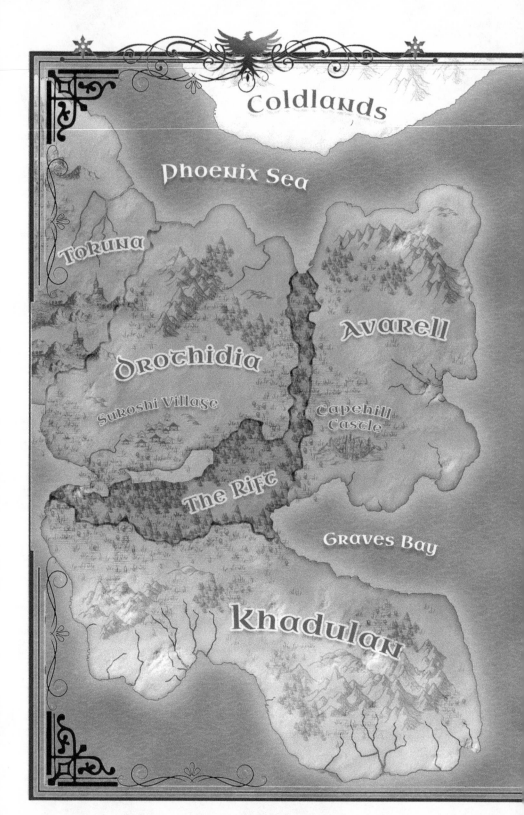

Creoca

Gadleish

Maudric
Ocean

Mirror Sea

Crystal Islands

Hammer Sea

Nostidour

Hellcrest
Bay

CHAPTER ONE

Surging water penetrated Hira Kaliskan's lungs like a brutal intruder. Her jaw was tight as she fought the urge to breathe. The current tossed her like a rag doll, and her vision wavered. Squeezing her eyes shut, the face of her mother appeared in her mind. The tormented look on her mother's face when she was attacked came screaming back at Hira. It was a warning. A plea. *Survive, Hira,* those eyes told her. *Stand strong and survive.*

That message stayed with her for fifteen years, and she wasn't about to stop listening now. She tightened her fists and thrust out her chest. Her body writhed in agony from lack of oxygen, and Hira struggled to free her leg from the stringy debris and seaweed that had tangled around it. The slimy restraints were stubborn to give in, but eventually, she loosened them enough to break free.

Just as she thought she couldn't muster any more strength to kick to the surface, two strong hands took hold of her arm and pulled Hira out of the water.

Hira gasped, the sound of it harsh and ragged. Zhadé pulled her tight against their body as they hauled her up the rope ladder with incredible strength. Hira begged her muscles not to loosen and give in to the relief of being rescued by her faithful companion. She had to hold on. She was the Pirate Queen of the Crystal Islands, and her people were counting on her. The ladder swung and swayed, causing Hira's head to swim, so she forced herself to concentrate on her rescuer. Their golden tattoos, intricately drawn upon their dark skin, glistened in the sun. With seemingly little effort, Zhadé continued to climb and didn't stop until they reached the deck.

Zhadé set Hira down and crouched over her, studying her face. "Nearly lost you that time," they said, stroking a hand over her wet cheek.

"You'll never be so lucky," Hira retorted, her voice still raspy as she struggled to get more air into her lungs. She pushed sopping wet hair out of her face and gestured with her chin. "Is he dead?"

Zhadé glanced over their shoulder at the man sprawled out flat on the deck. He didn't move. "Your dagger landed directly between his eyes just as you disappeared over the ship's edge."

Hira glanced at her own body, running her palm over the small scratch on her forearm. "Luckily his aim was not as good as mine. Shame I couldn't catch his spear, though. It was nicely crafted."

Holding back a grunt, Hira stood to examine the man she'd just killed. She recognized his face—his scar in particular. His name was Crogarn, and he was under King Grigori Stoneheart's command. How she wished it were Stoneheart himself, the savage king of Nostidour. The son of the man who'd led the invasion and attack on her realm over a decade ago. The son of the man who'd killed her mother.

Hira jumped to her feet and yelled to her crew. "This ship is dragging debris. It needs to be cleared."

A cacophony of replies—mostly "Yes, Your Highness!"— sounded around her. The crew scattered about, her top officers delegating orders to do exactly what their queen demanded.

Hira slicked back her wet hair and surveilled the ship. They'd spotted the Nostidourian vessel a couple hours after they'd undocked from the Crystal Islands. Despite a cautious approach, the Nostidour crew had fired their cannons. Hira had no choice but to retaliate. Her ship, the *Diamond Palm*, took some heavy damage, but not enough to sink her. When the ships were close enough to each other, Hira and her crew had managed to throw out hooked ropes, seizing the enemy ship. Hira had been first to swing on board, with Zhadé and some of her best crew following, swords at the ready. It wasn't an easy battle, and Hira lost two of her crew, but eventually they conquered the Nostidourians, the last triumph being Hira's dagger between Crogarn's eyes.

Now they had one of the enemy's ships. To some, it might seem like a big score, but it was nothing compared to everything the Nostidourians had taken from her people.

Hira absently scratched at her wrist before she was even aware of what she was doing. Her skin there still bore the reddish, uneven scar, a constant reminder of her last battle with Grigori Stoneheart. It itched more than it hurt, and sometimes when she caught a glimpse of it, her mind would flash with the gruesome memory of flames scorching her flesh.

With a hiss, she shifted her leather wrist band to cover the scar and pushed the thought of it out of her mind.

"Your Highness," Zhadé said, their beautiful face stoic. "There's something you need to see."

"Did you find something interesting?"

"You could say that."

Zhadé whistled, a signal to Hira's officers to bring forward their find. Hira narrowed her eyes when she found their discovery to be a man.

"He was beneath deck." Zhadé hit their dagger against the shackles at his wrists. "And he was wearing these."

The officers pushed the big man forward. Hira studied him, her fingers tapping as her palms rested on her waist. She found his ears particularly interesting, as they came to points near the top, a certain sign of his Khadulian origin. He also appeared to have recently caught a fist to his right eye.

"What's your name?" the pirate queen asked.

"The name's Goran."

She looked again at his pointed ears. "What brings a Khadulian to a Nostidour ship? Have you been kidnapped?"

He shifted his shoulders as if chasing away an itch. "I was caught as a stowaway."

She raised a brow. "Stowing away on a ship is a serious crime. It is common law that stowaways be punished."

"I wasn't aware that pirates adhered to laws."

Hira drew her sword. "I wasn't aware that Khadulians were so eager to be slain."

Goran clenched his jaw as if assessing his next words. "Allow me to explain. The Nostidourians have my wife. What you see before you is a rescue mission gone awry."

Hira deliberately dragged the tip of her sword over the wooden planks of the deck as she paced, the sharp blade carving a shallow line between her and Goran. "How was it that they acquired your wife?"

"She was sold into slavery by the queen regent of Avarell."

Hira pursed her lips and shook her head. "I am aware that Lady Maescia is ruthless with her reign. It's no secret that the nation of the Crystal Islands has not been pleased with the politics of Avarell for quite some time. As their queen, I feel I must take action before the twisted dogmas of Avarell begin to plague my people."

Goran's eyes widened. "So it's true; you live. The infamous Hira Kaliskan, Queen of the Crystal Islands."

She smirked and lifted a brow. "Either that, or I'm simply a very determined ghost. Or perhaps I did die but have risen again, like a phoenix."

She wasn't surprised by his comment. There had been rumors of her death ever since the infamous standoff against Stoneheart. Nostidour had the upper hand, and the Crystal Islands' army had lost dozens of officers. Hira had been captured and tortured with fire. It was skill and a stroke of luck that she managed to escape alive amongst the bloodshed. The Crystal Islands had retaliated to regain their strength—and to allow time for Hira to heal—and many had thought her dead.

Now she was ready to stand strong, and she vowed to ruin the realm of Nostidour. They were monsters, every one of them, and they deserved to die.

A loud shriek pierced the air, and Hira squared her shoulders just as a phoenix swooped down toward her. It landed gracefully on her shoulder, where a piece of armor was affixed to protect her from the bird's talons. The phoenix spread its wings, its gold and orange feathers almost iridescent as they caught the sun. The beautiful bird seemed to shudder, its feathers ruffling as it positioned itself more comfortably on Hira's shoulder.

Goran's eyes were fixed on the bird.

"Do you fear the phoenix, Sir Goran?" Hira asked, knowing full well how the phoenixes across the sea had been infected with disease.

"Fear? No. Such a magnificent beast should be respected."

She narrowed her eyes. "And you are not troubled over the risk of disease?"

His brow furrowed. "No, Your Highness. I have been immunized against the phoenix fever."

"Ah yes, the immunity that Avarell exclusively *sold* to the other eight realms. I believe even Khadulan—the mining lands that manufactured the cure—had to pay the queendom of Avarell to receive it."

"That is correct, although I do believe the offer was not extended to Drothidia."

She crossed her arms over her midsection and eyed him up and down. "And if we did not pay Avarell's outrageous fee, we were left to our own devices to deal with the disease. Which is possibly why Drothidia was not offered the cure. The forest dwellers are not big on gold and would bring no profit to Avarell."

The Khadulian nodded solemnly. "I do believe those were the terms."

"No doubt an underhanded ploy to wipe out the citizens of Drothidia in order to take their land." Hira pet the long feathers of her phoenix. "Would it surprise you to know Fury here does not carry the disease? None of the phoenixes from the Crystal Islands do."

He narrowed his eyes, as if finding it hard to believe.

Instead of explaining further, she motioned to Zhadé. "Let's remove his shackles."

Zhadé stepped forward. With one swift swing of their sword, the shackles were cut from Goran's wrists.

Goran swallowed hard, staring at his unscathed wrists in disbelief.

"Sir Goran, I will see to it that you have help in your quest. I shall have one of my best officers bring you to Nostidour on this ship and help you find your wife."

He studied her for a moment. "How is it that the infamous pirate queen is so generous?"

"Let's just say I detest everything about Nostidour, and I especially abhor any crimes against women. We will help you get your wife back. And in return, you shall owe me a favor."

CHAPTER TWO

A dove cooed outside Tori's window, its gentle cry causing her to open her eyes. She reached up with curiosity to touch the cold cloth that had been placed upon her forehead, arching her back in a long overdue stretch. It ached to move, as if she hadn't put her muscles to use in a long while. How long had she been asleep?

Then she remembered: she hadn't fallen asleep; she died.

At least, she'd thought she had died. It certainly had felt like her heart had stopped and the blood in her veins had been on fire. It was slowly coming back to her. The night of the Queen's birthday celebration…

Removing the cold cloth and turning her head to the side, she found herself under the merciless glare of Finja, who sat in a chair by Tori's bed. Judging by the scowl on her face, Finja was furious. But that didn't surprise Tori. One of the key points of their plan had fallen through, so disappointment was expected.

Tori sighed. "I know what you're going to say."

"You've messed up."

"See, I was right."

"Don't get cocky, girl."

Tori pursed her lips. "I haven't messed up. Not entirely. The Queen is dead. Well, Undead. I don't believe even Goran could have expected such an outcome, and it wasn't my fault she attacked me."

"But it was your fault that she got away."

Tori was about to retort, but she snapped her mouth shut and averted her gaze. She couldn't deny it. If she had only seen that Queen Callista was Undead before she had unchained her, the Queen would still be locked up in the high tower instead of roaming through the Rift, perhaps never to be seen again.

Tori bit her cheek, hesitant to admit she was disappointed in how things had evolved. She had carried out every other step of Goran's plan to dethrone Lady Maescia without fail. She'd found

Hettie—Goran's daughter who was being kept as Duke Grunmire's handmaiden against her will—and helped her to escape. She'd stolen the book of slave sales and managed to get it to Goran so he could locate his missing wife. But the last step, the step that was supposed to end in saving the imprisoned Queen Callista in order to restore balance to not only Avarell but the nine realms, had been a failure before she'd even known it. Instead of rescuing the Queen, Tori had found Her Royal Highness had become a monster, and that her sister, Lady Maescia, had kept her chained in her secret chambers all this time, with the citizens of the queendom none the wiser.

"Don't dwell on it," Finja said in a scolding voice. "We have no way to prove that the Queen is neither dead nor Undead. How do we build a case against Lady Maescia if we can't prove her treason?"

Tori attempted to sit up, but her vision swam. Spots appeared and disappeared wherever she looked. She squeezed her eyes shut. And as she moved, the area on her chest over her heart ached.

Finja let out a frustrated sigh, pushing Tori's shoulder down. "Lie down, child. You're still recovering."

"I'm fine," Tori insisted, her eyes still shut. She took a number of slow, deep breaths, using the skills her trainer had taught her to will the pain away. She made herself think of something else. "Have you… have you seen Takumi?"

If anything had brought her peace—aside from the love of her family—it was her fox. Though those who had seen the animal had thought it was her pet, Tori thought of him more as a friend. He was the most clever animal she'd ever known and loyal to the core. He was the best sidekick anyone could ask for. And the last time she'd seen him was when he was chasing after the Undead queen through the secret passage tunnel that led to the Rift. She squeezed her hands into fists, hoping he was okay.

"No." Finja held her chin high, but Tori saw a frown flash over her lips. "He hasn't returned."

"Oh," was all Tori could think to say.

There was a pause, and then Finja finally spoke. "I'm sorry."

Tori lifted a brow. "Truly?"

Finja let out the smallest of grunts. "The foul beast may not be my favorite, but I do not wish him any harm." She removed the wet washcloth and dumped it in a bucket of water, wringing it out and placing it back on Tori's forehead.

Despite the uncomfortable feeling of water dripping toward her ears, Tori gave Finja a small smile. "Thank you."

"Yes, well, he was quite insistent that I promise to take care of you, and I always keep my promises."

"Who was? Goran?"

"No." Finja narrowed her eyes. "Master Stormbolt."

Tori's breath caught in her chest for a moment, like a tiny implosion that left her temporarily stunned. She sat up slightly. "Bram?"

The side of Finja's mouth pinched, as if in disapproval. "Yes, Master Stormbolt has paid a few visits, expecting your recovery.

He stayed a bit to watch over you when I couldn't be here."

The thought of Bram sitting vigil gave Tori a fluttery feeling in her stomach, though she wondered how much Finja might have divulged to him, if anything. She'd been in Avarell under the guise of being a High Priestess of Tokuna in order to infiltrate the court. Had he found out she'd been lying? Was he simply waiting for her to wake so he could berate her?

She worried the edge of the blanket and averted her eyes. "Does he know the truth about me?"

"I can't say for certain, but I don't think so."

Tori wondered if it would make a difference.

"He saved my life. I mean, he stabbed me in the heart with a needle, but he saved my life."

Finja let out an exasperated sigh. "Don't let a thing like that make you fall for the boy. There's no time for that."

To that, Tori didn't respond.

Finja studied her. "How are you faring?"

"I don't know." She pinched the bridge of her nose. "I feel weak. And quite dizzy. But I'm not in extreme pain. It's more as if I've gone without food for a couple days."

Ever since she had contracted the phoenix fever, it gave her symptoms of an acidic stomach, a fire-like burn through her veins, and the feeling of having been throttled over the head with a heavy object. But Tori didn't feel any of those things now. She wondered if the serum Bram had injected into her heart had been the cure, but she didn't want to hang on false hope.

She suddenly remembered the horrified look in Bram's eyes when she begged him to stab the syringe into her heart. She also remembered feeling like it had killed her.

"You should rest some more then," Finja said. "There's no telling if the chemical did any damage to your body."

"No, I have to get up. We need to get the news about the Queen to Goran. We need to usurp the queen regent. And I need to make sure my family is all right."

"Rest, child. Goran's ship doesn't come in for two days. Until then, we're alone."

CHAPTER THREE

*T*he dank smell of mold and urine hovered in the air like a fog that made Wrena's eyes sting. She tugged at her hood, pulling the material as close to her nose as possible. She was glad the handmaidens had used a pleasant-smelling lavender soap. If she could mask the ungodly stench by breathing in the smell of the borrowed cloak she wore, perhaps she could survive the dungeon. But there would be no point in surviving if she couldn't find Aurora.

She readied herself as she passed some guards, ducking her head so they wouldn't recognize her. She was almost past them when one turned her way.

"Hey, you there."

She froze. She had thought she could get away without being recognized. She should have known that even in a borrowed handmaiden's cloak, there was no way of disguising her glorious blond hair and glowing skin. If only she had thought to smudge some dirt on her face and tie her hair back, then she might have gone by undetected.

"Oh! Your Highness," the guard said, his thick brows plunged to his small eyes. "What are you doing here?"

She pursed her lips, wishing she needn't speak with him. He had slowed her progress, and every minute that passed without knowing if Aurora was all right was torture. She cleared her throat, demanding his respect.

The two guards bowed, but continued to gape at her, as out of place as she was.

"I'm investigating the dungeons," she said. "Making sure they are secure."

"Begging your pardon, but shouldn't that be a job for a soldier, or at least the duke?"

She held her chin high, her hood almost slipping off. "I don't believe it is your place to assess my whereabouts or the reasons behind them. Now let me pass, or I shall have your head."

His shoulders sagged slightly. "Sorry, Princess—uh, Your Highness. Of course."

As they stepped aside, one of the guards smacked the other on the back of the head. "What's the matter with you," he whispered. "Questioning royalty? I swear you've lost your gob."

They marched forward, leaving her to carry on with her search. She waited until their footfalls grew quiet before she continued forward.

Digging her fingernails into her palms, she trudged on, disgusted by the conditions the jailed prisoners had to endure. Some of them looked up at her and stared in confusion. One bared his teeth at her, letting out a sound between a hiss and a growl. Others she wasn't even sure were alive as they lay sprawled out on the filthy floor. Some of them deserved their imprisonment, of course, but there were others whom her aunt had unjustifiably sentenced, citizens who had not committed crimes, who were merely jailed on her aunt's word.

Of course, she now knew that her aunt hadn't been the mastermind behind this political movement at all. It was Duke Grunmire who had been destroying the reputation of the queendom. She didn't know on what grounds he was blackmailing her aunt, but whatever it was, her aunt bent to his every whim.

He was the reason Aurora was imprisoned, claiming it was a threat to the queendom. So long as Aurora was in Wrena's life, there could be no heir.

At long last, Wrena came upon Aurora's cell. She recognized her small form and brunette waves. Wrena's eyes jetted around Aurora's surroundings, and she almost burst into tears at what she saw.

Aurora, crouched in a dingy corner, stared up at her with wide eyes.

"Aurora." Her voice was small as she said it, her inner strength seemingly depleted.

"Wrena?" Aurora sounded parched and robbed of sleep. "Oh stars, is that really you?"

At first she stood, a shuddering breath escaping her, but then she pulled dirty fingers through greasy hair, her back hunched and her face lowered in shame.

"Aurora, please, let me see you."

Aurora wrapped her arms tightly around her midsection, the sadness in her eyes almost palpable. "I don't want you to see me like this."

Wrena wrapped her fingers around the cell bars. "I've been so worried about you. I can't imagine what you must be going through down here."

"Wrena, you shouldn't be here! If we're seen together—"

"Do not let it worry you. I won't let anything happen to you." She waited for Aurora to come closer. "Please, Aurora. Would you come to me?"

Aurora bit her lip and slowly moved forward. As their gazes locked, Aurora let herself draw nearer until their fingers intertwined.

"It's frightening down here," Aurora whispered. "The rats. The noises from the other cells. It's awful. I'm so afraid."

Wrena looked her over. "I'm so sorry."

"No, don't say that. Saying that means our relationship isn't worth it."

Wrena stroked her hand. "It is worth it, you know that. I'm going to get you out of here."

"How? Isn't the duke forcing you to marry Eleazar?"

She averted her eyes for a moment, not wanting to make any promises she wasn't sure she could keep. "I don't want you to worry. I will figure out a way."

They stared at each other as if they wanted to say more but couldn't organize their thoughts. The silence surrounding them was almost as thick as the musty smell of the dungeon.

"I heard Jasmine was injured," Aurora finally said, breaking the silence. "What happened?"

"I don't know, but she's very ill. They're keeping her under bed rest."

"Have you seen her?"

"No, not yet."

Aurora nodded. "How is Bram? Has he asked about me?"

"Yes, of course he has. But the duke is making us lie about your whereabouts." She didn't have to add that he threatened to have Aurora killed if Wrena told anyone where she was. They both knew it to be true. "I wish I could tell him. Truly I do."

"I understand. As long as you know where I am."

They squeezed each other's hands and pressed their heads together, despite the bars between them. And Wrena couldn't for the life of her figure out what good it was to be a princess if she couldn't keep the love of her life out of danger.

CHAPTER FOUR

*B*ram hesitated before knocking on Lady Tori's door. Wringing his hands, he took several paces down the hall before turning around and standing before her door again. Perhaps she wasn't awake yet. Perhaps running that needle through her heart did some kind of irreparable damage. She'd been asleep for days. What if she never woke up? What if it was his fault?

He scrubbed a hand through his hair and ruffled it at the back of his head, muttering to himself. Then he held his breath and knocked.

The door swung open, leaving Bram scurrying for a breath. When it was Tori at the door instead of her handmaid, he couldn't hold back his smile. His head felt light and his heart swelled, seeing her standing there clutching her robe.

"Lady Tori."

"Master Bramwell."

Though she looked pale and brittle, he swore there was a sparkle in her eyes when she saw that he was at the door.

He cleared his throat and squared his shoulders. "I wanted to check on you. I didn't expect you to be awake. That is… Is your handmaid not present?"

"I'm sorry, were you expecting an audience with Finja?"

He let out a small laugh. "No. No, of course not. I only assumed—"

"She's out fetching some food for me," she said, seemingly holding back a smile.

Bram was, of course, glad Finja was not there. He hadn't had a moment alone with Tori since the stabbing incident. In the time he had carried her to her rooms—keeping to the secret passageways as much as he could so they wouldn't be spotted— things had been a blur. Feeling her lifeless form in his arms had drained the hope from him, leaving him an empty shell with no purpose to hold on to. Finja had answered the door when he brought her in unconscious. He recalled the suspicious look she had given him. He had tumbled over his words as he tried to explain what had happened, and then she had dismissed him. He had insisted he should stay, but she wouldn't let him. Despite that, he returned the next day and she took pity on him, letting him in to see Tori, even if it was only to watch her sleep off her illness. So long as she was breathing, he didn't mind.

"I don't mean to disturb you," he said, feeling suddenly awkward and not aware of what he should do with his hands. "I was just wondering if you were feeling better."

"Of course." She nodded once. "Come in."

Tori stepped aside and allowed him to enter the room.

He watched her walk to her couch, her gait a sign she was still weak. Behind her, the balcony doors were open, the sun casting a glow around her dark hair. Taking a step closer, the familiar smell of lilac soap welcomed him. He placed his hands on his hips, then shifted them to behind his back, and then clenched his fists in frustration with himself.

Internally telling himself to stop fidgeting, he finally let his arms drop to his sides. "How are you faring, Lady Tori?"

She wrapped the robe tighter around her, studying him. "Why aren't you in uniform?"

At first, he could only blink, thrown off by her question. But then he realized it was her way of avoiding his question.

He rubbed his hand under his jaw, trying to be patient. "Lady Tori, I am concerned about your well-being."

She gave him the smallest of smiles. "You are very kind, Master Stormbolt."

He moved closer, resting on the arm of the couch. He dipped his head slightly and hoped she would stop toying with him.

She shifted and sighed, obviously recognizing his impatience. "I'm regaining strength, Master Stormbolt. Thank you for your concern. Finja remains positive that I will survive."

He let out a huff of a laugh. "That's good to hear. You do look better. The color seems to have returned to your skin."

She placed a hand on her cheek, which reddened at his words, and then cleared her throat. "I haven't had a chance to thank you for saving my life."

He felt the urge to move even closer. Instead, he stood from the couch and took a moment to gaze out the balcony doors. "I never thanked you for saving mine."

He glanced her way and caught her eyes dropping for a split second.

"Beg your pardon?"

His hand slipped inside his pocket. He kept his gaze on her as he took a shuriken out of his pocket. It was the one he found when he chased the mysterious woman in black through the town. It was similar to the one the girl in the Rift had thrown to save him from the Undead. He knew he was taking a chance guessing the weapon belonged to her, but in his heart, he was certain.

Her eyes widened for a moment as she stared at the weapon,

but then her face sobered, blinking away the expression. "Why, is that a shuriken? I haven't seen one of those since I was a child growing up in Sukoshi."

He carefully turned the metal shuriken around in his hands, as if admiring it. "Something tells me you've seen one more recently than that."

She appeared flustered for a moment. He held back a smirk.

Straightening her clothes, she averted her gaze. "Perhaps during my travels. Weapons are, of course, forbidden in Tokuna." She seemingly gathered her composure and looked at him again. "It is a place of worship, of peace and faith."

He studied her, wondering how to approach the subject of her true identity. Returning the shuriken to his pocket, he turned and took a few steps behind the couch and paced near the balcony door. "Yes, faith. Conviction and trust. You know, when you begged me to stick that needle in your heart, you told me that you saved me once. That it was my turn to save you."

She shook her head. "Master Stormbolt, I was delusional, of course. I didn't know what I was saying."

He leaned closer to her, his hands on the back of her sofa. "I know you are the girl that saved me when I fell into the Rift as a boy. What I do not know is why you are lying about it."

Their gazes were locked for what seemed like forever, Tori's lips parted slightly, seemingly taken aback by his statement. The intensity of her eyes suddenly overwhelmed him. Like if he looked at her any longer he might not be able to resist kissing her.

He straightened, begging his head to clear, and turned toward the balcony. "What I'd really like to know is—"

He stopped talking when something caught his eye from the courtyard below. The sight of Lady Raven, traversing through the garden caused him to remember that he needed to speak with her.

He faced Lady Tori and bowed slightly. "I beg your pardon, Lady Tori. It has been a delight to see you, and I'm very glad you're faring better, but there is something I need to do, and I'm afraid it can't wait."

She stood, looking confused.

He bowed again and marched toward the door.

"Oh. All right. I understand," she said.

He turned to look at her and found that she had followed his gaze. No doubt she had spotted Lady Raven and gathered the wrong idea.

"Lady Tori, it's not what you think. I can't find my cousin, Aurora. I thought perhaps Lady Raven might be able to shed some light on where to find her."

A crease formed between her brows. "You can't find her?"

He shook his head. "She doesn't answer the door to her rooms, and no one seems to know where she is. It seems amidst the chaos from the Queen's Birthday celebration, Aurora has gone missing."

CHAPTER FIVE

*L*ady Maescia hoped the dark circles under her eyes from lack of sleep weren't too apparent. Her handmaidens could do miracles with her dress, her hair, and her lips, but they couldn't erase the evidential traces of the insomnia that plagued her. Now more than ever, she felt trapped. To anyone who might have witnessed her at the moment, casually sipping her wine in her private lounge, one would think she was a cold-hearted ruler with no cares in the world. But in reality, here she sat with Duke Grunmire, feeling as if he were pressing her under his boot, prisoner to his blackmail, and there was little she could do about it.

She nervously tapped her fingernails upon her goblet, averting her gaze and praying that he wouldn't find out about the escape of her sister, the Queen. Her sister, who was now Undead and loose in the Rift instead of locked up in the high tower.

"It's incredulous that no one knows anything about the attack," the duke said. "I lost four of my best guards —including my most efficient executioner."

The muscles in her neck tightened. "Don't you mean *my* executioner?"

He looked as if he were about to laugh. "Yes, of course."

"With the Queen's birthday celebrations masking any signs of intrusion, my men are at a loss as to what occurred."

"A mystery," Lady Maescia said, feigning bemusement. "Perhaps it was one of the guests at the feast. Do you suppose we have enemies in our midst?"

The duke looked down his long nose at her. "I'm sure there are plenty who would seek to dethrone you, Your Grace. The question is: where have they gone? And why did they flee?"

"Yes, very good questions. Of course, the obvious reasoning was that they fled when they heard approaching guards."

"How fortuitous of the assailants to have escaped without witness. But it does make one wonder why they didn't continue their attack on any approaching guards. What could they have gained by such a small strike of viciousness?"

"I cannot say, Duke Grunmire." Lady Maescia took her time sipping her wine. "There is rumor that some rebels escaped the celebration. They must have been the ones who killed your soldiers."

He scoffed. "Those children? How is it that they were able to escape so easily? And what were they after? Had they simply entered the castle to mock the queen regent, kill a few guards, and then leave?"

"Perhaps they wanted to send a message. Or perhaps they had bigger plans but were usurped in their execution. So to speak."

"Perhaps." He stood and began to pace, his hands clasped behind his back. "I shall need to implement a stronger strategy to protect the castle."

She lifted her cloth napkin and dabbed at her mouth, looking away from him.

"Have you checked in on your dear sister as of late?" he asked, his teeth practically clicking as he enunciated his Ts.

"Yes, just last night," she lied, lifting her chin and forcing a smile.

"My sources tell me you had brought in an apothecary last week to have a look at her."

She stiffened. "The curtains were kept drawn, with only a candle to light the room. He saw nothing of consequence."

"Are you so foolish to think anyone can help her?"

She scowled inwardly. "My family is all I have. I will do anything for them."

"How commendable." He snickered, refocusing his gaze out the window. "You do realize that any apothecary you commission is followed by one of my men and disposed of to assure their silence."

"I hardly find that necessary. Even if they were to suspect Callista's true condition, I always pay them handsomely not to mention their visits to anyone. After all, it is I who would be accused of treason for keeping the news of the Queen's demise from the queendom."

"One can never be too careful, Your Grace."

She slowly pushed her chair back and stood. So long as he wasn't suspect of her sister's disappearance, she wouldn't press the matter. Moving closer to the window, she caught sight of the Queen's Guard on their rounds. "You haven't informed me of any progress of the negotiations with Nostidour since the feast. Have you abandoned that course of action?"

"On the contrary, we've made some progress. In fact, the Nostidourian king will be arriving soon to discuss details of our deal, face-to-face."

"Stoneheart? Here?" The thought of the Nostidourian savages setting foot in Avarell scared her to the core. "How can you trust him or his… people?"

"It is a matter of establishing authority. So long as they know I am in the position of power, I have nothing to fear."

"Even from a bunch of savages?"

"It's all about being smarter than your enemies, and the last I checked, the Nostidourians are not known for their brain power."

She fidgeted, the crushing pressure of his domination closing in on her.

"By the way, have you heard the good news?" The duke grabbed his goblet and lifted it, a fiendish smile stretching his lips. "The happy couple has chosen a date!"

"Which happy couple might you be speaking of?"

"Why, your niece and my son, of course. Or has all the chaos of the Queen's birthday celebration clouded your mind to the fact that they are engaged? We need to begin the preparations of ceremony."

Her throat went dry. "Wrena agreed to this?"

"Yes, I'd say she's more than ready to begin the union. We should announce the wedding date at the Harvest Moon banquet."

Her stomach roiled with acid, knowing the duke had orchestrated the entire deal. Wrena did not wish to marry Eleazar. Her niece only knew one love; her heart belonged to Aurora. But the duke would never allow that love to be. Grunmire could only continue to control the throne if Wrena married Eleazar.

"Why do I feel as though there is more to this than meets the eye?"

"My dear Lady, why ever would you say such a thing?"

"Perhaps because I know how you can manipulate people

into doing your bidding."

In one swift move, he grabbed her by the wrist and held her in place, his face mere inches from hers. "Lady Maescia, I'd be careful if I were you. Need I remind you that a simple slip of the tongue would not only get you removed from the throne but executed as well."

Even under the sick feeling of the threat, she lifted her chin. "Duke Grunmire, your presence in my sister's court is the only reminder I need."

His eyes narrowed, a smirk playing on his lips. "Good."

CHAPTER SIX

Though Wrena's worried mind was on Aurora, she found joy in holding her brother's hand as they made their way to the banquet hall. He was the only other person she held so closely to her heart. It bothered her that she couldn't be more upfront with him about her suspicions regarding their mother, especially since Theo had been complaining for days about how their mother was supposed to join them at the birthday celebration but had never shown.

She knew someone—most likely the duke—was hiding the truth from them. Though it pained her to even think it, she doubted her mother was even alive. Suspicion or not, she didn't have the heart to tell Theo.

"How come they wouldn't let us see Mother if she was feeling better?" he asked, looking up at her with wide, innocent eyes.

Hiding away her sorrow, she put on the most neutral face she could manage. "I don't know, Theo. Sometimes when someone is sick, they might think they are feeling better but then it turns out they were wrong. I'm sure Aunt Maescia simply didn't want us to catch anything."

Her mind flashed back to the night Aurora had been arrested and how the duke hadn't denied he'd been blackmailing her aunt. What was he holding over her head? What could she have possibly done that would have given the duke so much power over her?

They reached the grand corridor outside of the banquet hall, and the smells of freshly baked rolls wafted around Wrena, making her stomach growl with hunger. The morning sun cast a bright golden light upon the entrance of the hall, where servants bustled in and out, carrying huge trays of waffles and muffins filled with fruit, assortments of steaming meats, and platters of various cheeses.

"Oh, my favorite," Theo exclaimed as one servant hurried past them with a tray of chocolate-filled croissants.

Wrena let out a laugh as he released her hand to chase after the servant.

The banquet hall was already full, the painted murals of seraphim and cherubim watching from above as the Lords and Ladies of the court filled their plates and goblets with the finest foods and wines. A waving hand caught her attention, and she smiled back at Raven, who gestured for her to join her. A pang of guilt shot through her as she thought about Jasmine, their mutual friend and Lady of the court. She wished she had found the time to visit with her. She knew Raven had frequented the infirmary, so the least she could do was sit with Raven and ask her about Jasmine.

No sooner had she taken two steps toward Raven than a figure appeared before her, stopping her in her tracks. At the sight of Eleazar, she held back a sneer and deliberately took a step away from him. He mirrored her shift in position and blocked her progress.

"Your Highness," he said, his smile sickly sweet. "My dear."

Her jaw was clenched so tight she couldn't acknowledge him.

"My father tells me we are to announce our wedding date at the Harvest Moon banquet. But between you and me, there are already quite a few individuals at court who have caught wind of the information. Needless to say, a great excitement is rising in the castle."

"I'm sure there is," she replied, her tone full of venom.

"Now, now, we are supposed to be in love." He reached for

her hand, but she recoiled. He cleared his throat. "It would be best for all parties involved if we each acted our part in this, such as allowing me to escort you to your table. Or taking a walk with me in the gardens after breakfast. We need to appear delighted about our upcoming wedding, as if we are all too anxious about our eminent bond."

Her lips pinched into a tight line as she fought to control the roiling heat of hatred burning beneath her skin. "I can barely look at you without disgust; how am I supposed to feign adoration?"

His smile almost faltered. His gaze went left and right before he pierced her with an ice-cold glare. "My dear, when I say 'all parties involved,' you must realize to whom I refer. Perhaps for Aurora's sake, you will learn to play along."

For a second her jaw hung slightly open, taken aback by his behavior. This wasn't the Eleazar she thought she knew all these years. "I… I thought we were friends."

"We are." He shook his head slowly, looking down at her with what she could only interpret as pity. "Trust me, it's better this way. I know how you feel about your little plaything, but marrying me serves the queendom."

"How can you even speak of serving the queendom when one of its citizens—a member of the royal court no less—is locked in the dungeon for the simple act of loving someone?"

"You know the answer to that, Wrena. She's a threat to the queendom."

"She's no more a threat than you are."

"I can give you an heir," he said through clenched teeth. "That is what Avarell expects from you."

"I would think Avarell expects an honest ruler. And if you think for one moment I would let you get close enough to produce an heir—"

"Your Highness," came a voice from behind her.

Wrena bristled when she turned her head to spot the duke.

"The court has eyes," he said. "Let us adjourn to our seats and have breakfast in peace, yes?"

Wrena glared at him, taking a step away from both of them. "You'll have to excuse me, but I have lost my appetite." Gathering her skirts, she turned on her heel and stormed out of the banquet hall.

Bramwell and Logan handed their practice swords to the page, who carried them off to the casemate. Inside, Bram's nerves felt as if they were melting in acid. He had put off telling Logan about his offer from Gadleigh, but he had to inform his friend now before Logan found out from someone else.

"Logan, before we part, there's something I need to talk to you about."

Logan wiped the sweat from his brow and nodded. "Sure. But I can't dwell too long. Azalea awaits in the courtyard. I promised her a walk under the full moon tonight."

"Certainly," Bram said, clearing his throat. "In all my years in Avarell, you have proven to be the one person I could rely on, the one person I could truly call my friend. So, I feel I need to be upfront with you. I've been offered a commanding position in the Gadleigh army, and after much deliberation, I've decided to accept."

Logan's jaw hung agape for a moment. Bram felt incredibly small under the high ceiling of the training hall, waiting for Logan to respond.

It felt like ages, but soon Logan's expression of shock turned to pride for his friend. "They are truly lucky to have you, my friend." Logan slapped his hand into Bram's and shook it. "Your father would have been proud. Though it would be a lie to say you won't be missed."

"It won't be the same without you, either." Bram smirked. "Who else is going to tell me how poorly I swing my sword?"

"I'm certain some young soldier who finds themselves jealous of your skills won't hesitate to warp your mind to such lies." Logan smiled as he patted Bram's shoulder. "Thank you for telling me, my friend."

Bram nodded. "I didn't want you to think I was abandoning you."

"Never. It isn't in your character to be untrue. Gadleigh is your true home, and home has finally called on you."

Bram rubbed at his jaw. "I hope the duke sees things the way you do."

Logan let out a small chuckle. "I wouldn't bet on it, but I wish you luck. Now if you don't mind, I have a damsel in the courtyard who needs to rescue me from this dreary mood you've put me in."

Logan delivered a friendly punch to Bram's arm before leaving the training hall. Bram took a deep breath, straightened his jacket, and headed for the queen regent's lounge, where he knew the duke would be. Telling Logan about his plans was the part he had dreaded most, and now that it was taken care of, he had to do his duty and hand in his notice to his captain, the duke. He wasn't expecting a pleasant reception, but he reminded himself that he no longer had to be manipulated by Grunmire, that he would be free of his tyranny once and for all.

As they had conspired, Lady Maescia awaited Bramwell's arrival in her lounge, unbeknownst to the duke. This was part of the bargain between her and Bram, established the night her sister fled the castle. Bram had promised to keep Lady Maescia's secret about the Queen being Undead, and Lady Maescia would grant Bram an easy dismissal from Avarell's Queen's Guard. The queen regent gave Bram a subtle nod as he approached, setting down her wine and smoothing out the skirts of her dress. The duke clasped his hands behind his back, brows sunken down to his narrowed eyes.

"Master Stormbolt," the duke said, his tone low and expression cautious. "To what do we owe the pleasure?"

"Your Grace," Bram said, bowing to the queen regent. "Duke Grunmire, I have come to inform you of my official notice of leave from the Avarell army."

One greyed and bushy brow shot upward as the duke glared at him. "Notice of leave?"

"Oh, yes." Lady Maescia stood graciously and rounded the table to stand between them. "It was on my agenda to inform you, Duke Grunmire. Master Stormbolt is to return to his homeland. I have already accepted his request and granted him full emancipation from Avarell ties, exempt from any retribution. The papers were signed this morning."

The duke's stare fled from Bramwell and focused upon Lady Maescia. "Did you not think to consult with me on this matter, Your Grace?"

"I didn't find it necessary. We certainly cannot keep a young soldier here against his wishes, can we?"

Duke Grunmire chewed at his lip for a second, and then began to pace. "Master Stormbolt, does this perchance have something to do with a denied promotion?"

Bram suspected the duke would touch upon the subject. Instead of answering directly, he decided to stick to the facts. "I have been offered a commanding position in the Gadleigh army that any man would be a fool to turn down. Not to mention that Gadleigh is my birth home. My father was a well-respected officer, and in honor of his service to King Adam and Queen Layla, they wish to pay tribute by incorporating me into their brigade."

"Do you not find this entire situation traitorous? Some might consider you a turncoat. Who is to say you wouldn't use Avarell's military secrets against us?"

"There is no need for dramatics," Lady Maescia said, waving a dismissive hand in his direction. "The agreement signed includes a clause that forbids Master Stormbolt from divulging any secrets to Gadleigh under the punishment of death."

The duke let out a humorless chuckle, turning to Bram. "But how are we to know what you divulge and what you do not? By the time any hint of war may arise, it will be too late."

"I give you my word as a soldier, Duke Grunmire, as I have given the queen regent." Bram forced himself to give the duke a respectful bow of the head. "And I am still at your service for a week's time."

The duke studied Bram. Bram felt as if the duke's eyes were boring into his soul. "Yes, well, I'm sure we'll make good use of you in that time."

"Thank you," Bram said. He offered another bow of the head and turned to leave.

"Tell me, Master Stormbolt," the duke said just as Bram was about to exit the lounge. "How has your cousin, Lady Aurora, taken the news of your departure?"

Bram turned toward the duke. He could have sworn there was mischief playing in his eyes. He clenched his fists together at his sides and attempted to keep his expression neutral. "I haven't had a chance to tell her yet."

"I see."

Bram could have sworn a smile reached the duke's lips before he took a sip of his wine. The duke offered no further words, and Lady Maescia's eyes were averted elsewhere, so Bram turned once again and took his leave.

CHAPTER SEVEN

*T*ori could have ventured to Lady Maescia's chambers like anyone else in the castle, taking the main corridors and requesting an audience with her, but somehow, she felt taking the secret passageway was more fitting. After all, they had both kept secrets from each other, both told enormous lies, and now, as a result of both of their deceptions, the queendom was without a queen.

She wrapped an old cloak Finja had lent her around her High Priestess dress in order to keep the dirt and grime off her elegant clothes. Donning the dress was a precaution should she need to slip out of the secret passage and into the main corridors. In such a case, she would dispose of the cloak, should she need to merge into the flow of people in the castle.

Tori had been concerned that she might be too weak to make this journey, but surprisingly she felt stronger. Her energy had been renewed. She hadn't felt any pangs of pain or bouts of dizziness in the last day, and if it hadn't been for Finja's incessant reminder to take her medication, she would have forgotten that she needed it at all.

When she reached the secret door that connected to the queen regent's chambers, Tori pushed gently on the spot that popped the panel out of place, careful not to make too much noise. Peering through the crack in the door, she spotted Lady Maescia's handmaidens tending to her nightly ritual. Tori waited patiently until the servants finished their duties and were dismissed for the night. At long last, they left the queen regent with her evening tea, her dress for the morrow hung on its rack, and the door shut properly behind them.

The queen regent made deliberate strokes as she brushed her hair, gazing into the mirror with a crease between her brows. Tori used the flat of her hand to gently push the secret passage door open another few inches. Lady Maescia's gaze went to the door in the reflection of the mirror. She spotted Tori and froze.

Swallowing visibly, she set down the brush and turned to meet Tori's gaze, her hands sitting in her lap and her lips pinched together.

Tori hesitated a moment, wondering if Lady Maescia meant to call on her guards to come in and arrest her. But after a moment of silence from the queen regent, Tori stepped out of her hiding place.

"Lady Tori. I'd say this is a surprise, but I've been wondering when you might drop by."

Despite the unorthodox entrance, Tori gave Lady Maescia a bow. "I would have been by sooner, but I've been ill."

"Yes, I know. I've had one of my handmaidens ask your handmaid for updates on the progress of your health. I'm glad to see that you're back on your feet." She studied Tori, the crease in her brow still present. "Please, come sit."

The queen regent motioned to a settee near her vanity. Tori hesitated a moment, speculating what the queen regent might have in store.

"Please," Lady Maescia said.

There was something in her voice that made Tori let down her guard. Something like exhaustion mixed with desperation.

Tori strode toward the seat and set herself down, weighing the words she wanted to speak. "Your Grace, I'm afraid I'm at a loss as to what has really happened. I don't just mean the night of the celebration. You've been lying for years about your sister. The Queen is dead, and Princess Wrena should be on the throne.

Honestly, I'm having difficulty coming up with a reason not to report you to the court."

The queen regent shook her head, a sadness changing the shape of her eyes. "This whole thing, it wasn't my idea. In order for me to explain, I need to ask you for your utter confidence."

"I'm afraid I cannot offer it until I know precisely what the situation is."

Lady Maescia took a deep breath and let it out slowly. "I'm… I'm being blackmailed by the duke."

Tori took a moment to let the words sink in. "How do I know you're not lying to me now?"

"I swear to you. I swear by the Divine Mother's faith. I would never have done any of the things I've done in the last few years unless my hands were tied."

Tori shook her head in disbelief. "What is the duke blackmailing you for?"

"For something that happened years ago. It pains me to relive the memory, but if I must, to prove to you I'm telling the truth, I will divulge my deepest secret."

Lady Maescia rose from her bench and went toward the door to her chambers, checking the corridor to make sure it was clear. She closed the door but did not return to her seat. Instead, she paced, wringing her hands together. Tori held her breath, wondering if Lady Maescia was about to reveal her hand in the death of the last High Priestess.

"The truth," Lady Maescia began, "is that I killed the King."

It felt as if time had stopped. Tori simply stared at the queen regent for the better part of a minute, not knowing how to react. "What? You… you killed King Henry?"

"I didn't do it on purpose. The King… he liked to have his way, as most kings do. When it came to power, to riches, to women, it was King Henry's need to have as much as possible. He was a gluttonous, greedy, lust-filled man who couldn't keep his pockets full enough or keep his hands to himself. There was more than one occasion when he pressured himself on me. I'm sure I was not the only one, but to push yourself on your wife's sister? To say the least, he was repulsive."

Tori put a hand to her neck, astonished.

"This night in particular," Lady Maescia continued, her voice wavering as she went on pacing, "he was drunk—more drunk than usual. He had always been a forward man, but this night, he'd made advances on me, advances that were hard for me to escape from, in the west wing tower. I was frightened, but too afraid to call for help. I didn't know what would happen if I were to act against the King. Perhaps no one would have helped me anyway. He had forced himself on me, even ripping my dress, cornering me against the wall and…" She shuddered. "And in my efforts to free myself from his rough, aggressive hands, I accidentally pushed him out the window."

Tori's mouth hung open, staring at Lady Maescia.

"It was self-defense, but that's why he fell to his death."

"Why didn't you tell anyone it was an accident?"

"There were no witnesses. I had no proof."

Tori blinked as her words sunk in. Slowly, she nodded. "And Grunmire knows about this."

"Yes, I went to him thinking he would help me. He was the King's cousin; surely he was aware of his ways. I thought he would protect me. But he had other ideas. He used this information to his advantage. He was diligent in reminding me that no one would believe me. So when my sister—when she became ill, when it was clear she could no longer rule, that is when he used this information to blackmail me. He told me to accept the position of queen regent, as my niece Wrena was not yet old enough to take the throne. But he would be the one making the real decisions. I became his puppet. He made me reign the way he would want, he made me act as if all these horrible ideas were mine. They were not. I don't agree with him. But I have to. Otherwise he would have me executed for treason—for killing the King."

"And what of the Queen?" Tori asked. "Keeping her locked up in the tower like that?"

"It's not what you think. I couldn't give up on her. I was determined to find a cure."

"There is no cure for being Undead."

Lady Maescia rubbed at her eyes with the palms of her hands, her exhaustion apparent and her sorrow tangible. "I'm beginning to believe you're right. It was just so hard for me to come to terms. I loved my sister, and I didn't want to let go."

"And so why don't you tell the queendom the truth now? Or at least tell them that the Queen has passed."

"Because now the duke is threatening the princess."

"What do you mean? How has he threatened her?"

She shook her head and crouched in front of Tori, taking her hands into her own. "I can't say, and I'm afraid if you know, you'll be in danger too."

Tori wanted to say she had lived in danger for years but held back.

Lady Maescia stood, wringing her hands again and waiting for Tori to speak.

Tori rubbed at the space between her lip and her chin, her chest tightening as her mind fought to find a solution. She wished her mentor from Sukoshi village were there to give her advice, though she doubted that even he would have a simple solution to the situation.

"I'll figure a way out of this," Lady Maescia said. She came forward and took Tori's hands again. "Please, trust me. Be patient, and I'll come up with a way to free Wrena from his grasp. When she's free, I will gladly step down and let her take the throne."

"There must be a way for me to help."

The memory of following the duke's carriage to the Rift struck Tori. She had the opportunity that night to have the advantage over him. He had delivered two frightened handmaidens to the Rift as punishment for their refusal to divulge the whereabouts of his runaway handmaiden, Hettie—

Goran's daughter, whom the Duke forced to work for him. She could have killed him then and there, at the edge of the Rift. She could have slit his throat and then pushed him into the ravine for the Undead to have. But she didn't. She wasn't even sure she had it in her to carry out such a cold and heartless act. Could she set aside her morals for the sake of the queen regent? For the princess? For the queendom?

She looked up at Lady Maescia and held her gaze. "Your Grace, if you want to get rid of Duke Grunmire, I would be more than willing to help."

CHAPTER EIGHT

*T*he sound of hammering and sawing reverberated through the *Diamond Palm*. Hira's chambers, nestled in the belly of the ship, remained untouched of any damage. Golden tulle hung from the ceiling to the walls, bunched together with thick sashes of fuchsia velvet and lime green silk, creating a tent-like atmosphere that made her think of home. The scent of sage and hibiscus filled the room. A number of oil lanterns sat on various pieces of dark wood furniture, spreading a soft honey-colored glow upon the ceiling and floors. Finely crafted swords and spears were displayed on areas of the walls that were not covered in cloth, and a collection of rum and ale sat bunched on one corner of Hira's desk.

Gazing upon the giant map splayed out on a worktable, Hira ran her fingers along the sea bordering the Crystal Islands and Nostidour. The anger she held on to for all these years grew at a steady pace now that talk of war was making its rounds. Her army was strong and skilled—which was her goal after Nostidour had ravaged her land and her people, killing all the men and keeping women and children as captives. The horrible things she and her young friends witnessed happen to their mothers were deplorable. When she had become old enough to fight back, she did so with relentless drive. Leading her friends to take back their land took verve and might she hadn't been sure they had, but in the end, they won the battle, driving out those too cowardly to stay and killing the rest. But in the end, they had lost their mothers and only had each other to rely on.

The movement of something small skittering across the floor caught her eye. The mouse was quick, most likely frightened by all the commotion above deck, but found itself at a disadvantage when it stopped to nibble on a crumb found on the floorboards. Hira stealthily unsheathed her sword. It only took one attempt to stab the mouse in the back, its writhing body stuck to the sword's tip. Fury, perched on a rope swing hung from the ceiling, let out a loud squawk at the sight of it. Hira lifted the dying mouse and offered it to Fury, watching the hunger in the bird's eyes as he snatched the rodent from the tip of the sword.

"There you go, Fury. Enjoy your dinner."

She smiled at her feathered companion, not realizing until it was too late that she had scratched open the burn wound on her wrist. Hissing in through her teeth, she retracted her hand and turned toward her desk. The wooden drawer wouldn't open smoothly, which frustrated her all the more. When she could finally reach inside, she pulled out a small green tin. She unscrewed the top and dug her fingertips into the smooth yellow cream within. There was a moment of relief, but it didn't last long. Instead of dwelling on the pain—or the fact that the reddened skin of the wound seemed to be spreading—Hira grabbed a bottle of whisky and poured herself a shot. It probably wasn't the best way to deal with the agony, but for now, it would have to do.

The door to her chambers opened after a double knock. Hira lifted her head to find Zhadé entering, with one of her top officers at their heels.

"Your Highness," Zhadé said. "Word from the front."

The soldier marched forward, bowed to Hira, then straightened.

"Yes, Mai. What have you found out?"

"Your Highness," Mai said, her shoulders squared. "The man I hired has informed me that Avarell's captain of the guard is arranging a meeting with Grigori Stoneheart, king of the Nostidour nation."

"Did he mention the purpose of this meeting?"

"He said that negotiations have gone forward to combine their efforts and work together to conquer the remaining realms."

Zhadé paced, their hands linked behind their back. "So, the information Goran gave us was true."

Hira nodded, her eyes narrowed. "The old fool was telling the truth. But Nostidour becoming an ally to Avarell is extremely disconcerting. What happened to Avarell's ties with Gadleigh?"

"Ties were cut upon Gadleigh's last visit to Avarell," Mai said. "Negotiations with Gadleigh have been terminated."

"And the engagement between Princess Wrena and Prince Liam?"

"Severed."

Though Hira nodded, she still couldn't quite grasp the sudden change in alliance. "Thank you, Mai. Good work."

"Thank you, Your Highness." Mai nodded and left the room.

Hira resisted the urge to scratch at her wrist as she paced, her mind swirling with the newly confirmed information.

Zhadé approached and handed her a silver goblet. "Have a drink, my queen. You do your best thinking with a drink in your hand."

Hira let out a small chuckle and did as her partner said. She had been so lost in thought, she hadn't even realized they had poured the drink for her. Zhadé motioned to the small couch in the room, and Hira dropped her weight into it. After taking a hefty sip of spiced rum, Hira closed her eyes. Zhadé came up behind her and rubbed expertly at her shoulders.

"I can sense the wheels whirring in your mind."

Hira opened her eyes and let her gaze drift over to the painted portrait of her mother on the far wall. She felt as if her mother's eyes were filled with so many emotions, the same emotions reflected in her own. Hira was determined to overcome the apprehension she felt, to push forward with the drive to succeed and the need to lead her people. They were once a battered nation, and she was resolute to keep that from happening again.

"I feel a shift in the realms," Hira said, letting out a deep breath. "Like a boulder bounding downhill, ready to strike. I also feel that we need to act soon, or we could fall under that boulder."

"Good," Zhadé said, continuing the massage. "Let us start there. What are our choices?"

Hira gestured with her goblet, tilting it left and right. "Should we attack Avarell? Cut into their negotiations? Or should we approach Gadleigh?"

Zhadé stopped rubbing. "Approach Gadleigh? You mean make them an ally? I thought we didn't side with anyone but our own."

Hira patted Zhadé's hand, pressing her lips together in a straight line. "Times are changing, my love. We must think about what will keep our people alive, and I'm afraid we won't be able to do that on our own."

CHAPTER NINE

Settled on the floor at the small table in her sitting area, Tori examined the assortment of herbs spread out before her. It was all she had left from the collection she had brought with her, plus a few specimens she'd found in the courtyard gardens and in the nearby forest. She could do plenty with the variety she had, but she wasn't positive any combination of ingredients would be ample to make a poison.

Tapping her fingers against her chin, she considered travelling out to the Rift to see if she could find some acidic herb that would surely poison him. Though, chances were that such an herb would prove so bitter that the duke would most likely spit it out and not ingest enough to render him dead.

She wasn't quite sure if she even had it in her to use a poison against him. She didn't fancy herself a murderer. But she found the task of creating a poison a challenge, even if it were just to have one on hand. Just in case.

Finja suddenly let out a high-pitched scream and ran into Tori's apartment from the balcony. With a hand on her heart, she let out a labored breath. "That beast will be the end of me," she grumbled.

Tori stood, a smile exploding on her face as she caught sight of Takumi prancing upon the balcony's railing. The fearless fox sniffed at the air, then jumped down onto the balcony and skittered toward Tori.

Tori crouched down, letting him crawl into her lap, his wet nose sniffing around her cheek as if he were kissing her in greeting.

"Where have you been, old friend?" Tori smoothed a hand over his head, stopping to scratch between his ears. "I feared the worst."

Finja was backed up against the fireplace, a hand patting her chest as if to get her heart to match the slow rhythm. "I know I'm not one to give that creature credit for being smart. But I'm pretty sure he was tracking the Queen."

Tori thought back on the night Takumi chased after the Queen. Knowing the fox, he had made it his mission to find out where she ran off to. But he had been gone so long she feared he had run into trouble in the Rift.

"I think you're right," Tori said. "And his return means either he lost her, or something has happened to her."

"You think her dead?"

"Or whatever the term may be for 'dead' beyond being Undead."

"Finja pursed her lips. "There's no way for us to find out for sure aside from trekking out to the Rift ourselves. You'll have to excuse me if I'm not jumping up to take part in that right away."

"Dead or Undead, she's gone. It should be Wrena on the throne, not Lady Maescia."

Takumi nuzzled against Tori's hand. She opened it for him, and he gently let something slip out of his mouth into her palm, like he'd been hiding it there for some time. Tori lifted her palm to inspect it.

"Kinofuji?" she whispered, gazing at the tiny twig dotted with tiny greenish-white flowers.

"What is that?" Finja asked, coming closer.

"It's a flower native to my village." Tori's head shot up and leaned closer to Takumi. "Were you in Sukoshi?"

Takumi gekkered in response, lifting one of his front paws.

"Did you see them? Did you see my family?" Her eyes filled

with tears at the thought of her beloved parents and siblings. She knew Takumi couldn't actually answer, but as he nuzzled against her, she hoped it was a sign that they were all right. Tori squeezed her eyes shut and pulled Takumi into an embrace.

When a knock came at the door, Tori wiped her tears away and stood.

"I'll get it," Finja said.

Tori wasn't sure whom to expect, but it took her by surprise when young Prince Theo strode into her rooms. The little boy of eleven smiled first at Tori, then rushed forward and dropped to his knees to pet the fox.

Finja clasped her hands in front of her. "If you'll excuse me, I need to run some errands."

"Thank you, Finja," Tori said. She then focused on the prince, who was busy stroking the fox's fur.

"I knew I saw him," Prince Theo said.

"You saw him, Your Highness?" Tori placed a hand over her heart. "That can't be good. Perhaps you weren't the only one who spotted him."

"I don't think so, Lady Tori. Everyone else is busy with decorating for the Harvest Moon Festival. Plus, I only spotted him because I was playing with my spy glass."

"I do hope you are right."

"Will you be coming to the festival?" he asked.

"No. Not this one, I'm afraid. I will be returning to my duties very soon though."

Takumi turned in a circle and placed his front paws on the prince, sniffing at his face. The prince let out a delighted laugh.

At first, Tori smiled along with him, but then her mind flashed with the image of his mother, the Queen, Undead and racing down the secret tunnel to the Rift with a savage rage in her eyes. Her heart felt as if it were pinched in a vice, knowing the young prince wasn't even aware that he was an orphan and that he would never see his mother again. She reached out, wanting to comfort him, but retracted her hand.

Prince Theo looked up at her. He tilted his head. "Do you have time to play a game?"

"I do owe you a game, don't I?"

"That's all right," he said. "I know you've been sick. I'm just glad it's not so bad you'd need to be quarantined."

"No, I'm much better," Tori said, trying not to let the pity she felt show in her expression. "And I happen to be free now, so if you're up for the challenge, I'd love to play with you."

His smile lit up the room. As the prince pulled a satchel out of his pocket and laid out the game, Tori's heart ached for the young boy's loss. And it made her miss her family all the more.

Garlands of tiny red and orange flowers hung above the banquet hall, creating a colorful and fragrant canopy. The inviting smells of pot roast and succulent duck wafted through the enormous room. Decorative cornucopias sat as centerpieces on every table, overflowing with gold coins. The Lords and Ladies of the court galivanted around, showing off their Harvest Moon outfits, complete with capes of deep orange silk or plum purple velvet. Their faces were adorned with glitter and sequins, and hairpins fastened behind their ears sported feathers of every color of the rainbow. The Lords and Ladies spilled over each other, laughing and drinking and taking advantage of everything the queen regent set out before them.

They seemed full of cheer, and though Lady Maescia felt she was at the lowest point of her life, she forced herself to pretend she was as happy as they were. She plastered on a smile and complimented Ladies of the court on their choice of dresses. It wasn't until she spotted Duke Grunmire coming her way that she was unable to keep up the ruse.

"We have a few announcements to make," he said to her. The serious expression on his face dragged Lady Maescia's mood even lower. "Three, in fact."

"Yes, of course," she replied. Then she blinked a few times. "You'll have to forgive me. I know the most pressing announcement is the wedding date for Wrena and Eleazar, and the second announcement is Lady Tori's return to her duties. But what other announcement did you plan on me delivering tonight?"

He straightened the cuffs of his cashmere-silk tunic. "I've

gone over the testaments from my men about the night of the Queen's birthday celebration. Though none of them bore witness to the attacks on my guards, it occurred to me that all the Lords and Ladies of the court were present that night."

"You expect me to give an inquiry during a feast?"

"They are all present," the duke said. "Here and now. What better time to take care of this unfortunate matter?"

"Do you really think anyone will come forward? All this time has passed, and they haven't approached us yet. If they haven't done it privately, what makes you think they would do so here, so publicly, in front of all their peers?"

"Because I have an idea of how to persuade them." The duke drew nearer and whispered in Lady Maescia's ear.

As he spoke, she began to shake, her skin growing cold and her head feeling dizzy. She clenched her fists and swallowed hard. It was all she could do to keep tears from spilling out over her cheeks.

After he had told her his plan, he glared at her. "Don't think of going against my wishes, Your Grace. You know the consequences."

Her fingers wrapped around the material of her skirts. She had no choice. She had to do as he asked.

"And don't forget," he added. "You're supposed to be happy about your niece's wedding."

Trying to control her breathing, she nodded once and turned toward the raised platform where the royals' tables were set. She held her chin high, begging her knees to stop wobbling. The duke was a mere three steps behind her, no doubt to make sure she would deliver his message to the letter. And convincingly enough to make it seem as if it were her idea.

"Dearest members of the court," Lady Maescia began. The rumbling of voices slowly quieted until all eyes were on her. She took a deep breath and smiled, making sure her teeth were showing and her eyes cooperated. "I know you are all dying with anticipation to hear news about my sweet niece's upcoming vows."

She let her eyes slide quickly to Wrena. But seeing the gloomy look on her face, she had to avert her eyes. It was bad enough her niece was being forced into this wedding; she would now have to endure the entire court congratulating her on something she didn't want.

"I am pleased to announce that the royal wedding will take place in three weeks' time."

The room erupted with joyous gasps and quiet squeals. Lady Maescia seriously considered leaving it at that and escaping from the stage, but the duke was quick to clear his throat.

"I am also happy to tell you that Lady Tori is feeling much better and will be returning to her duties as High Priestess in two days' time."

She was met with nods and smiles, and the Lords and Ladies exchanged quips of gratefulness.

"Yes, I too am delighted for her return. Now that the happy

news has been announced, I'm afraid I need to address a more regrettable matter."

The room quieted again, and even Wrena's expression changed to one of curiosity.

"As you all know, there was an attack on some of my guards during the Queen's birthday celebration. It has come to my attention that there is a witness among you who has not come forward. Perhaps this person had not seen the vicious act take place, but they had surely seen something of suspicion and have not yet reported it. I do not know the identity of the person in question, however. Therefore, until the witness comes forward, I will start arresting members of the court, beginning with the youngest."

She had never seen so many jaws drop at once. Lady Maescia was still trying to wrap her head around the situation herself, when two Queen's Guard soldiers hauled a young girl from the crowd. She couldn't be more than fifteen. Lady Maescia held back a cry of protest, forcing herself to remain unaffected by the girl's pleas. The girl shrieked and struggled to free herself from the two soldiers, but to no avail. They dragged her onto the platform and threw her at Lady Maescia's feet.

"Young Lady, what is your name?" the queen regent asked.

The girl swept her hair out of her face, sitting up and smoothing out the silken skirts of her sunflower-yellow gown. "It's Lady Felicity, Your Grace."

"Lady Felicity," the queen regent repeated, keeping her

mouth in a straight line. She turned to the crowd. "Will no one spare young Lady Felicity from being thrown in the dungeon? Will no one who bore witness to even the slightest hint of the traitorous act come forward and give her mercy?"

At first, no one moved. No one spoke. But then, the duke instructed his guards to grab the girl and haul her to her feet. A woman rushed forward then, dressed in her finest dark green gown. Glittering jewels were set in her hair and around her wrists. The unmistakable look of panic was ablaze in her eyes as she moved closer to the stage.

"P-please, no. Don't arrest her."

Lady Maescia held her reserve, her hands clutched in front of her. "Lady Theresa, do you have something to say?"

"I saw something that night. I couldn't be sure, but the longer I think about it... yes. I saw something."

Lady Maescia begged her heart to slow down. It occurred to her that not only could someone have witnessed whoever it was that attacked the guards, but someone could also have witnessed her and Bramwell chasing down her sister. She said a quick, silent prayer to the Divine Mother that this woman had seen the former rather than the latter. "What is it you saw, Lady Theresa?"

"I heard a noise in the corridor perpendicular to the one I was in," Lady Theresa said, her voice shaking. "You know, the one by the kitchens. And I started to go toward the noise. I saw a guard yelling at someone. He was holding one of the dancing performers from the celebration. But suddenly, it got dark in that corridor, as if someone had turned off the light. And then the guard was struck with something, directly in his neck. It looked like some sort of small blade. And he dropped to the ground, and the young girl ran off."

"Did you see who threw this blade?"

"No. I was so frightened by the commotion that I turned around and fled through the kitchens. That's all I saw. I swear."

Lady Maescia pretended to study the woman, but really, she was buying her time. "Is there any reason for you to tell untruths, Lady Theresa? Are you related to Lady Felicity in any way?"

"No."

"Is she perhaps a friend's daughter?"

"No. I mean, I know of her mother, Lady Gertrude, but we don't run in the same circles."

"And why did it take you until this moment to come forward?"

Lady Theresa shook her head. "I was frightened. I hadn't actually seen what happened, and I—"

"That's quite enough," Lady Maescia waved a hand in the air.

The guards dropped the young girl, who slumped to the ground in surprise, and marched down to capture Lady Theresa.

Sliding across the floor, Lady Felicity made her way off the stage in tears. She ran into the crowd—no doubt to her mother—and disappeared. On the stage, the guards held Lady Theresa in place. Joining them was Nils, the new executioner.

Lady Theresa blubbered. "What are you to do with me? I did

nothing wrong."

"Lady Theresa, you withheld important information about a crime against the crown. According to the laws, that is considered an act of treason."

Lady Theresa's eyes were locked on the executioner. On his belt were strapped a battle axe and a dagger. Crying out her protests, the woman flailed to free herself from the soldiers' grasp, losing her footing and almost falling to her knees.

"Since you could not bear witness to the event of treason that night," Lady Maescia said, fighting to keep the authority in her voice, "then you shall not bear witness to anything else. Ever again."

With one swift move, Nils slid the dagger out from his belt and swiped his arm out horizontally. The blade swept across Lady Theresa's eyes, blinding her. She let out a scream that echoed off the walls. Blood poured down her face, and her wails ascended in pitch. The crowd gasped and groaned and mumbled in shock, backing away.

"You may take her to the infirmary," Lady Maescia announced to the guards, using all her effort to keep the contents of her stomach down. She turned to the crowd and forced a smile. "Now that this matter is taken care of, let us return to the celebration."

As soon as she turned away from the crowd, her smile disappeared, replaced by a frown of repulsion as she glared at the duke. She headed past him, needing to sit down and calm her nerves.

"You did well," he said in a low voice before she could walk by.

Instead of answering him, she picked up her pace and ran to a washroom to throw up.

CHAPTER TEN

*B*ram strode toward lady Raven, his heart heavy for what they were about to see. Lady Raven offered him a smile, but it didn't reach her eyes.

"Thank you for coming with me, Bramwell," Lady Raven said.

"Of course." Bram walked alongside her. "Lady Jasmine is my friend as well."

"I do hope she fares better today." Lady Raven wrung her hands as she stepped quickly toward the infirmary. "Any word on Aurora?"

When Bram had approached Lady Raven a couple days earlier, he was disappointed to find that she had been too busy attending to Lady Jasmine to have known that Aurora might be missing.

"No, there's still no sign of her."

"I'm sorry. I tried going to her chambers as well, but I had no luck. Though her handmaiden informed me that Aurora was simply under the weather and wished not to be bothered. I don't see any reason not to believe her."

Bram wondered if Aurora's handmaiden would have any reason to lie. Or to hide the truth. Of course, with a discreet exchange of gold, a simple handmaiden could be convinced to do almost anything.

"I hear you've given your notice to the queen regent and the duke."

"Yes, just last night."

"So I gather you will be leaving us soon."

"I will still be here for a short while. And I meant what I said, Lady Raven. We will remain friends."

As Lady Raven's gaze fell to the floor, Bram remembered the pain in her eyes when he broke her heart. He had offered his friendship, but she had contended that she didn't want to stay friends. It seemed that cutting ties with him would suit Lady

Raven better than being friends with someone who didn't return the amorous feelings she had for him. She had been angry at him. So angry that she had told the queen regent he was leaving Avarell to join the Gadleigh army. And though that was true, Bram had divulged that information in confidence, and Lady Raven had betrayed that confidence.

If anything, he should be angry with her, but with all that conspired since that night, there was no longer time or space for anger. Right now, he could see that Lady Raven's upmost concern was for that of her dear friend, and it wouldn't be like him to deny her of his support.

They entered the infirmary, and Bram took notice of the dimming of light. Heavy drapes covered the windows, practically blocking out the sun. The bulbs that burned in the sconces on the walls did not provide much illumination at all, casting a dreary glow on the patients in the room.

Bramwell followed Lady Raven to one of the sick beds, where a number of nurses tended to a very grey-skinned Lady Jasmine. Maintaining complete silence, Bram and Lady Raven waited patiently until the nurses finished changing the cold cloths on Jasmine's forehead and applying ointment to the bite mark on her arm. Bram winced at the sight of the swollen and blistering bite, holding back a shudder. The Queen had been the one who attacked Jasmine. But the only ones who knew the truth about it were Lady Maescia and himself.

As the nurses stepped away to tend to the other patients,

Bram put a hand on Lady Raven's back to urge her forward. Lady Raven took a deep breath and let it out, rubbing at her arms before getting closer to the bed.

"Hello, dear friend," Lady Raven said, her voice noticeably shaky. She slipped into the chair beside Lady Jasmine's bed. "Look who I brought with me. Good old Bramwell, looking as handsome as always, of course. How I wish that you would open your eyes to greet him."

It broke Bram's heart to hear Raven speak to Jasmine as if there was no hope left for her. In truth, it was just a matter of time before Jasmine either died or turned into an Undead. There was no avoiding the fate that awaited her. As far as he knew, anyone who had ever been bit by the Undead turned and became like them. Judging by Jasmine's pale and grayish skin and her labored breathing, he had to believe she would turn. He just didn't know when.

Lady Jasmine let out a gurgled, raspy breath. Raven put a hand to her chest and bit her lip.

"Oh, Jasmine. Please get better. I'm sorry if I was ever mean to you. I know I acted as if I was better than you, but it was just my insecurities playing up. I do hold you to be a very dear friend. My best friend, actually." She sniffled and wiped at her cheeks. "I pray you fare better. I miss you."

Lady Raven leaned closer and lay her cheek against Lady Jasmine's hand, her shoulders shaking from her sobs.

Just as Bram was about to place a gentle, consoling hand on

Lady Raven's back, Lady Jasmine opened her eyes. Bram froze in place. Lady Jasmine's eyes were glazed over, and the irises were as white as fog.

Bram couldn't find his voice, putting his hand on Raven's shoulder. She hadn't noticed the change in her friend and was still cheek-down on the bed.

Jasmine let out a slow groan, and Raven lifted her head, gasping.

"Lady Raven," Bram said quickly. "I need you to move away from the bed. Now!"

Raven jumped back, her jaw agape. She took in the sight of Jasmine's eyes and let out a whimper. Jasmine growled and bared her teeth, lifting her head from her pillow. Raven scurried behind Bram, her hands covering her mouth in shock.

The nurses in the infirmary let out shrieks of shock and fear. Bram kept his focus on Jasmine as disorder ensued behind him. He unsheathed his sword and held it between Jasmine and himself.

"Bram, no," Raven said, her voice quivering.

"I'm sorry, Raven. I have no choice. She's an Undead."

Jasmine shifted, lifting herself from the bed, her fingers extended like claws. Bram knew what he had to do, though it pained him to the core. "Look away, Lady Raven."

With a wince, Bram thrust his sword through Jasmine's head, ignoring the squishy sound it made as it pierced her brain. When he withdrew the sword, Jasmine slumped to the floor.

Lady Raven let out a muffled cry, her head still turned away. "Oh, Divine Mother. Is she… is she dead?"

It took a moment before Bram could speak, the sight of his friend now dead on the floor unsettling him. "I'm afraid so."

Tears trailed down Raven's cheeks and the color drained from her face. "How did this happen?" Her voice was a whisper. "Undead?" She dissolved into sobs.

"I'm so sorry, my Lady." Bram painstakingly wiped his sword off on Jasmine's bedsheets. "I had no choice. For your protection, and for the queendom, it had to be done."

CHAPTER ELEVEN

ori opened the door on the second impatient knock.
Bramwell barely waited for her to open the door before
he barged into her room. She watched him as he passed her, his
fingers raking through his hair. He looked pale and shocked, and
her concern for him was so daunting she almost forgot to close
the door.

"I'm sorry, Your Holiness. I just… I wasn't sure where to go."

"What is it? What happened?"

He took a deep breath. "It's Lady Jasmine. She's dead."

"Oh no. I hadn't realized she was so ill."

"No, you don't understand. She was an Undead."

Tori bristled. "What? How?" But before he could answer, her mind whirled back to the night the Queen escaped through the castle. "Oh. I remember. I passed her when I chased the Queen. I saw Lady Jasmine lying to the side, but I had assumed she was merely knocked over. That the Queen had bounded into her while making her escape. I hadn't realized she had *bit* her."

"No one knows, of course, aside from you, I, and Lady Maescia."

"So, she turned." It wasn't a question. Tori was all too familiar with how the Undead turned their victims into copies of themselves. She knew there was nothing anyone could do for them but put an end to their days of walking dead. "You... Did you have to kill her?"

His gaze fell to the floor as he nodded. "Yes. I accompanied Lady Raven to see her. I needed to find out how she was faring. I knew she had been bitten, but I guess part of me hoped that nothing would come of it. But as I had suspected, it was too late."

"I'm so very sorry."

He worried the hilt of his sword. "Living in Avarell, feeling safe all these years and so distant from the Rift, I never thought the terror of the Undead would truly reach me. Now I've encountered them twice in the past week. It makes me think back to when I first saw an Undead. Back when I was a lad."

He lifted his head to look at her. She felt as if he were trying to get her to admit that she was the girl from the Rift. She cleared her throat and shook her head, her eyes trained on the floor. "I shall mourn Lady Jasmine's loss."

The pattering of swift, little feet sounded in the room, and Bram jumped back, arms spread and eyes wide. Tori almost laughed when Takumi skittered around Bram, sniffing in the air. As Takumi finally stopped in front of Bram and sat on his haunches, Bram's expression relaxed.

"I remember you." Bram glanced at Tori. "He looks like he wants to be properly introduced."

"I suppose so. Bramwell Stormbolt, allow me to *properly* introduce you to Takumi. Takumi is a very dear friend of mine and practically smarter than most people I know."

"Is that a fact?"

"I'm afraid so."

Bram raised a brow. "I see."

"Takumi, this is Master Stormbolt of the Queen's Guard."

Takumi stood on his hind feet for a moment, raising his paws before plunking back down on all fours. Bram let out a laugh.

"How did you get to meet such an interesting fox?" Bram asked.

"Oh, we became friends when I was fora—" Tori stopped short and cleared her throat, ignoring the fire in her cheeks from almost giving herself away. "—when I was meditating near the forest in Tokuna. He, um, came up to me and sat beside me. Almost as if he were meditating with me."

Bram's eyes were locked on her. Slowly he shook his head. "Are you really going to continue to deny it?"

She blinked rapidly, taken aback. "What do you mean?"

"You are the girl from the Rift. I have no doubt it was you. And you didn't meet this fox when you were meditating; you probably came upon him when you were fighting off the Undead." He pulled out the shuriken again. "With this. Or at least ones similar to it."

"Master Stormbolt, I'm sure you are still confused about that girl. We have some things in common, that is all."

"I would say you still hold things in common with your younger self, of course. You are still confident. Smart. Beautiful. I do hope your knowledge of herbs and plants has improved, however, because you very well could have killed me. That leaf you made me eat was poisonous."

She scoffed. "It was not. Klamath weed has a sedative effect but is not poisonous."

He smirked, catching her in the lie.

She set her jaw and turned away from him. He had confused her with the compliments and made her forget to keep up her ruse. And now she was backed against a wall with no retreat possible.

He moved closer to her, his brow furrowed. "Why did you lie?"

She let out a slow breath. "I'm afraid if I tell you, you will be an accomplice to treason."

For a moment, he blanched. But then he straightened his shoulders and tilted his head. "Perhaps you did not hear: I'm leaving Avarell."

"Leaving?"

"Yes, in a few days' time."

"Where are you to go?"

"Back home to Gadleigh."

"I see." She studied his face. She wasn't sure how to feel about this news. It wasn't as if she were staying in Avarell indefinitely. She was there on a mission, and once the threat of Duke Grunmire was removed and Princess Wrena crowned queen, she would return to Drothidia. It wasn't in the cards for them to become anything more than acquaintances. "I will tell you the truth, but it does not leave these walls."

"You have my word." He gave her a bow, but the slight smile that played with the corners of his mouth did not go unnoticed.

She worried at the sleeve of her dress, gathering the courage to tell him her story. Taking a seat on her couch, she gestured for him to sit beside her. "I was hired by a man named Goran, a Khadulian. He needed three things from me—two of them personal and the third of a worldly concern."

"All right," he said cautiously.

"First he needed me to find and rescue his daughter. She was taken hostage by the queendom as payment for a damaged shipment and put to work as a handmaiden."

"The handmaiden that escaped the duke's services?" The look in his eyes told Tori he was putting the pieces together.

"Yes. I helped her escape and delivered her to her father at the docks. Next, he needed a book. A record of sales. He was told his wife had been killed, but he believed that she was sold into slavery by the queen regent."

"So you stole a book."

"I don't believe anyone even knows it's missing yet. But yes, I brought Goran the book as well."

"And was his wife sold into slavery?"

"That, I do not know."

He nodded. "All right. What was the third assignment?"

"To find the Queen and have Lady Maescia dethroned."

"I see. And I know now how that task unfolded. But what now? The Queen is Undead and loose in the Rift. Lady Maescia is still on the throne."

"It seems I've uncovered the true miscreant behind the undoing of Avarell," she said. Bramwell looked as if he were holding his breath until she spoke again. "Duke Grunmire."

His shoulders slumped as if he had expected to hear the name. They stayed silent for a moment, contemplating the fate of Avarell, the conundrum of how to save the nine realms from falling under Duke Grunmire's bloody boot.

Bram gave Tori a sideways look, his eyes narrowed. "So, you're not really a High Priestess."

She shook her head. "No."

His gaze seemed to penetrate her, reaching down into her heartstrings and plucking them gently. She was frozen in place, wondering what he would do next, and what she might do in response. But then suddenly, he stood and pulled his fingers through his hair, waltzing to her fireplace and leaning on the mantle.

"Why did this Goran fellow hire you? I can't imagine it was gold you were after." he asked.

"Not gold, no. It's the cure to the phoenix fever. My family is... sick."

He paused. A flash of realization dawned on his face. Tori gathered that he remembered her telling him she had the sickness right before she handed him the syringe.

"Does Drothidia not have access to the inoculation?" he asked.

"If we were ever offered the opportunity, I have no knowledge of it. My father said that the people of Drothidia do not have a place of importance in Avarell's eyes. Probably why my mother taught me never to trust anyone outside our village."

There seemed to be a spark of anger in Bram's eyes. "This man from Khadulan, he must have access to the cure. You've done your part; he should deliver what he promised."

"His ship is due in tomorrow. I will deliver the news, and that should be that."

He nodded, his jaw tight and his hand on the hilt of his

sword. "I shall go with you to meet his ship. I owe you that much. If anything, I can stand as a sign of strength, to make sure he makes good on his promise. Your family will get the cure. I vow it."

CHAPTER TWELVE

Ninja pulled at the strings of Tori's corset, readying her for Jasmine's funeral. As long as Tori was to stick around and help Lady Maescia usurp the duke, she had to continue to blend in as High Priestess. Tori took a deep breath, pressing the palm of her hand against the silky material of her dress and begging her stomach to stop churning.

"I hate doing these," she said. "Not only are they depressing, but I feel like I'm robbing the family of a true blessing, not allowing a real High Priestess to send the departed soul to the land of eternal peace."

"I understand, but we have no choice."

"Poor Jasmine."

"She won't be the only one dead if we don't figure out how to get the queen regent out of the duke's control." Finja held up the traditional gold cloak that High Priestesses donned for leading funeral rites. "Did you figure out that poison?"

"No." Tori tied the cloak, the heavy material pushing down her shoulders. "I don't have the proper ingredients. Pending a trip to the Rift, I won't be able to get them anytime soon.

"Well, one step at a time." Finja handed her the book of prayers. "For now, you've got funeral rites to read."

They left Tori's chambers together, taking their strides in silence. The air in the castle smelled of approaching rain, and the sky was muddled with clouds. The castle staff scurried about, tending to their daily duties, but the Lords and Ladies of the court could be spotted making their way to the chapel, their heads bowed and eyes full of sorrow.

Tori was about to walk through the chapel doors when a figure stepped in front of her.

"Your Holiness, how good to see you up and about." The duke bowed his head to her, but the straight line of his mouth made Tori uncomfortable. "I had heard you were ill. I'm pleased to see you have recovered."

Tori didn't bother to bow in return. "Thank you, Duke Grunmire. The Divine Mother has seen to it that I remain resilient in my mission. With her grace, I will prevail."

"Yes, well, it's unfortunate that your first day back falls under such solemn circumstances."

"I believe in the circle of life and that balance shall be restored." The fact that the duke didn't flinch told Tori he was unaware of the double meaning in her words. "If you'll excuse me, I have a service to lead."

"Yes, of course, Your Holiness."

The chapel was filled with the somber faces of the Lords and Ladies of the court, and in the front pew sat Jasmine's family. A little girl, whom Tori assumed was Jasmine's sister, clutched a doll and cried into its hair. Jasmine's mother wept so hard her shoulders shook, but her father could only stare, his eyes red and his shoulders hunched.

Jasmine's body was laid out on a long slab on the altar platform. She was wrapped in a family cloth with traditional silver cord tied around the material. There were flowers and trinkets from her childhood placed on her still form. Candles burned at the foot of the slab.

Tori brought the book of prayers to the altar, barely able to focus on what she was supposed to say. All she could see was Jasmine's little sister, sobbing at the loss of her sibling. If Tori blinked, she could imagine it was Taeyeon sitting there, crying for her family. Tori felt a pinch in her heart. She longed to see her sister. She longed to go home and be with her family. If things went badly, it could be her who was placed upon that slab—or her mother or Taeyeon. It could happen so easily, and her family might never get a chance to say goodbye to each other.

"In the name of the Divine Mother, I wish you peace," Tori began.

The congregation murmured the words to wish their High Priestess peace in return. She only spared a second's glance at Lady Maescia and Princess Wrena, both sitting in their places of honor beside the altar with their heads bowed.

She went on to recite the words she had memorized, praying for Jasmine's soul, for her journey to the land of eternal peace, and blessing the castle to protect it from malevolence. She prattled out the verses, almost not hearing herself as her mind swirled with the impossibility of what her life had become. Before she knew it, it was time for the procession to travel outside to the cemetery.

As she stepped off the altar, she lifted her head to see Bram, whom she only just realized was there. He took his place behind his friend Logan, with Azalea—the only female soldier in Avarell—stepping opposite them. Joined by three other Queen's Guard soldiers, they stood around Jasmine's body and lifted the wooden board it lay upon from the slab.

With a deliberate gait, the six soldiers carried Jasmine's corpse out of the chapel and toward the castle's cemetery. As a Lady of the court, Jasmine was entitled to a burial plot on royal land. Her family followed closely behind the soldiers. A few of the Lords and Ladies, including the duke, joined as well, but many of them parted from the procession, choosing not to take part in the burial ceremony. Bringing up the rear were Tori, Lady Maescia, and Princess Wrena. None of them exchanged words during the entire march.

As they stepped onto the cemetery grounds, the darkening clouds finally released the anticipated rain. The soft sprinkling of drops matched the tears in Jasmine's mother's eyes.

A grave had been dug prior to their arrival, and the Queen's Guard went to great lengths to place Jasmine's body gently inside it. Once her corpse was settled, Logan and Bram backed up to where Azalea stood.

Azalea, though a strong soldier who could hold her own, broke down and cried on Logan's shoulder. Though not a Lady of the court, Tori knew Azalea was a part of their clique, and she had also lost a good friend.

Raven glanced at Bram, but then lowered her eyes. Tori knew Bram had been forced to kill Jasmine in front of her, and Tori wondered if Raven might despise him for it.

Finja held the book of prayers open for Tori to recite the final prayer. Her voice barely carried over the rain. Servants with shovels began to cover Jasmine's body with dirt, and her mother's sobs grew louder.

With a final blessing of peace, the book of prayer was closed, and the service ended. For a moment, no one moved.

Ignoring the falling rain, the queen regent stepped forward. Shadowing her was Duke Grunmire, his chin lifted and his mouth in a straight line. Tori noticed that he appeared more bored than sad. Perhaps he felt above the Lords and Ladies of the court. Perhaps nobody's death was worth his time.

"I would like you all to know," the queen regent began, "that we are conducting an investigation as to how such a tragedy might have befallen one of Avarell's prominent members of court. To contract the disease of the Undead is entirely impossible within the walls of the castle. Though we were not aware of any journey Jasmine may have partaken in, we have to assume that she ventured near the Rift and was bitten."

A few gasps sounded, and Jasmine's mother shook her head.

"Our speculation at this time is that she hid any signs of becoming ill until her disease progressed to the point that she could no longer conceal it. Though the investigation continues, we will mourn her loss and ask the Divine Mother to keep watch over her soul."

Suddenly the duke stepped forward. He had brushed up against the queen regent's arm with such unexpectedness that she bristled.

"All things considered, we, as a nation, must carry on. We need a light in the darkness to lift our spirits, which is why the wedding of Princess Wrena and my son, Eleazar, has been moved up. They shall marry within a week."

Tori's eyes went to the princess. The slight drop in Princess

Wrena's jaw did not go unnoticed. Lady Maescia's expression did not change, though Tori wasn't convinced she knew about the duke's announcement in advance.

He turned to the queen regent, looking down his nose at her. "Isn't that wonderful news, Your Grace?"

Lady Maescia blanched for a split second before adopting a forced smile. "Yes, of course. Wonderful news."

The duke motioned to his son, who stepped closer to the princess. The princess's hands were clasped in front of her, her gaze trained on the ground. Tori caught a sudden flinch of the princess's shoulders when Eleazar put his hand on her back.

This much she figured out: the duke was somehow forcing the princess to marry his son. But she could not yet figure out what the duke could be holding against her to make her do it. And if the queen regent wasn't going to tell her, she wondered if Finja could find out.

"I'm going to escort Azalea back to her rooms," Logan said to Bram. This time, there were no innuendos in his words. He was obviously afflicted by Jasmine's demise along with everyone else. Bram nodded and clapped Logan on the shoulder, glad Azalea and Logan had each other for comfort in a time of loss. Their closeness made him think of Tori, but when he turned toward her, she was already walking away with Finja, her gold cloak almost black from the rain.

The muffled sound of harsh voices caught his ears. He turned to see Eleazar hovering over the princess's shoulder. She was obviously distraught by whatever he was saying to her, but Bram couldn't make out the words. It then occurred to him that the princess might know where his cousin was. After all, it was no secret to him that they shared a bond closer than friendship.

"I beg your pardon, Your Highness," he said to her.

Eleazar looked up at Bram and took a step back, feigning a small smile as though everything was fine between him and Princess Wrena.

"Yes, Master Stormbolt?" the princess answered.

"I apologize if this is a bad time, but I'm quite desperate. I haven't seen Lady Aurora in a long while. In fact, I can't imagine why she would miss Lady Jasmine's funeral. I've asked practically everyone, and no one seems to know of her whereabouts. I'm sorry if this seems brash, but I'm quite concerned. Have you seen her, Your Highness?"

Wrena opened her mouth, and Bram was filled with a sudden sense of hope. But when she closed her mouth again and shook her head, his hope depleted. The whole situation was odd and frustrating, and he couldn't understand why everyone seemed to be keeping secrets. He hoped against hope that Aurora was somewhere safe, but if something had happened to her—even something like what had happened to Jasmine—he wished someone would tell him.

"She has been absent from court," Lady Maescia said, gracefully moving between them. "But with all the recent events, I haven't had a chance to address her absence."

His brows cinched together, and his fingers worried the sheath at his side. "How could she simply disappear?"

"Disappear?" Lady Maescia let out a laugh that didn't sound genuine. "No, no, she is around somewhere, I'm sure."

"Ah, yes," the duke said. "I remember some of the handmaidens mentioning Lady Aurora. I believe they said she was feeling ill and was resting in her rooms."

Since when did the duke keep tabs on Aurora? "I've visited her rooms, but there was no answer."

"Perhaps she'd been so ill that she slept through your visit without rousing," the duke suggested.

"Worry not," Lady Maescia said, placing a gentle hand on Bram's arm. "I shall have her handmaiden inform us of how she is faring and let you know. But for now, let us get out of this wretched rain before it starts coming down any harder."

The answer didn't please him, but he had no choice but to concede. Still, something in Lady Maescia's eyes told him she knew more than she was letting on. "Yes, of course. Thank you, Your Grace."

CHAPTER THIRTEEN

Wrena had been weeping into her pillow for at least an hour when the gentle sound of footsteps roused her. At first, she refused to lift her head, but then she realized that whoever entered her room hadn't understood her silent request to be left alone. Expecting a nosey servant or even an intrusion by Eleazar, she was pleasantly surprised to find her brother, Theo, standing at the foot of her bed.

"Theo." She did her best to wipe her tears away. "I'm sorry. I didn't know it was you."

He tilted his head at her. "What's wrong?"

"Dear brother, I lost someone and had to say goodbye to them today." She wasn't sure he had heard about Jasmine, but she couldn't bring herself to say her friend's name.

"I'm sorry."

She smiled at him and gestured for him to come sit by her. As soon as he was close enough, Wrena wrapped him in her arms and squeezed him, kissing the top of his head.

"I wish things could go back to how they were when Mother was around. It was so simple then. Easy. And I was surrounded by people I loved all the time."

"I'm here, Wrena."

She hugged him tighter. "I'm very grateful. I don't know what I'd do without you."

"You never have to be without me," he said. He squeezed her hand and tilted his head. "I promise."

Tears formed in her eyes, knowing that it was an impossible promise to keep. None of them could give anyone any kind of guarantee. Not with the world in the state it was now, with deceptive rulers calling the shots and manipulating everyone to do their bidding. She wondered if there was any hope left at all.

A broad woman peered through the doorway, then let out a sigh and straightened. "There you are, Your Highness."

Theo faced Wrena and rolled his eyes. She held back a laugh, knowing he was getting tired of being looked after by a nursemaid. But she had suffered the same fate when she was growing up, and it hadn't done her any harm.

"Come on now, sire," the nursemaid said. "Off to get ready for bed."

He leaned close to his sister and gave her a kiss on the cheek, making her smile. "Goodnight, Wrena. I love you."

"I love you too, Theo," she whispered. "Sweet dreams."

He jumped off her bed and dragged his feet as he went with his nursemaid, leaving Wrena alone in her quiet room.

Sweeping her hair away from her face, she stood and wandered toward the window. Hanging on a dress hook near the window, her wedding dress caught the light of the moon. She ground her teeth and wrapped her arms across her stomach, thinking about the upcoming wedding she was being coerced to agree to. She couldn't wrap her mind around the fact that she would have to go through with it. Though she wasn't a highly religious person, she clasped her hands together and begged the Divine Mother to help her find a way out of it.

When she opened her eyes, something shiny on her windowsill caught her eye. It was in the corner, hidden from view, and when Wrena realized what it was, a sense of wistfulness overcame her. She picked up the jeweled hairpin, remembering how she had slipped it out of Aurora's hair one day when they were alone in her rooms. She wrapped her hand around the pin and held it to her heart, wondering if it was a sign.

Moving closer to the window, she pressed her forehead against the glass, thinking she might be able to see the part of the castle where the dungeon was. But she couldn't see anything, especially in the rain.

"We will find a way out of this," she whispered. Though the promise could not reach Aurora, she intended to keep it.

Spinning toward her desk, she rushed to find a pen and parchment. Aurora might be the one in the dungeon, but they were both prisoners as long as they remained in Avarell. Leaving might mean she would have to give up the throne but staying meant giving up her livelihood. Careful with her words in case someone got ahold of it, the princess penned a letter to her uncle, King Rainer, in Creoca. She would request a visit, so he would know to expect her. But for all accounts and purposes, it would be more than just a visit. First, however, she needed to break Aurora out of the dungeon.

Tori ran a finger over the detailing of the mask in her hands as she and Finja waited in the cold rain for Goran's ship to dock. The rain had calmed to a drizzle, and the bay was filled with the sounds of the waves and footsteps through puddles. The thrashing waves rocked the boat as it approached, and it seemed to take forever until they anchored. As the crew finally set out the gangway and began unloading their shipment, Tori craned her neck, searching for Goran.

For a moment, she remembered that Bramwell had said he wanted to accompany her to meet the ship, his determination to make sure Goran would hold true to his promise to get the phoenix fever cure to Tori's family driving his motives. She purposely did not tell him when she and Finja would be meeting the ship for fear that Bram might want to harm Goran. She knew there would be no way to get the cure to her family if Goran was killed.

"I don't see him," Tori said, but it was more to herself than to Finja. The more she scanned the crew without seeing him, the deeper the crease in her brow grew.

"Well, this is ridiculous," Finja said. "Pardon me. You there!"

A burly crew member who carried a crate set it down on the dock and swiped rain-soaked hair off his brow. "Yes, miss."

"We're waiting for Goran. He was supposed to meet us."

"Sorry, miss. He's not on board."

"What?" Tori exclaimed, blinking in confusion.

"Where is he?" Finja asked.

"We're not sure, to tell the truth. He took two of his best men and left without letting us know where they were headed off to."

"And he didn't say when he would be back?"

"No, he didn't. He told us to keep on schedule, that was all."

"How long ago was this?" Tori asked.

The man carried on with his work but spared Tori a glance.

"A little more than a week ago."

"And you've heard no word from him?"

"No, not yet."

Tori felt light-headed. She opened her mouth to speak, but her throat was as dry as the desert. Gathering her wits, she grabbed Finja's hands.

Finja raised a brow but did not pull away.

"Finja, he had the book. The book of sales that might have been a record where his wife was sold into slavery. I think he's gone to rescue her."

She fought off the panic that seized her heart. With Goran gone, how would her family get the cure to the phoenix fever? What if Goran was killed before he could instruct his people to bring the cure to Sukoshi as they had agreed? Would he return? Perhaps he had gotten himself into more trouble than he anticipated. With her skills, Tori would have been able to assist him in his quest. Why hadn't he asked her?

"Do you think he's gone to Nostidour?" Tori asked.

Finja's lips pressed together as she shook her head. "We didn't take a single peek into that book. We don't know where he's gone. And if your theory is correct and his wife has been enslaved in Nostidour, there's no telling if he would be able to rescue her. Or if he would even still be alive."

CHAPTER FOURTEEN

inja entered tori's chambers, carrying a steaming pot of hot water. Another handmaiden followed with a second pot. Tori glanced at her as she brushed her hair, preparing herself for a much-needed hot bath. The look Finja gave her in return made Tori's brow furrow. Still, she waited until the other handmaiden left before questioning her.

"What is it?" Tori asked, her fingertips dipping into the tub to test the temperature.

"I may know a man available for hire who can go into the Rift and get the missing ingredient you need."

At first Tori didn't respond. A part of her was relieved she didn't have all the ingredients. She wasn't sure she could carry out actually poisoning the duke. But then she nodded, steeling herself.

"All right. What do we need to do?"

"He'll need a description of the plant, to the finest detail."

"I can do better," Tori said. "I'll draw it for him as well. But is this man able to fend off the Undead?"

"He showed no signs of fear when I mentioned the Rift."

"Good." She swallowed hard but tried to compose herself. This was a necessary evil. And perhaps their only way to get Lady Maescia out of the duke's grasp. "I'll give you the drawing this eve."

⁕

Tori could not find Lady Maescia in the throne room or her private sitting room, so she ventured toward the lounge. She knew the queen regent would frequent the private space before dinner, but she did not know if she would find her alone.

When the guards opened the door for her, she was surprised to find that the duke and queen regent were not alone.

Concentrating on a parchment map laid out on a strategy table, Prince Theo tapped his fingers against his bottom lip. The duke hovered over him like a vulture waiting to snatch up its prey. Upon the map were dozens of tiny iron pieces molded into the likeness of soldiers. Some of the pieces were painted other colors, and Tori gathered they were to represent the other realms.

Tori's eyes were then drawn to the queen regent, who scratched at her neck. It occurred to Tori that it wasn't the first time she'd caught Lady Maescia's nervous tick.

"Your Grace," Tori said, bowing her head. She locked gazes with Lady Maescia, hoping she would see that they had a matter to discuss in private. "I was hoping we could find the time to discuss the upcoming Holy day."

A wrinkle planted itself upon Lady Maescia's brow for a solitary second. "Oh. Oh yes. Perhaps we should adjourn to my sitting room to speak in private."

The duke lifted his head from the strategy table. "Don't mind us, Your Holiness. Feel free to discuss your plans here. As the queen regent's advisor, it would probably be fitting that I am briefed on the plans as well."

"It's simply plans for the sacred celebration, Duke Grunmire," Tori said. "I wouldn't want to trouble you, especially when there are no strategies or politics involved."

"If it's such a simple conversation, then I see no reason you can't discuss matters here." He motioned with his hand for her to begin her discussion with the queen regent.

Tori forced herself not to show her frustration. "Very well." She turned to Lady Maescia. "You will, of course, be asked to read a passage of the celebratory verses. Perhaps you'd like to review the Book of Prayers to choose one? I could have my personal copy delivered to your chambers, if you'd like. Later tonight, perhaps."

It was a quick lie, but she hoped Lady Maescia understood that Tori meant she would discuss matters with her later.

"That would be perfect." Lady Maescia gave her a knowing nod. "Thank you so much, Your Holiness."

Tori nodded to the queen regent, then turned toward the young prince. His fingers were wrapped around an iron soldier. He looked up at Tori and smiled.

"Hello, Lady Tori."

"Hello, Your Highness." She came nearer. "This looks complicated."

"The duke is teaching me how to be king."

Before Tori could respond, the duke let out a chuckle. "There's still time, of course. First the princess and Eleazar will be wed, making *him* king. But it is wise to brush up on strategy and matters of conquest for when your time comes. Not to mention it is quite exciting. Don't you agree, Prince Theo?"

Theo responded by knocking down a Gadleigh soldier figure and letting out a laugh.

Tori took a deep breath. "Your Highness, I wanted to tell you: I heard some of the staff mention they made the chocolate truffle pudding today, but there wouldn't be enough for everyone. Perhaps if you got to the banquet hall early…"

Theo threw down his iron figure, a huge smile on his face. "Yes!"

Theo raced out of the lounge, and Tori stepped closer to the strategy table. Duke Grunmire straightened as she looked at the map.

"I've heard about your idea to negotiate with Nostidour," Tori said.

"Not that it's any of your concern, but it is more than just an idea. Negotiations are in full swing."

"I wonder, though, if it's a wise plan to involve Avarell with barbarians."

"I take it you don't agree."

"No. I think Nostidour has no qualms about stepping on others' toes—or worse—to get what they want. Perhaps negotiations with a more peaceful nation would prove beneficial. It would make sense to form a lasting bond with other realms. Realms who strive for amity and harmony between the nations."

The duke shook his head. "Your Holiness, we tried that strategy. It did not give Avarell an advantage."

"It's not about having an advantage; it's about forming a unity."

He looked down at her, his chin lifted. "May the Divine Mother forgive me for saying you are wrong." With an iron figure in his hand, he swiped the map of all other figures, making Tori flinch. "What do you know of politics? I'm confident enough to say you know very little, if not nothing. Political strategy is not a topic for a holy woman. That is why I am captain of the guard, and you are the deliverer of cheery words."

Her fingers brushed against the area of her skirt where her kunai was hidden. It took all of her resolve to not take out the blade.

"You might be wary of where you meddle, Lady Tori. You wouldn't be the first person to stick their nose where it didn't belong. Perhaps the time has come for the queen regent to consider seeking a more reasonable High Priestess."

"You mean blindly compliant."

"Call it what you will. As her advisor, I think it wise to consider."

She almost laughed to herself. He had no idea that she wasn't relying on this job. She decided to turn the conversation on him. "Duke Grunmire, I do have a question—nothing to do with politics, of course. One of the Ladies of the court seems to have been absent for quite some time now. Would you happen to know where Lady Aurora is... or perhaps what's happened to her?"

He studied her. "Don't trouble yourself over a simple girl, Your Holiness. I'm sure she's around."

"I'm not troubling myself. As a High Priestess, it is my duty to care for all members of the court. She's also cousin to a dear friend of mine, and it pains me to see him suffering."

"I'm afraid I cannot help you."

A smile played upon her lips. "It's all right. I'm not worried. The Divine Mother will see fit that Lady Aurora is found and that any evil will be rightly punished."

CHAPTER FIFTEEN

*B*ram stopped in his tracks in the hall leading to his chambers. Pacing in front of his door was Lady Maescia, wringing her hands. She looked as if she hadn't slept in a fortnight. Her pacing came to an abrupt halt when she spotted him, and a hand flew quickly to her neck, where she gave it a quick scratch.

"Your Grace?" Bram looked over his shoulder to make sure

no one else was around.

"Master Stormbolt, I need to ask you a favor."

"Of course. What is it?"

"The Queen's Guard plans to partake in a hunt before the wedding feast. I need you to join it."

"I do not think I will be asked to join, since I've given my notice to take leave from the Queen's Guard."

"The duke will not be along for the hunt, and he need not know you will be there. If anyone asks, you may say I gave you permission to join. The duke will know nothing of it, and even if he finds out later, you will have already returned."

Bram rubbed at his chin, already dotted with stubble. "May I ask what you need me to do on this hunt?"

"Two things." She placed a hand on her stomach and took in a deep breath. "I know you have friends in the guard. Perhaps friends who have inside information on the duke's plans with Nostidour."

"I thought you were aware of his plans."

"There are things he's not telling me. I'm sure of it. But he is known to boast to his favorites in the guard, and my hope is that they will in turn leak this information to you."

Bram nodded. "I can't make any promises, but I can try." He studied the queen regent. "What is the second thing you need?"

"I know the hunt usually brings the guard close to the Rift. Although it is probably impossible, I would like for you to keep an eye out. Even if there is the slightest chance of spotting the

Queen… if I just knew if my sister was alive…" She scratched at her neck again. "Please. Please do this for me. I'm at a loss of what else to do."

He placed a hand on her sleeve. Though he agreed that it was improbable he would spot the Undead Queen, he felt he needed to placate Lady Maescia, who was clearly troubled. "Your Grace. Of course. I'll do as you ask."

The sound of footsteps pounding into the dirt echoed all around. Bram's adrenaline pumped through him, causing him to run faster. There was a time, when he was younger, that he was slower than Logan. Back then, he had to exert more energy than he knew he had just to keep Logan in his sights on a hunt. But now, he could outrun him. It took him a moment to remember that wasn't the purpose for his presence on the hunt this day.

Distracted by thrown glances into the Rift, Bram missed his opportunity to take down a stag. Logan's quick reflexes and precise aim with his bow and arrow won him the game. Instead of being jealous of his friend's skill, as had often been the case when they were younger, Bram clapped Logan on the back and congratulated him. It was enough satisfaction to take part in the hunt one last time, and the thought of never running with his friend again made his heart ache.

The rest of the Queen's Guard nodded to Logan and continued the hunt, seeking more game for the wedding. Bram and Logan stayed behind, approaching the dying stag. Logan unsheathed his sword and thrust it through the stag's heart to put it out of his misery. Bram unhooked the rope from his belt, and he and Logan began tying up the stag to bring back to the castle.

"I'm surprised you missed this one," Logan said, binding the stag's legs together over a long branch. "Or are our Avarell stags no longer good enough for a Gadleigh soldier?"

Bram let out a small laugh. "Perhaps I've just been too distracted as of late. What will I do without you to keep me on my toes?"

"If you'd like, I can send you letters twice a month reminding of your poor skills and lack of discipline."

Bram bit back a smile. "You're a true friend, Logan."

"And now, your sworn enemy," Logan teased.

Bram's smile broke free. "Never."

"You know, I was wondering, if I were to get married, would you be able to part from Gadleigh for a day or two to serve as my groomsman? That is, if you're allowed back on Avarell soil after being labelled a traitor."

Bram finished his knot in the rope and studied his friend. "Are you and Azalea to marry?"

"Perhaps. I haven't asked her yet. But it's something that's crossed my mind as of late."

"So, the infamous scoundrel Logan Rathmore is considering

marriage. I think I've heard everything now."

Logan removed his hunting gloves and wiped at his brow. "Well, dear Bramwell, between the princess's upcoming wedding and the untimely death of Lady Jasmine, I've been inspired to seize the opportunities set before me and start living. Life's too short, my friend."

"Too true," Bram replied, his meaning tangled in his own thoughts. "Tell me, have you heard any discussion about the negotiations with Nostidour?"

"Nothing more than you've heard, I'm sure. Why?"

"It worries me." Bram wiped sweat from his brow. "I've grown up learning not to trust that realm. Feels odd to be inviting them to join us in what I can only assume is a provocation of war."

Logan nodded. "It is strange. But I haven't heard any details. If I do—and you haven't left yet—I'll let you know."

A groan and a rustling of leaves caused the two young men to stop and turn. Though Bram hadn't made a sound, Logan held up a finger to shush him. Ever so slowly, the two moved closer to the source of the sound. It wasn't until they were peering into the Rift that they realized where the sound was coming from.

Below, in the cavern, five Undead roamed. At first, it didn't seem any more unusual than the Undead Bram had seen before. But then he had noticed the one Undead at the head of the group. Bram held back a gasp as he realized it was the Queen.

He pulled Logan back, hoping his friend wouldn't recognize

her. "Come on," he whispered. "It's just a bunch of Undead."

"But that one is… doesn't it appear as if she's *leading* the others?"

Sweat formed at Bram's temples. "I'm not well versed in how the Undead congregate," he said, still pulling on Logan's arm. "Perhaps that is normal, and we just never realized it."

"She looks as if she's communicating with them, signaling to them."

"That's ridiculous. They haven't the capacity." But Bram knew Logan was right. Though he tried not to stare, the Undead Queen was more or less in command of the group. And they were actually following her instructions. Bram could barely wrap his head around what this could mean. "Come on, we've a stag to get back to the castle."

Logan wouldn't budge. "It looks as if they are an organized unit."

"Organized in what way? What could they possibly be doing down there?"

"This may sound crazy, but I think they're trying to find a way out."

Bram watched for a moment, unable to tear his gaze away. The Undead Queen was instructing the group—with mere grunts and hand gestures—to move rocks and boulders closer to the embankment.

"We need to stop them."

Before Bram could respond, Logan nocked an arrow and

aimed it into the Rift. Bram wasn't sure how to feel about the possibility of Logan actually killing the Queen. Of course, she was already technically dead. Bram wondered if the queen regent would forgive him if he let Logan take her down. Still, he couldn't just stand there while his friend did all the work. It would look too suspicious.

Shooting into the Rift was difficult. The arrows lost momentum before they reached down far enough to hit their targets. Bram managed to take out one of the Undead in the rear of the group, while Logan hit one in the front. The Queen—whom Bram was glad Logan still hadn't recognized—looked up at them and bared her yellowed teeth, her fingers bent like claws as she growled. She ducked out of sight, camouflaging herself among some thick bushes.

In Logan's effort to take out the last of the group of followers, he slipped on wet leaves. Bram was quick to catch his friend before he fell into the Rift. He dropped his bow and used both hands to lift Logan. Breathing labored, Logan nodded his thanks to Bram.

By the time their gazes went back to the Rift, the remaining undead were nowhere to be seen.

Logan raked a hand through his hair, his eyes still searching for Undead.

"I think we got most of them," Bram said.

"What about the leader?"

"I'm sure my arrow took her down." Bram hoped Logan

couldn't tell he was lying. "We should get back."

Logan hesitated for a moment but finally nodded. "All right. Let's go."

He and Logan lifted the branch the stag was tied to and trudged back toward the castle. Bram was sure Logan would mention this encounter to Duke Grunmire. He was still a loyal soldier, after all. Try as he might, Bram couldn't think of anything to say to change his mind.

CHAPTER SIXTEEN

ori stood at the pulpit, her hands placed upon the Marriage Divinities, fingers traveling along the lines of scripture. Beside Princess Wrena stood Lady Maescia, her mouth in a straight line as the princess and Eleazar rehearsed the exchange of vows. The queen regent spared her a knowing glance, but only for a moment. She had agreed with Tori's plan to make the poison when they had met in secret the night before. She even seemed a bit relieved. Now it was just a matter of waiting for Finja's hired man to deliver the missing ingredient.

"After I've read the second passage," Tori explained to the princess and Eleazar, "you will both kneel."

Eleazar eased down so that his knees lay on the thin silk pillow at the base of the platform. The princess took her time doing the same, her eyes still trained on the floor. She looked lovely in her light blue gown, but her face was full of sorrow. Eleazar seemed a bit lost, as if he continuously needed an extra few seconds to figure out what to do. As if he were overwhelmed to be in the situation he found himself in.

"I will then lay the sacred wedding sash over your joined hands and bind you in the name of the Divine Mother. After this, I will have you each drink from the golden goblet, which will contain blessed wine."

Eleazar nodded. The princess did not respond. Tori noted she had the pallor of someone who was about to be sick. But the look she received from the duke made her press on.

"At that time, you will both stand and face the pews, and I will announce you husband and wife."

Eleazar stood, and then extended a hand to Princess Wrena. She stood without his help and turned toward the pews. Tori noticed the duke's tightening of his lips, obviously holding back abrasive words. She tore her eyes away from him to finish the rehearsal instructions.

"With joined hands, raised for everyone to see, you will both exit the chapel, followed by your wedding party."

Tori could see the reluctance in the princess's actions as she placed her hand upon Eleazar's. They held a steady gait as they headed out of the chapel, and as soon as they reached the archway that led into the hall, Princess Wrena snatched her hand away and crossed her arms.

Tori knew that most royal marriages were arranged, but the princess's demeanor showed more than simple reluctance. She was being forced into this against her will.

The princess and Eleazar re-entered the chapel, but they no longer walked together. Princess Wrena came over to stand close to her aunt. Without looking at her, Lady Maescia placed a hand on the princess's back.

"Well, let's hope the actual ceremony has more feeling to it," the duke said. "I felt as if I were awaiting my own execution."

"My feelings exactly," the princess mumbled.

"Beg your pardon, Your Highness?" The duke raised a brow at her.

"Nothing."

"You'd do well to mind your posture," the duke said, glaring at her. "You're supposed to look like a queen, not some limp dishrag. Avarell will need someone as strong as your aunt... and your mother. You would let them down with an ill-mannered disposition. This should be the event of the century, a spark of hope for the next generation. The festivities will be grand, and you and my son—" He clapped Eleazar on the back. "—will be celebrated by all."

Eleazar straightened his shoulders, a cocky smile playing on his lips.

The queen regent appeared as if she held back a sneer, but otherwise kept still and silent.

"Your Highness," Tori said, her voice kept low. "Are you all right?"

The princess glanced at the duke and her aunt, then bowed her head to Tori. "Apologies for my poignant mood. I'm just still struck by Jasmine's death. But I know she would have wanted me to continue with this... joyous event."

"Your Holiness." The duke's voice was loud in the chapel. "Thank you for the rehearsal. I look forward to tonight's ceremony."

At his poor attempt to bow his head to her in respect, she half-heartedly returned the gesture, her fingers dwelling at the spot where her kunai were hidden. Every minute she had to spend in his presence made her lean more and more in favor of poisoning him.

As the chapel emptied, Finja followed Tori into the vestry to store the Marriage Divinities book and the other items they would need for the ceremony. With the last of the items put away, Finja turned to Tori.

"I overheard something," she said. "I thought I should let you know."

"What did you overhear?"

"Just before the rehearsal, one of the duke's men approached him. Most of their conversation was whispered, but I did hear Nostidour mentioned. His guard also said something about how 'they' would be arriving soon."

"What does that mean? You think representatives from Nostidour are coming to Avarell?"

"If they are, that can't be good."

Tori chewed on her thumbnail and began to pace. "We've never had the Nostidourians present on this side of the ocean. I have a bad feeling about this."

Finja scowled at her. "Would you stop pacing? You're going to wear a rut in the floors."

It wasn't Finja's words but a knock on the door which caused Tori to stop.

Finja gave Tori a warning look before she opened the door. A hand on her chest, Tori was relieved to see Bram enter the room. Other than appearing a bit disheveled, he looked as handsome as ever.

"I'm sorry if I'm interrupting," he said. His brow was creased, and his jaw was set.

"What is it, Master Stormbolt?"

He glanced at Finja, obviously deliberating whether he should continue.

"It's all right," Tori said. "You may speak freely in front of Finja."

He hesitated before nodding his head. "I joined the hunt with the Queen's Guard, and I spotted… I spotted the Queen in the Rift."

Tori felt as though her heart had momentarily stopped. "You're sure it was her?"

"I could never forget how she looked. It was her."

"What happened?" Finja interrupted. "Did anyone else see her?"

"Logan was there, but he didn't seem to recognize her." He rubbed at the back of his neck. "Also, I'm concerned that she isn't like the others. She seems smarter. Organized. Like she's planning something."

"Planning what?" Finja asked, her eyes narrowed.

Bram shook his head. "I don't know. I think she's trying to get the Undead out of the Rift."

"No," Finja said. "That's impossible."

"I can't explain it. I wouldn't fathom it either if I hadn't seen it myself."

"It's too risky to leave her out there," Tori said, her heart beginning to race. "Perhaps I should go to the Rift."

"And do what?" Bram asked. "Could you really kill her? Do you think Lady Maescia would accept that as her fate?"

She simply stared at him, unable to answer.

"I need to talk to the queen regent," Bram said. "She's the one who asked me to keep an eye out for her sister. Maybe she'll have an idea of how to handle this."

"All right," Tori said with a nod.

He gazed at her for a moment, a look on his face as if he was weighing his options. "May I speak to you privately, Lady Tori?"

She glanced at Finja and then nodded. "Of course."

"I'll see to the preparations." Finja strode past them and left the room.

"What is it?" Tori asked. "Is something wrong?"

"I don't know. I feel a little... lost? A strange feeling of desperation, perhaps. I don't know what to do."

"About what? Can I help?"

"When I was out with Logan today, he got me thinking. He said something about life being short and seizing opportunities lain before him. And I was contemplating why I wasn't doing the same."

"What opportunities?"

He locked eyes with her. Suddenly it felt as if the room melted away. She could almost hear her heart beat. He reached for her. She backed away.

He looked puzzled, dropping his hand. "I'm sorry."

She cleared her throat. "No, I'm sorry. It's not that I don't... I'm here on a mission. And I'm afraid it leaves no room for... for romance. I've got a world to save."

He was silent, his eyes roaming her face. He didn't seem upset, but still, she couldn't breathe, waiting for his response.

"Let me help you then. At least I'd be by your side."

"Bram, you're leaving for Gadl—"

He reached out and took her hand before she could pull away, but in the next second he released her, his jaw hanging open.

"Lady Tori, you feel as if you're on fire."

She reached up and placed the back of her hand upon her head. "Do I?"

"Is it the phoenix fever?"

"No. I know how that usually makes me feel, but I... I feel fine." Her brow wrinkled. "In fact, I feel better than I have in years."

CHAPTER SEVENTEEN

Snow-white peonies covered in silver glitter lined the arches in the chapel. The candles that stood in every corner were adorned with baby roses and honeysuckle, and wreaths of vibrant daisies hung at the end of every pew. The setting sun shone through the windows, casting a glow on the altar. Tiny butterflies, rumored to be a special gift from Lady Raven, floated around the room, landing on sleeves and skirts and making the Ladies of the court laugh.

Everything would have been perfect, if only the princess was marrying the person she was actually in love with. Lady Maescia imagined her niece must have felt as if her union with Eleazar was more like a death sentence. She placed a hand on her churning stomach and took in a deep breath. This union would change the fate of the nation. But there was nothing she could do to stop it.

The duke marched in, his eyes scanning the room as if to make sure everything was in place. Lady Maescia had to force herself not to roll her eyes. Why did he care so much about the small details? Ultimately, he was getting what he wanted. Did it matter that the flowers or candles or any of it was here? His son would be in line to be the king. The rest of it was simply trivial.

When he caught sight of her, he sauntered over, pausing occasionally to greet the Lords and Ladies of the court. Little did they know they would soon be deeper under his thumb than they already were.

"Lady Maescia," he said simply.

"In case you were wondering," she said, not bothering to look him in the eye, "gloating does not become you."

He leaned closer. "Let me just remind you that this ceremony must go as planned. If it does not, I will be forced to reveal what you did to King Henry. Additionally, I'll be sure that when Aurora is killed, *you* will be the one your niece holds accountable."

The pews filled with members of the court and other

prestigious citizens of Avarell. A quartet began to play lilting music, and two servants scurried to accomplish some last-minute sweeping.

One of the duke's men approached them, and it took a moment before Lady Maescia remembered his name.

"Duke Grunmire," Logan said to the duke before turning to the queen regent. "I beg your pardon, Your Grace."

Lady Maescia put on a fake smile. "Yes, Master Rathmore?"

"I wonder if I could have a quick word with you."

"Could this wait?" the duke asked. "This is an important moment in the history of Avarell. Isn't that right, Lady Maescia?"

The duke glanced at Lady Maescia, raising his brow. She wished, in that moment, she could lop off his wretched eyebrow and throw it in the Rift. "Yes, it is," she replied. "Happiest day of my life. My darling niece is getting married."

"Yes, it's quite a match," the duke added. "Extraordinary."

Logan looked frazzled. "It's just that there seems to be something strange going on in the Rift. The Undead—I think they're trying to get out. I think one of them is leading the effort."

"Now, now, Master Rathmore," the duke said, smiling despite his teeth clenching together. He placed a heavy hand on Logan's shoulder. "There is always something strange happening in the Rift. That is why we stay clear of that area. Now if you'll please take a seat, my son's wedding is about to begin."

Lady Maescia kept her eyes on Logan, letting his message sink in. Her heart felt as if it were in a vice. Could he have been speaking about her sister?

Logan pressed his lips together, clearly frustrated with the duke, but backed away with a nod. "Yes, of course," he said. "My apologies."

Tori let out a shuddered breath. She'd been pretending to be something she wasn't for some time now, but what she was about to pull off was huge. This was a royal wedding. A royal wedding that was being forced upon the princess against her will. How did she get herself into this mess? She shook out her hands, not able to wipe off her sweat on her ceremonial gown or cape. She searched the vestry, hoping to find a hand towel, or even a stray handkerchief.

Finja straightened Tori's cape and clucked her tongue. "Calm down. You do realize that you are not a High Priestess, yes? This wedding will not be official in the Divine Mother's eyes."

"But they do not know that."

"You only need to make it *look* real."

Tori nodded, letting out another breath. "All right. Yes, I can do that."

Finja's fingers were still untwisting the hem of Tori's cape when Tori swiped her hand away.

"Stop fidgeting," Tori said. "You're making me more

nervous."

Finja's eyes were narrowed. "Girl, you are burning hot."

She felt for Tori's head, but Tori pushed her away. "Will you stop? I'm fine."

"You don't feel feverish?"

"Not at all." She pursed her lips. "I mean, I'm worried about my family, and I'm frustrated with the situation here, and I'm confused about where Goran could be. But physically, I actually feel great."

Finja studied her. "Have you been taking your medicine?"

Tori bit her lip. "Would you be furious if I told you I've forgotten a few times?"

Finja's brow furrowed. "How can you be feeling well if you've skipped your medicine?"

"I don't know." Tori shook her head. "I think… I think it has something to do with that syringe and whatever was in it. Do you think Goran put the cure in there?"

Finja swiped a hand over her brow. "It's possible. That man is rather unpredictable."

Tori stared at Finja, her mind whirling. "Finja. I need to get the cure to my family. Without Goran, I'm at a loss at what to do. That is, unless you could help me."

Finja let out a deep sigh. "I suppose you have done everything you were asked to."

"And I'm not abandoning the effort, either. I'm here to fight. To set things right. I just want what Goran promised my family."

Slowly, Finja nodded. "I'll send word to someone who can get the message to one of Goran's soldiers."

"Really? Truly?" Tori's eyes were wide, and she thought she would collapse to her knees.

"You've proven your worth, girl; it's due you."

Tori pulled Finja into an embrace so quickly, Finja didn't have the chance to dodge it. "Thank you! Thank you from the bottom of my heart."

Finja hadn't pushed her away immediately, Tori noted. So when she did struggle to free herself from Tori's arms, she let her go without a word.

"Come on now," Finja said. "We've got a fake wedding to perform."

CHAPTER EIGHTEEN

Wrena gazed into the mirror. Her handmaidens had made her stunning. Her hair was perfect. Every inch of her wedding gown was pure perfection. Even Raven had looked genuinely amazed by how she looked. But no part of it could bring a smile to her face.

"It's time," Raven said. "Are you ready?"

Wrena turned to her and nodded solemnly.

"What's wrong, Your Highness?" Raven asked. "You're supposed to be glowing; it's your wedding day."

The corner of Wrena's mouth twitched. "I... I wish my mother could be here."

It wasn't a lie. If her mother were here, she might not be in this situation. Her mother would surely stomp out any efforts the duke made, ended any acts of manipulation the duke attempted to carry out. Instead, she was a pawn in a game of politics and lies.

Raven took hold of Wrena's hand and squeezed it. "I'm sorry, Your Highness. I wish she could be here for you as well."

Wrena placed a hand on her stomach and breathed deeply. "All right. We can go now."

Raven took hold of Wrena's train. "Ready when you are."

With a small bouquet of calla lilies in her hand, Wrena walked into the chapel, her gait in time with the music. She spotted Eleazar at the end of the isle but had to avert her eyes. Her gown, though soft, made her feel weighed down. But she knew it wasn't the gown causing her discomfort. She did her best to not even look at the duke as she stood beside her aunt.

The only thing keeping her from turning and running away was the horrid thought of something terrible happening to Aurora. Remembering what the duke made her aunt do to Lady Theresa, how she was forced to ruthlessly order the executioner to maim her, and the way the duke smirked at her afterword— no. She wouldn't let anything like that happen to Aurora.

If only there was a way to get Aurora out of her cell, she would rescue her, hire a ship, and take her far away. Anywhere away from the duke and his corruptness, anywhere where they could be together without fearing for their lives.

But that was impossible.

In the back of her mind, she wondered if Aurora could hear the music. If she knew the wedding was taking place today. She swallowed back the sour taste in her throat and held her chin up.

Finally, she stood before Lady Tori, putting up a front so that the High Priestess wouldn't notice her fear. Eleazar leaned over and whispered how lovely she looked. Aside from flinching away from him, Wrena offered no response.

While Lady Tori read the verses, Wrena felt as if she were watching the whole thing from outside her body. What would happen if she simply decided to run out? What would they do? Would the duke really stop her? Would he go so far as to use force to keep her in the chapel? Surely, he wouldn't make such a spectacle of himself in front of the Lords and Ladies of the court.

Or would he?

No, it would be much worse. He would kill Aurora.

Everything in the next few moments were a blur. Before she knew it, Lady Tori was already asking Wrena and Eleazar to kneel. As the High Priestess lay the wedding sash over their hands, Wrena couldn't keep her hands from shaking.

Her stomach soured as she drank the blessed wine. And she didn't even realize, until Tori wrinkled her brow at her, that tears were streaming down her face.

Lady Tori bowed her head and gave them a blessing, and then Eleazar took her hand, placed a kiss upon it, and turned her toward the pews.

Before Lady Tori could announce it, the duke had the audacity to step forward.

"Lords and Ladies of the court, may I introduce to you the newly wed couple, husband and wife, Princess Wrena and my son, the Prince consort of Avarell, and future king."

CHAPTER NINETEEN

Eleazar and Wrena were accompanied to their wedding chamber by the Queen's Guard. The duke, of course, marched behind them, no doubt to make sure Wrena didn't flee. Wrena felt flushed. Her body was cold, and she fought off shivers. But it wasn't the drafty corridor. As protocol, the newly wed royals were expected to enter the wedding chambers and consummate the marriage.

Wrena's stomach churned at the thought of Eleazar even coming near her.

The grand doors were opened by the guards. Eleazar had a sickly smile on his face as he placed a hand on Wrena's back.

"After you, my bride."

The duke stepped in beside his son. "Congratulations, my son. The queendom is lucky to have you as their future leader." He cocked his head in the direction of the wedding chamber. "Do me proud. The queendom expects an heir."

Wrena's eyes went straight to the windows as if she could find a way to escape. To the right, an enormous canopy bed stood, draped with dark red curtains, white flower petals sprinkled upon the sheets. The doors closed behind her with a *bang*, and suddenly she felt trapped.

Eleazar sauntered over to a table in the middle of the room and picked up a bottle of wine. "A wedding present," he said, setting it down. "Probably from your aunt."

She rubbed at her arms, feeling like prey caught in a snare.

"You seem so tense. Perhaps a drink will loosen you up. And look; there are strawberries as well. How lovely." He came nearer. "But not as lovely as you."

He traced the back of his hand over her arm. She shivered and wrapped her arms around her stomach. He let out a chuckle, obviously finding her reaction funny. She ground her teeth and clenched her fists. She didn't know she could have so much hate for one person.

"You can't fight me off forever," he said. "You heard what the duke said. Avarell expects an heir."

She glared at him. "I want to make something perfectly clear. I will never in my life let you lay a hand on me."

His eyes narrowed. "We'll see about that."

Before she could move away, he grabbed her by the arms.

"No!" She struggled, nails digging into Eleazar's skin. "Get off!"

She managed to pull away from him, but in doing so, her dress ripped at the shoulder.

Instantly, he pushed her against the wall, smirking. "You can make all the noise you want. I told the guards it might get loud in here and they are not to interrupt."

She slid sideways, trying to slip out of his grasp, but he grabbed her by the waist and pulled her so that her back was to him, his arms wrapped around her stomach. She thrashed, trying to claw at him, but he was out of reach.

"I love a good fight. Makes the reward all the greater." He pushed her forward toward the table in the middle of the room, trying to bend her forward.

He pressed his body into her, and her hand shot out and grabbed the bottle of wine off the table. With a force she didn't know she had, she pivoted and swung the bottle. But she missed, and the bottle caught the edge of the table. The wine bottle shattered in half, clattering to the floor.

Eleazar grabbed her arms and turned her around, and before

she could push him away, he slapped her hard in the face. She fell to the floor among the broken glass. For a moment she was shocked, unable to do anything but hold her cheek.

Seizing the opportunity, he lowered himself on top of her, lifting the skirt of her gown. She tried to fight him off, but he was strong and heavy, pushing her down to the floor. She reached out, feeling desperately around her. And then her hand touched something. Turning her neck slightly, she spotted the broken wine bottle, glinting in the candlelight.

She grasped for it, her hand stinging from it cutting her flesh, and rammed it into Eleazar's collar.

He stopped moving, his hand dropping her skirt. His eyes widened, his mouth agape, as he clutched at his wound, blood spurting out and all over the both of them.

CHAPTER TWENTY

*W*rena shook as she opened her blood-soaked palms and backed away from Eleazar. His face was streaked with purple veins as he reached a hand out toward her, a gurgled cry escaping his mouth.

Her breath hitched. Her mind raced. But battling the panic that threatened to fracture her was the loathing she felt for the man.

"You can make all the noise you want," she said, her voice flat. "The guards were told it might get loud in here and they are not to interrupt."

Eleazar bared his teeth at her, but she turned away from him.

Gathering her skirts, she raced for the wall panels, searching. There had to be an entrance to the secret passageway in here. With shaking hands, she felt along the grooves of the panels, praying to the Divine Mother she could find a pressured latch. She almost let out a cry of defeat when the first three panels yielded nothing but wallpaper. But as she pressed upon the edges of the fourth panel, it sprung back.

She pulled it open without hesitation and raced down the passageway. Not familiar with this wing of the castle, she was lost, but it didn't matter. She had to keep running as far away from Eleazar as she could. She didn't have time to wrap her head around what had just happened. There was only looking forward now. She needed to get Aurora and leave Avarell, out of the duke's control. Once the duke found out about his son, not only would her life be in danger, but Aurora's as well.

She had no choice but to go to the one person who would help her free Aurora. She only prayed that no one would spot her as she made her way to Bram's rooms.

Tori's hands were clenched the entire journey to Bram's rooms. She couldn't stop thinking about what he told her about the Queen. It was her fault the Queen was in the Rift, and if it was true that the Queen was somehow organizing a way for the Undead to get out of the Rift, if the Undead were to somehow manage to climb into Avarell, lives of the citizens would be in danger. She was apprehensive about what to do, and it was taking a lot of resolve not to throw on her black disguise and charge into the Rift to stop any of their efforts.

She knocked on his door, her mind swirling with indecisiveness.

"Lady Tori." He opened the door wider and stepped into the hall. "What is it?"

"Have you spoken with Lady Maescia?"

"No, but not for lack of trying. She's been in her lounge with the duke almost entirely since the wedding. There was a short period when the duke escorted the princess and Eleazar to the wedding chambers, but even then, there were guards stationed at the lounge door who wouldn't allow anyone access. It was as if she was being protected. Or as if the duke was preventing her from leaving."

"But why? What kind of threat would she serve?"

Before he could respond, a shadowed figure in the hall drew away their attention. Tori gasped as she took in the sight of Princess Wrena. She was shaking, and her once pristine wedding gown was now soaked with blood.

"Your Highness!" Tori took quick strides toward her with Bram close behind. The princess's face was streaked with tears. "Whose blood is that?"

"S-some of it is mine." Wrena shuddered, her eyes darting between Tori and Bram. "But most of it is Eleazar's."

"What happened?" Bram asked. "Should I fetch a guard?"

She held out her palm. "No. No, don't. Please. I'm so sorry, Your Holiness. I didn't mean to involve you in this."

Tori studied her face, noting the desperation. "Princess Wrena, you can confide in me. I promise to help you."

The princess let out a sob. "He attacked me. He hurt me. I had no choice."

Bram visibly swallowed. "Eleazar hurt you?"

With another sob, Princess Wrena nodded.

Bram's hands balled into fists. "I'll kill him myself if you haven't already done the job."

"No, no. I have to go." She looked over her shoulder and shook her head. "I have to leave. But I need Aurora first."

Bram stiffened. "Aurora? You know where she is?"

"Yes." She drew in a sniffle, nodding her head. "I'm sorry I couldn't tell you. The duke threatened me."

"Your Highness, where is she?"

Tori noted that Bram struggled to keep from losing his patience.

"She's in the dungeon."

Bram blanched. "What?"

"I can't explain fully. Not at the moment. Duke Grunmire arrested her. We need to somehow break her out of the cell. The duke knows about my love for Aurora, and when he finds out what I did to his son, he'll kill us both."

The princess seemed to be holding her breath, waiting for Bram and Tori to respond. Shock froze Bram's features, but he nodded.

"We can help you," Tori said, placing a gentle hand on Princess Wrena's arm. "I have an idea."

"Oh, blessed High Priestess," the princess said, a new set of tears breaking free. "How?"

"Being a High Priestess can open some doors for me. Along with the help of Bram—and a little friend of mine."

"Right." Bram disappeared into his room. Tori and the princess exchanged a look, confused. A moment later, Bram reemerged, setting a traveling sack just inside his door frame. "Stay here, Your Highness. Hide in my rooms until we return. They won't think to look for you here. Be ready. When we get back, we'll need to move fast."

CHAPTER TWENTY-ONE

Tori kept her eyes on the guards at the entrance of the dungeons, her High Priestess cloak billowing around her as she walked. It was anger that drove her, the need for justice snuffing out any ounce of uneasiness or fear. Aurora did not deserve to be locked up in the dungeon, especially not for simply loving someone—royalty or not.

Takumi kept his pace with her, but stayed hidden in the

shadows, bounding behind columns and plants and statues.

As Tori came closer to the entrance, a subtle movement of shadow caught her eye. Bram gave her a nod, signaling he was ready for his part of the plan, before slipping back to his hiding spot. Above her, the night sky was full of stars, and the smell of the ocean wafted around her from the winds of the bay.

One of the guards looked up, straightening to his full height as his eyes narrowed. The second guard followed his gaze to find Tori standing a mere ten feet in front of them.

"Your Holiness," the taller guard said, giving her a slight bow. "What brings you here?"

"One of the prisoners has come to realize the severity of his crimes." Tori placed her hands together as if praying. "He would like to repent and has asked for a prayer from the Divine Mother."

"I'm sorry," the shorter guard said. "No one is allowed into the dungeons after sundown."

"Alas, is it not the Divine Mother who said that time is but a curve in the map of the universe?"

"What?" the shorter guard asked, his bushy brows scrunched together.

The taller guard smacked him in the arm with the back of his hand. "Of course it was. Didn't you do your studies, Martin?"

"Oh, r-right." Martin scratched his head. "I forgot."

"I'm sorry, Your Holiness," the taller one said. "But those are the rules. You'll have to come back in the morning."

"I understand your instructions," Tori said. "But this prisoner may not have that much time. It would be against the laws of divinity to deny him a prayer of exculpation. Instead, the Divine Mother would smile upon your sanction."

"I'm afraid the duke would be far from smiling, Your Holiness," Martin said with a soft chuckle.

The taller one smacked him on the back of the head and then turned to Tori. "As much as we would like to help—"

"If it were you," she said over the end of his sentence, "would you not want to be admonished from your sins?"

"That's a lot of sins," the shorter one said. "Especially for you, Ergald."

"Would you shut your hole?" Ergald whispered through clenched teeth.

Tori held up both palms. "Let me propose something. If you let me pass, I can say a special prayer for you both now to admonish you from any sins or wrongdoings you may have committed. It will be like starting with a clean slate."

The two guards eyed each other and shrugged.

"I guess it couldn't hurt," Ergald said.

"It's not like she's bringing weapons into the dungeon," Martin replied.

Ergald nodded. "All right. We'll let you pass."

"The Divine Mother smiles upon you." She took one step closer to them. "If you would close your eyes, I can deliver your prayer."

"Close our eyes?" Ergald blinked in confusion.

"The light of the Divine Mother is best seen when your eyes are closed to the material world."

"Right," Martin said, closing his eyes right away.

"I don't know." Ergald rubbed at his chin, looking over his shoulders.

"It will take but a small minute," Tori said.

Ergald let out a breath and closed his eyes.

"And remember, the Divine Mother will know if you're peeking."

As Tori delivered her rehearsed prayer to the unsuspecting guards, Takumi came up behind Martin, a large velvet pouch between his jaws. Taking the pouch in his paws, he stealthily wrapped it around the ring of keys latched to Martin's belt to prevent the keys from making noise. He then unlatched the key ring and skittered away to where Bram hid. Bram made his way into the dungeon, quietly but quickly. When she was sure they were out of sight, Tori ended her prayer.

The guards opened their eyes. Tori smiled at them and bowed her head.

"Thank you, Your Holiness," Ergald said. "I feel... cleaner."

"You could still do with a bath," Martin said, landing him another smack on the back of the head.

As they scuffled with each other, Tori slipped into the dungeon entrance, picking up her pace to catch up with Bram and Takumi.

It took a few minutes before his eyes could adjust to the lack of light. If anything, it was the stench that kept him moving. The prisoners in the cells were barely recognizable as people; most of them appeared as small, boney clusters of dirty clothes and greasy hair. Takumi ran out in front of him, and Bram had to wonder if the fox knew for whom he searched.

He came upon a cell with a dark-haired woman crouching on the floor, facing away from him. Takumi didn't stop, but Bram had to be sure.

"Aurora?" he whispered into the darkness.

The woman craned her neck around, her long, crooked nose peeking out of her curtain of dirty hair. Wide eyes that appeared almost white stared back at him, and a grunt sounded from between a gaping mouth of rotted teeth.

Bram took a step back.

"Bram?" came a voice from farther down the corridor.

Bram's head swiveled in the direction of the voice. Takumi stood on his hind legs, gekkering and seemingly waving a paw before he lowered back down to all fours.

"Bram?" came the voice again. Aurora's voice, Bram realized, though a bit scratchy, as if she were parched.

"Aurora?" Bram raced forward and grabbed the bars of the

cell. He stared for a moment, appalled. He almost didn't recognize his cousin. Usually glamourous and pristine, Aurora stood before him in a stained, torn dress, her face and hands covered in grime.

"Bram, is it really you? Am I being set free?"

He pushed down his emotions. "We're getting you out of here. But we need to hurry."

Tori finally caught up and took a ring of keys out of the pouch in Bram's hand.

Aurora narrowed her eyes at the sight of Lady Tori. "What's going on? And is that a fox?"

Bram turned the lock and opened the cell door. "Come, cousin. Something's happened. We need to leave."

"What happened? Is it Wrena? Is she all right?"

Tori took her hand. "I promise everything will be explained. But not now; it's time to go."

"How do we get past the guards?" Aurora asked, clinging to Bram's arm.

"Leave that to Takumi," Tori said. She then bent down and handed the key ring to the fox.

Takumi took off, apparently not caring that the dangling keys were making noise. As they darted by cells, prisoners were roused by the ruckus, some of them drawn to the bars with curiosity. Bram held up his hand for them to slow down as they neared the entrance, where the guards stood sentry. Takumi ran past the guards, skidded to a stop, and then turned to face them so they could see the keys hanging from his teeth.

"What in the—?" Martin shouted.

Takumi spun around and took off, making his way toward the castle walls, which he then ascended and jumped over.

"How did it get the keys?" Martin felt around his belt as if expecting to find the key ring there.

"Little bastard. You go that way," Ergald yelled to Martin. "I'll try to cut him off on the other side."

Bram and the others waited as the guards took off after the fox. They slowly moved forward together when the guards were out of sight, and Bram double checked to make sure they were in the clear.

"Okay, let's go," he said, his arm around Aurora.

Their footsteps were quick but silent. Aurora's breaths came out in shallow gasps, and she looked over her shoulder, checking that no one spotted them. But she hadn't watched her step, and although Bram led her, her foot caught on a decorative vase along the pathway. It toppled over and smashed into pieces, the noise echoing around them.

Bram muttered a curse and pulled Aurora along. "Come on, before one of them comes back."

"Hey, who's there?" Ergald shouted as he rushed back.

"Quickly," Bram whispered, ducking his head.

"You keep going," Tori said, side stepping into the shadows. "I'll hold him off."

"You?" Aurora asked. "But—"

"Just go!" Tori waved them away, and Bram noticed her slip one of her shuriken out of her skirts before she disappeared into the darkness.

They made it to an alcove before they stopped to take a breath. Bram pressed his cheek against the wall and peeked around toward Tori and Ergald.

Ergald stood in the middle of the pathway, his sword drawn. As he came nearer to Tori's hiding spot, he suddenly started. He dropped his sword as his hand reached for his neck, where Tori's blade had landed. Aurora must have witnessed the hit as well, because she slapped a hand over her mouth to keep herself from screaming.

Ergald dropped to the ground, but Tori kept herself hidden.

"Come on," Bram said. "We need to get to my rooms."

"But what about Lady Tori?" Aurora asked.

"Don't worry. I'm quite certain she can take care of herself."

CHAPTER TWENTY-TWO

As soon as Bram opened the door, Wrena jumped up and gasped.

"Oh, my stars, you've done it!"

Aurora, dazed and anxious, hurried to her and was immediately enveloped in her embrace. Wrena swept Aurora's hair back and kissed her on the lips.

For a second, Aurora smiled, but then she took in the sight

of Wrena. Her eyes widened, and her face paled. "My love, you're bleeding. What happened?"

Wrena squeezed her eyes shut, as if wanting to erase the memory. When she opened them again, they were glassy with tears. "It was Eleazar. He... He a-attacked me." She pressed a palm against her temple. "So I defended myself."

"He attacked you? Did he...?" Aurora clenched her fists. "I'll kill him."

Wrena shook her head. "I may have already done so. I couldn't be sure, though. I had to get out of there. But no, my love. I hurt him before he could get that far."

"We need to leave," Bram said. "The duke won't care if it was an attack initiated by his son; he'll want someone's head. The sooner we get you two out of Avarell, the better."

He grabbed two cloaks from his dressing cabinet and wrapped one around Aurora.

"Your Highness," he said, handing the princess the other.

"We're leaving Avarell?" Aurora asked. "How?"

"I've hired a boat. However, we need to move fast. I didn't mention who would be aboard, but once word gets out about Eleazar, there's no doubt in my mind the helmsman will take off without you."

Aurora grabbed Wrena's shaking hands, worry in her eyes.

Wrena nodded. "Yes, yes, we need to leave."

"We'll need to keep to the shadows to get to the docks unseen." Bram grabbed the packed sack he'd set by the door.

Stepping into the hall, Bram heard footsteps coming toward them. He tensed and put a hand on the hilt of his sword. Wrena and Aurora squeezed each other's hands.

When Tori appeared in front of them, Bram released the breath he'd been holding. Takumi skittered up to them, sniffing around the princess.

"Lady Tori!" Aurora pressed her hand against her chest. "Are you all right?"

"Yes, Lady Aurora. Do not worry."

"What happened to the other guard?" Aurora asked.

"Taken care of," she replied, a look of remorse on her face. She then studied Bram, looking pointedly at the sack on his back. "You're going with them." It was more of a statement than a question.

He let out a quick sigh, nodding. "Yes. I was leaving anyway. It seems things have just moved along a lot quicker than I anticipated."

"Okay," Tori said. "Let's go then."

"Wait. What are you doing?" Bram asked.

"You'll need help getting to the dock. I can at least offer a source of distraction in case you run into trouble."

"All right," Bram said. "We're off."

"Is that your fox?" the princess asked.

"He's my partner," Tori said, turning hastily to lead them out of the castle.

PARAGON RISING

Before they even arrived at the dock, they were puzzled by the amount of noise. At first Tori thought it might be the Queen's Guard searching for the princess. But then she realized soldiers were running from the direction of the dock. As they drew closer, taking in the scene of people scurrying about, they were still unsure of what, exactly, was happening. Queen's Guard soldiers marched about, raising their voices. Boatmen were fleeing. But what caught Tori's attention the most were the large, muscular, half-naked men pushing their way through the people and knocking over crates and pieces of machinery. They carried massive swords and axes and other weapons Tori had never seen before.

The Nostidourian army had arrived.

Tori, Bram, Aurora, and the princess hid behind a stack of barrels, pulling their cloaks tightly around them. A colossal ship was anchored at the dock, the crew reeling in its dark sails. More of the Nostidourian savages jumped from the ship's deck, landing with loud thuds on the wooden planks of the dock, a feat that would have surely broken the legs of the average Avarell soldier.

Their attire consisted mostly of animal hides and leather, barely enough to conceal their massive muscles and hairy chests. Most of the Nostidourians had shaved heads, but one of them donned a thick, long braid which fell from the center of the back of his head. He was almost twice as large as most of his peers, and he carried an authority with him that was almost palpable.

A Queen's Guard soldier approached him, holding his chin up and squaring his shoulders.

"King Stoneheart, in the name of the queendom of Avarell, we request that you cease this uproar you are causing and respectfully adhere to the laws of courtesy while on our land."

The large, braided man snickered. Appearing next to him was one of his men, carrying a club with spikes hammered into it. On King Stoneheart's command, his soldier swung the club sideways. A scream filled the air as the Queen's Guard was knocked off the ground, soaring past the edge of the dock and landing in the sea.

The savage king let out a booming, mischievous laugh and clapped his soldier on the back. "Excellent, Chod."

"Grigori Stoneheart," Princess Wrena whispered, a mixture of fear and repulsion in her voice. "King of Nostidour. He's come to meet with the duke."

"And kill anyone who steps in his path, it seems," Bram added. "Looks like he brought his entire army."

Tori watched in awe as a few of the Queen's Guard fled from the docks in fright.

"What are we to do?" Aurora asked.

Bram pointed. "Just beyond that barge is our boat. It doesn't appear to be disturbed by the chaos, but getting there will prove complicated."

Takumi pawed at Tori, chittering. Before she could respond,

he took off, zigzagging through the people and the crates at full speed.

"Where is he going?" Bram asked.

"He must have a plan," Tori said.

The princess scoffed. "A fox? With a plan?"

Tori didn't answer. Instead, she watched with bated breath as Takumi climbed up a crane and onto a crate that hung from it. Sitting upon the crate, he began chewing through the rope from which it hung.

"He's going to cause a distraction," Tori said. "On my count, we run for the boat."

"Are we seriously trusting an animal?" Princess Wrena was barely able to finish her sentence before Tori shushed her.

"Get ready." Tori held her hand up, her eyes trained on Takumi's progress. "Now!"

Their heads ducked, they darted for the boat. Tori heard a rip and cast a glance over her shoulder to see that Aurora's cloak had caught on a pile of fishing equipment. She quickly slipped a shuriken out of her skirts and whipped it at the cloak, splitting it so that Aurora was free.

An ear-splitting crash boomed around them as the crate Takumi loosened burst open on the dock. Both the Nostidourian army and the remaining Queen's Guard turned to investigate the fallen crate, not noticing the fox that had jumped off and out of sight.

Tori reached the gangplank of the boat first and turned to

help the others. Bram's eyes locked with hers as he climbed aboard, their hands joined for longer than she had anticipated. He looked as if he were about to say his goodbyes.

"Tori, I—"

"Hey!" came a low voice.

They both turned to see one of the Nostidourians stomping toward them. His axe was raised in one hand.

Tori pushed Bram onto the boat just as the axe flew through the air. It missed Bram by a hair.

The soldier growled as he grabbed the end of the gangplank and lifted it. Tori spread out her hands, fighting to keep her balance. When the soldier lifted the plank higher, Tori fell to one knee. She grabbed a shuriken and lobbed it at his head. It struck him between the eyes. As he shouted in pain, he dropped the gangplank, which landed askew. Tori leapt back and grabbed for the boat, missing by a centimeter. Bram caught her hand. Tori's heart hammered through her chest.

She heard the engine start. Kicking her feet up on the side of the boat, she used Bram's hand and heaved herself upward. As soon as she was high enough, Bram grabbed her by the waist and lifted her onto the safety of the deck. She let herself fall into his arms, gasping for breath and begging her heartbeat to slow.

The boat was already yards away from the dock before Tori released him.

"What happened?" Aurora asked. "Lady Tori, were you meant to leave Avarell?"

PARAGON RISING

Tori gazed back at the dock, at the brutality of the Nostidourians making their mark on the queendom. She shook her head. "Looks like I don't have a choice."

CHAPTER TWENTY-THREE

ori felt a tug on the hem of her skirt. She looked down, surprised to see Takumi pawing her dress, his nose twitching as he gazed at her.

"Takumi? How did you get here?"

"He jumped on board when we did." Aurora bent down and scratched him between his ears. "He's awfully fast."

Behind her, Princess Wrena wrapped her arms around herself

and shivered, her eyes trained on Avarell as the boat made its way farther into the Maudric Ocean.

"Your Highness," Tori said. "How are you faring?"

Wrena opened her mouth as if to speak, but no sound came out. She shook her head, blinking rapidly.

"I think the shock is finally hitting her," Tori said to Bram. She rushed forward and took Wrena's hand, studying the wound in her palm.

"It's from the broken glass." Wrena's voice was flat, like she was talking in her sleep.

Tori reached into a pocket in her cloak and took out a small tin. "This should reduce the swelling and kill the bacteria. But we'll need a cloth to wrap it."

Wrena slowly lifted her eyes to Tori's. "Take a clean piece from my gown, if you can find it. I'm going to burn this dress anyway, the second I have a chance."

Aurora approached, her moves cautious. "Wrena. It's going to be all right."

She turned to Aurora, but she seemed to be looking right through her. "I wasn't thinking clearly. Perhaps I left too hastily. I should have made sure Theo was safe first."

"They won't touch him," Aurora said, her shoulders hunched. "He's a child. And the future King."

Silent tears trickled down Wrena's cheeks. "If only I were sure."

"You had no other choice, Your Highness." Bram dropped

his sack on the deck. "It was the only opportunity to leave Avarell undetected." He glanced at Tori and gave her a nod, a secretive look in his eye. "I'm sure Her Holiness will pray to the Divine Mother for Theo's safety."

Lady Tori nodded solemnly. "Of course." She turned her sad eyes to Wrena. "It goes without question, Your Highness."

She turned away from them for a moment, reaching out to the railing as the boat teetered on the waves. The princess wasn't the only one experiencing the delayed onset of shock. Tori was on a boat in the middle of the ocean with a runaway princess and the only man she ever thought about while tyrants raged upon Avarell.

Takumi snaked around her legs, making noises as if he were concerned. He raised himself up and placed his paws on her leg. She stroked his head and reluctantly smiled.

"What's the plan now?" Aurora asked, wringing her hands.

At first, they simply exchanged silent glances.

"I'm going to Gadleigh," Bram said, breaking the silence. "It was my plan all along. I just got a big push forward, that's all."

Aurora set a hand on his arm. "I'm sorry, Bram."

"No, don't apologize. I would do it all over again if I had to. I'm just sorry it took me so long to find out where you were."

"I sent a letter to my uncle a while ago," the princess said. "After you depart at Gadleigh, Aurora and I will continue on to Creoca. That is…" She turned to Aurora and took her hand. "… if you'll join me."

Aurora squeezed her hand, glad it was the uninjured one. "I'll follow you anywhere."

Wrena nodded, a hint of a smile creeping onto her face for the smallest of seconds. "We will seek sanctuary with my uncle. I have a feeling I wouldn't be welcome in Gadleigh anyway."

Tori nodded, remembering that Gadleigh was the home of Prince Liam, who had been engaged to Wrena under a treaty that was later broken by Duke Grunmire. The royals of Gadleigh had left outraged when the duke rescinded the engagement along with their alliance.

"And you, Lady Tori?" Aurora asked.

She stared at Aurora. It was in that moment she realized she was lost, without a plan. She had unfinished business to attend to in Avarell, and she had a family to return to in Drothidia. But it seemed that this group needed her now, in this moment, and something inside her told her she was meant to help them. "I will sail with you to Gadleigh and assure your safe arrival. And then I shall return with the boat. I am still pledged to the queen regent, and with the Nostidour army wreaking havoc upon Avarell, she will most definitely need my assistance."

"How will you explain your absence?" Princess Wrena asked.

"I'm hoping my handmaid, Finja, will cover for me. Besides, I think the duke will have enough to worry about once he finds out about his son."

CHAPTER TWENTY-FOUR

All Lady Maescia wanted to do was go to her chambers. It had been a long, grueling day, and she'd been trapped in the lounge with the duke for hours now. Her eyelids were heavy, and her heart burned with shame. She hoped Wrena was all right. Remembering the look on her face when she took her vows, Lady Maescia had the deepest desire to fall to her knees in front of her niece and apologize.

She glanced at the duke, who stood at the window with a malicious smirk on his face, no doubt reveling in the fact that he had one more hand on the reins of the queendom. He swirled the contents of his glass and sipped at it loudly. Lady Maescia stood, wondering if she had it in her to push him from the window the same way she had King Henry.

A knock at the door interrupted her thoughts. Without waiting for a reply, a Queen's Guard burst into the room.

"Your Grace, Duke Grunmire, there's been an incident."

Lady Maescia clenched a fist against her heart. "What happened. Is it the princess?"

"No, Your Grace. It's Prince Eleazar."

The glass slipped from the duke's hands, shattering to the floor. He pounced upon the soldier and grabbed him by his uniform. "What happened? Where is he?"

"He's been injured, sire. He's in the wedding chambers."

The duke threw the soldier out of his way and raced out of the room. Lady Maescia hurried after him, her concern more for Wrena than for Eleazar. Eleazar might be injured, but what of her niece? If anything happened to her, she wouldn't know what she might do.

They sped through the corridors toward the royal wedding chambers, Lady Maescia's heart beating so hard she thought it would burst from her chest. It was hard to keep up with the duke and his guards, but apprehension pushed her forward.

When they reached the chambers, the duke threw open the

door and let out a curse. As he rushed to his son's side, Lady Maescia's eyes searched the room. But her niece was nowhere to be seen.

"My boy," the duke cried. He got down on the floor and pulled Eleazar's form into his lap. Blood covered the new prince. A thick cloth was pressed against his collar, already soaked through. His skin was pale, and his eyes drooped. But he was alive. "What happened here?"

Eleazar gasped for air. "She... she stabbed me." He grimaced, obviously finding it hard to speak.

"Stabbed?"

Eleazar tried to answer his father, but he was too weak and in too much pain.

"Guards!" the duke called. "Take my son to the infirmary. And be careful about it!"

Lady Maescia watched in shock as the guards carried him out of the chambers.

"What do you know of this?" the duke shouted at her as soon as they were alone.

"How could I know anything? I was with you the entire time. But if she did it, she must have had a reason."

The duke scowled at her, seemingly ready to retaliate, but another guard charged into the room.

"Sire, forgive me, but I have news."

"More news?" The duke clenched his jaw. "Well, out with it."

"Two guards have been found dead, my Lord. The ones tending to the dungeons."

A vein was visible in the duke's temple, and another one in his neck. His face turned red. "What about the prisoners? Are they all accounted for?"

"One cell is empty, my Lord."

The duke grabbed him by the shirt and pulled him closer. "Which prisoner?"

The guard swallowed, sparing a glance at the queen regent before he continued. "It was Lady Aurora, sire."

The duke released his hold on him, his face reddening with rage.

"Also, King Grigori Stoneheart has arrived with his army. They're headed to the castle as we speak."

The duke turned swiftly and let out a guttural scream, grabbing the edge of a nearby serving table and violently upending it.

"Prepare the throne room," he said to the guard. His breath came out in rapid bursts as he paced. "This was all your niece's doing." He stopped to point a finger in her face. "She attempted to kill my son and somehow broke her lover out of her cell. When I find her—*them*—they'll pay dearly for this mess."

"Could it really be a coincidence that all hell breaks loose the very night in which the Nostidour army is scheduled to arrive? It's *your* fault, Duke Grunmire. You've infuriated the Divine Mother and have invited evil unto the castle. I swear, if something happened to Wrena, heads will roll."

"Oh, I guarantee heads will be rolling, Your Grace." He thrust his finger into her shoulder. "But, mark my words, it will most likely be yours."

CHAPTER TWENTY-FIVE

*T*he voice of one of Hira's crew sounded from the crow's nest. "A boat, Your Highness! A small one."

Hira glanced up at her crew member, almost invisible against the night sky. Her lookout pointed in the direction of the spotted boat. Hira took out her spyglass and searched for the craft.

"Do you recognize it, Your Highness?" Zhadé asked from beside her.

"No, but the build of it does resemble Avarellian craftsmanship." She collapsed the spyglass and called to her crew. "Bring us around. Let's see who's on that boat."

It didn't take long for the *Diamond Palm* to catch up to the small boat. The late hour and the darkness helped to conceal their approach. Hira had to give the helmsman at the wheel credit for attempting to escape the large ship once he spotted them coming, no matter how futile the effort was. As soon as they were close enough, Hira's crew threw out grappling hooks, the ropes tugging the two seacraft together.

Hira surveilled the boat as the crew secured the ropes. The helmsman was visibly shaken. If there was anyone else on board, he didn't bother to alert them. Instead, he ran to the nearest railing and jumped ship.

At the sight of his reaction, Hira scoffed.

"Should we go after him, Your Highness?" Zhadé asked.

"No. Don't bother. But let's see if we can find out what this small boat is doing so far away from home port."

"What was that noise?" Princess Wrena whispered into the darkness of the room.

Takumi gekkered and sprinted out the room. Figuring he left to investigate the noise, Tori sat up straight, her eyes adjusting to the darkness.

The mixture of exhaustion and the rocking of the boat had caused them all to fall asleep. Though the room below deck was small and cramped, they had used their cloaks to lie upon, huddled together as they drifted off. Now, the repetitive thumping that sounded above deck woke them, and Tori had a feeling in her gut that something was wrong.

Bram shot to his feet. The thumping stopped, but they were now followed by hard footsteps.

"Get behind me," Bram whispered, drawing his sword.

Tori ignored his request, drawing her kunai and standing beside him.

Three female pirates swung down into the small room, brandishing weapons.

"Stay back," Bram warned them.

The pirate soldiers advanced, the one in the middle wielding her staff. Bram swung, but his sword did nothing to damage the staff. Momentarily paralyzed with shock, Bram missed his opportunity to block the pirate's next swing. His sword clattered to the floor.

Tori whipped her kunai at the woman, but she was quick to shift her staff. The kunai landed with a resounding thunk on the surface of the staff. She took a step back as the woman pried the kunai out of the staff and inspected it. The other two pirate soldiers held their weapons out in warning.

Another pirate descended into the room. This one taller and

darker than the others, donned with golden tattoos. The pirate who had caught the kunai handed over the weapon.

"Four, Your Highness," the tattooed one called.

"Four," came the voice from above deck. The source of the voice entered the room, joining her crew. "I always did like that number."

When she came into full view, Princess Wrena gasped. She leaned her head closer to Tori and Bram and whispered, "That's Hira Kaliskan, pirate queen of the Crystal Islands."

"What have we got here, Zhadé?" the pirate queen asked.

Zhadé handed her the weapon. "I believe it's a kunai, Your Highness. A weapon originating in Drothidia, popular among their military."

Queen Hira snickered. "I'd hardly call it military. From what I've heard, their army has been disbanded in the name of peace."

Tori wanted to speak up, to tell them that their army still existed, however small it was. Instead she tightened her jaw.

"Let's get everyone above deck," Queen Hira said, eying the group. "The stench down here is unbearable."

"I wouldn't try anything stupid if I were you," Zhadé said to them. "We've got reinforcements above deck. I'm afraid you're outnumbered."

The pirates urged them forward with their weapons, forcing them above deck. Bram kept his hand on the small of Tori's back, and Wrena locked hands with Aurora.

The hint of pink in the sky revealed that dawn was upon

them. Though the wind was cold, it was welcoming after being enclosed in the small room beneath deck.

A piercing squawk sliced through the air, and Tori's eyes widened in awe as she watched a phoenix swoop down to land on a metal plate on Queen Hira's shoulder.

"What an interesting mix we have here." The pirate queen paced, studying the group, who was surrounded by ten of her crew, each holding their weapons at the ready. The captees stood stiffly, all eyes focused on the phoenix. Aurora held a splayed hand against her bodice, seemingly holding her breath.

Queen Hira stopped in front of Tori and narrowed her eyes. "The origin of this weapon leads me to believe that either it belongs to you or it was given to this soldier as a gift." Queen Hira's head gestured at Bram.

"It is mine," Tori said.

Queen Hira smirked. "What is a High Priestess doing with such a weapon?"

She glanced at Bram. His eyes and the slight shake of his head told her to go along with the ruse. Internally, she had to agree. If they believed she was a High Priestess, she might be able to use the ruse to her advantage.

"I am not naïve to the dangers of the world. I carried the kunai for protection."

"Unfortunately, you don't seem to have the skills to use it." Queen Hira slapped the flat of the blade against her palm. "Therefore, deeming it a waste in your hands."

Tori bit back a rebuttal.

"Still, I'm impressed that a holy woman would appear ready to fight." Queen Hira slipped the weapon into her belt. "I love finding treasure."

"What have you done with our helmsman?" Princess Wrena asked, her chin held high.

Zhadé took a step closer, as if preparing to protect their queen.

"Ah yes, Your Highness," Queen Hira said, snickering when Wrena flinched. "Are you surprised I recognize you?"

"I suppose not, since I also recognize you."

"How could you not? I don't suppose there are many pirate queens sailing the Maudric Ocean, are there?"

"Our helmsman," the princess repeated. "Where is he?"

"I'm afraid he abandoned you, Your Highness. Jumped ship. It makes me question the loyalty of Avarellians to their royal leaders."

"And what do you want from us?" Princess Wrena asked.

"Now, now, princess. It can't be hard to figure out. After all, I'm a pirate. So, in keeping with pirate codes of behavior, I've captured your tiny little boat, and now I'm taking you hostage."

"For what purpose?" Bram asked, teeth clenched.

"The queen regent will never cooperate with you," Princess Wrena said.

"My apologies, Your Highness. Don't take it personally. But if you haven't heard, the nine realms are on the brink of a war, and I need all the aces my pockets can hold."

CHAPTER TWENTY-SIX

ira's phoenix circled the boats as her crew escorted the group onto the *Diamond Palm*. She led them to the forecastle, where they were placed in the sitting room. The Avarell soldier's brow furrowed at Hira.

"Look what I found, Your Highness," Zhadé said, entering behind them and holding a fox by the back of its neck. "It was on the boat."

Hira turned toward the group. "Does this little creature belong to any of you?"

The High Priestess tightened her lips for a second. "He's mine."

Zhadé set the fox down, and he ran to the High Priestess's feet.

Hira let out a chuckle. "I have to say, Your Holiness, you are full of surprises."

"Should I detain the animal, Your Highness?" Zhadé asked.

"No, that won't be necessary. I have a feeling he is faithful to our holy woman here. And I don't think she's a threat." Hira rested her hands on her hips and leaned against a serving table. "You're probably wondering why I haven't thrown you in the brig," she said.

"It crossed my mind," Bram replied, keeping his shoulders squared.

"First of all, you're surrounded by a hundred Crystal Island pirates. I doubt you'd be able to escape if you tried. Second of all, I'm in the presence of a royal princess and a High Priestess. I may be ruthless, but even I wouldn't tempt fate and enrage the Divine Mother by treating them with anything less than respect."

"You kidnap us yet claim to respect us?" the princess asked.

"It's all about knowing which lines not to cross, Your Highness." She motioned to the chairs in the room. "Please, make yourselves comfortable."

The group exchanged glances, unsure of what to do. Princess

Wrena was the first to sit, smoothing out her gown.

"If you don't mind me asking, Princess, is there a reason your dress is full of blood?"

Wrena opened her mouth, but it was clear by her expression she didn't know where to begin.

"Begging your forgiveness," the High Priestess said, "I suspect the princess is in no mood to relive what she's been through at the moment."

"Especially not in the presence of a kidnapping pirate," the soldier added.

Hira's glance flitted between them. "If you don't tell me," she said in a mocking voice, "I'll only suspect the worst."

"Well, you have your answer then," the princess replied.

Hira bit back a laugh, surprised by the princess's boldness. "Is that why you have a holy woman with you? So she can pray to the Divine Mother for your forgiveness?"

Princess Wrena gritted her teeth. "I had to defend myself. My... my so-called *husband* forced himself on me. And so I fended him off."

"Husband?" Hira crossed her arms over her chest. "I thought your wedding would be taking place at month's end. All the nations were invited, from what I heard."

"It was moved up."

The princess would not look up from her lap. Hira narrowed her eyes. "Is he dead? Your so-called husband?"

"I don't know."

Hira paced, exchanging a look with Zhadé. Her partner had to know how she felt, that she had a bit of compassion for the princess. After all, they both knew what it was like to suffer an attack.

"If there's one thing I despise, it's men who don't comprehend boundaries. If it were me, I would have killed him. And I would have made sure he stayed dead."

It was only then that Princess Wrena looked up. They locked eyes, and Hira could see the question in them.

"Do you know the history of the Crystal Islands?" Hira asked, strutting to the small bar at the side of the room and pouring herself a drink.

"Only what I've heard in tales," Princess Wrena said. "They are more like ghost stories, filled with monsters."

"Yes, monsters, indeed. We were once a peaceful nation. Bountiful. Beautiful. Full of love and light. Until Nostidour ambushed us. They staged a major attack, intending to conquer our land. They killed off all the men and… raped all our mothers."

Princess Wrena visibly swallowed. The brunette woman beside her snaked her arm through hers.

"We were prisoners in our own realm, suffering torture and torment. As we girls—the daughters of the island—grew up, our fear of what would happen to us as we got older pushed us to rebel. We banded together. We swore it would no longer go on as it had. So, we became strong and learned to fight. We sought revenge, and we took back what was ours. We eventually pushed out the Nostidourian savages from our home. Word got out of the battles, of course, and because of our brutal and merciless ways, we were labelled as pirates. Mostly because we didn't fear slashing their throats."

Hira felt her muscles tense up in her neck. Her pulse was elevated, and tunnel vision made it hard for her to focus on her captees. Zhadé was suddenly by her side and ran a hand slowly down Hira's arm. They tilted their head and locked eyes with her. Hira took a deep breath, nodding, and placed a hand on Zhadé's cheek.

Hira turned her attention to the group, noting how intently the princess gazed at them. It didn't go unnoticed how close the brunette in the dirty clothes sat to her. There was something more there. Yet another reason for Hira to sympathize with the princess.

"In the end," Hira said, "there is fear, and there is love. And in love, there is balance."

"And where there is love," Zhadé added, "there is no room for questions. It just is."

The brunette laced her fingers with the princess's. There was a small hint of a smile on her face. "Maybe we should become pirates."

Princess Wrena did not smile back. Instead, she nodded and squeezed the brunette's hand.

Hira clapped her hands together once. "Right. There's a

washroom in the back. I'll have one of my crew bring the two of you something clean to wear. You may be my prisoners, but I can't have you stinking up my ship, can I?"

CHAPTER TWENTY-SEVEN

In the belly of the banquet hall, Lady Maescia tried to keep her trembling to a minimum. Around her, the Lords and Ladies of the court wandered to their seats, their faces full of confusion. It no doubt puzzled them that a spontaneous welcome feast was being held, but what really perplexed them was for whom the feast was honoring.

Ignoring the usual plethora of meats and breads and

succulent dishes, all eyes were trained on King Grigori Stoneheart of Nostidour. He sat beside her at the head table, his second in command, Chod, at his side. The duke sat on the other side of Lady Maescia, making her feel trapped. She inched her plate away, acid roiling in her stomach.

"Lady Maescia," Stoneheart said, "your people stare as if we are animals uncaged who have not been invited to join you."

The queen regent reached for her wine glass, but her hands shook too fiercely. She withdrew and kept her hands in her lap. "I suppose you've arrived earlier than expected, and I had not had the chance to properly inform them of our much-anticipated unification."

"They will see, in time," the duke added, "that an alliance with your kingdom will greatly benefit all citizens of Avarell and bring order to the nine realms."

King Stoneheart eyed him warily. "Hmm. Yes, well, it is not their approval I seek, but rather their obedience."

"Yes, of course. Very well put." The duke dropped his eyes to his wine and took a sip.

"Tell me, where is your princess? I thought she would be joining us."

The duke and Lady Maescia exchanged a glance.

"She is otherwise preoccupied," Duke Grunmire said.

King Stoneheart slipped a curved blade from his belt and picked his nail with it. "Do you know what I enjoy most about carving out the tongue of liars, Duke?"

The duke visibly swallowed.

"The sound." The king stared at him a moment, seemingly letting his words sink in before he let out a humorless laugh.

"There's been an incident," Lady Maescia said, not wanting to be the victim of his blade. "It seems the princess and her new betrothed had a disagreement of sorts that ended very badly."

"How badly? Is one of them dead?"

"She stabbed my son in their wedding chambers," the duke put in. "Left him to die. Luckily her aim was not skilled. He is recovering in the infirmary."

"And the princess?"

"Escaped."

Stoneheart raised a bushy brow. "Some might question the integrity of a realm where a princess who has attempted to murder the prince consort slips through the hands of the Queen's Guard." He let out a chuckle and elbowed Chod. "This is what happens when a woman is in charge, right Chod?"

Chod grunted in response.

"And what of the ill-stricken queen?" Stoneheart asked.

"Quarantined." The duke had the audacity to let a small smile appear on his face, as if he were responsible for the Queen's state. "In the meantime, Lady Maescia is regent, and I her advisor. As for the fugitive princess, I believe she had help in her efforts; a number of our court have turned up missing as well, no doubt conspirators in her escape. And two of my guards were found killed. I can't imagine the princess would have done all of this on her own."

"Why not?" Stoneheart asked, smirking. "She attacked your son; what makes you think she wouldn't lash out on anyone else? This princess of yours sounds rather feisty. Perhaps I was wrong in not pushing for a union with her. I'm sure she would have been a lot of fun." He let out a mischievous laugh, making a vile gesture that Chod found amusing.

Lady Maescia subtly placed a hand on her chest, feigning the need to cough. In reality, she was straining to hold her tongue.

"Lady Maescia." Stoneheart leaned closer to her, and she did her best not to recoil. "Someone must have information. Perhaps a witness. Or someone who helped her escape. Chances are someone in this dreadful hole of a town saw something that could lead us to the princess's whereabouts." He took a swig of his wine, then turned to Chod. "What do you say we show the duke and queen regent how to hold a proper interrogation."

"I assure you," the duke began, "I can be very thorough in my—"

"Gather them now!" King Stoneheart rose to his feet so quickly his chair fell back from under him. "Ladies and Lords of Avarell, I demand your attention."

The room went silent, looks of horror marking the faces of the courtiers.

Stoneheart flexed his back muscles as he came around the table, planting himself center stage for everyone to see. Chod was close behind. Lady Maescia and the duke rose to their feet but remained on the far side of the table. A nervous twist formed in the queen regent's gut, and she wondered what the king of Nostidour had in mind.

"I have just been informed that the crowned princess, Wrena of Avarell, has fled the scene of a crime. Two dead and one seriously injured. In my experience, such circumstances usually involve a witness or two—not to the actual crime, per se, but perhaps to her fleeing. Now, I hate to start our relations on a sour note, but finding the princess is vitally important, both to you and to our progress. So that just leaves the question: which of you will come forward and tell me what I want to hear?"

The crowd rumbled with low mumbles, but no one spoke up. Lady Maescia said silent prayers in her head. She still felt guilty about having Nils slash out one of her Lady's eyes from the interrogation about the Queen's birthday celebration. She didn't want any more bloodshed.

"Not one," Stoneheart said. "Interesting. Duke Grunmire, send me your executioner."

The duke, pursing his lips, signaled for Nils to join Stoneheart at the front of the stage. Stoneheart then signaled for Chod to enter the crowd. Chod clomped into the masses, and if it hadn't been for his size, Lady Maescia would have lost sight of him. When he reemerged, he had Lord Canterley gripped by the arm. Nils reached the king's side, and Stoneheart clapped him on the back, almost making him stumble. Chod pushed Lord Canterley down belly-first on the stage and held him in place.

"Good man," Stoneheart said to Nils. "Cut off his head."

Nils furrowed his brow, looking back over his shoulder at the duke for confirmation. The duke, however, seemed to be too shocked to concur.

"Executioner," Stoneheart said. "I gave you an order."

Nils was at a loss of what to do. He undoubtedly found it against the norm to take orders from another nation's king. Nils hesitated, his fingers fidgeting with the axe handle on his belt.

Lady Maescia was sure Nils's heart was racing as fast as hers. Yet neither of them spoke up against the king.

Stoneheart let out a sigh and rolled his eyes. "Chod," was all he said.

Chod didn't spare a second. He raised his spiked club and hammered it down on Lord Canterley's head in a matter of seconds. The crowd, shocked by the unexpected move, took a moment before they could even think to react to the revolting act. The Lords and Ladies in the front of the crowd were tainted with splattered blood and brain matter. Lady Maescia's breath stuck in her throat, and she was afraid to move for fear of vomiting all over her dress. Beside her, the duke's face went pale.

"Still no one willing to come forward?" Stoneheart waited a moment, scanning the room. Dazed faces gaped back at him. "Then we shall try again tomorrow, at which time we shall take *two* heads. And the number will double every day until someone gives me a satisfactory answer."

PARAGON RISING

˚⊙⊛⊙˚

Lady Maescia instructed the nursemaid to pack a few more of Prince Theo's belongings. A hired man stood at the door, ready to escort the prince to a carriage that waited in the shadows to take him away.

Theo stood watching the whole ordeal, tears forming in his eyes. "What did I do wrong, Aunt Maescia?"

"Oh, darling." She pulled him into a hug. "You did nothing wrong. But you are no longer safe here. There are some bad people in Avarell, and it is with the deepest expression of love that I put you out of harm's way."

"I can fight too," he said.

She almost laughed, smoothing a hand over his hair. "You are very brave, my dear. And I have no doubt you will one day be the greatest warrior to ever exist. But things are extremely complex right now, and it is not in the best interest of the queendom for you to stay here."

He nodded, but she could tell he was not happy with her answer.

She turned to the man at the door. "You will head north and cross the Phoenix Sea to Tokuna. You are to seek sanctuary for him until I can send word that it is safe for him to return."

"Is that why Wrena left?" Prince Theo asked. "Because of the bad people?"

She bit her lip for a moment, contemplating what to say. "Yes, bad people made your sister leave."

"Why can't I go where she is?"

She squeezed his hand, fighting back tears. When Theo left, she would be alone, with no more family by her side. And she had no way of knowing if she would ever see them again. "I wish I knew where that was, dear Theo. But believe me, wherever she is, I just hope she's safe."

CHAPTER TWENTY-EIGHT

Tori watched as Queen Hira's phoenix swooped from the main topsail to the bowsprit of the ship. At one point, when it crossed the sun's rays, it cast a shadow on her face. When it landed, it let out a mighty cry, ruffled its feathers, and released a burst of fire. Tori blinked in shock. Instead of the normal golden-orange fire she had seen on the odd occasion when observing phoenixes, this one's fire was a hot blue.

"His name is Fury."

Tori turned to face Queen Hira, who had appeared beside her.

"I've never seen one that spat blue fire before," Tori said.

"Ah, then you've never seen an alpha. Until now, that is."

"An alpha?"

"When phoenixes are born, they are omegas. The omega phoenixes breathe golden fire. But at the end of their lifespan, when a phoenix bursts into flames and dies, one of two things happens. In most cases, the phoenix stays dead, passes on to the land of eternal peace. But on the rare occasion, when the phoenix's will is strong enough, it becomes an alpha. Alpha phoenixes are on their next life. They are stronger and more powerful, their fire—which now takes on the hotter blue hue— is more deadly. They are the leaders. Other phoenixes will follow the alpha unquestioningly."

"Why has no one ever taught me this?" Tori wondered out loud.

"Probably because it almost never happens. And there are few who have witnessed an alpha. And from what I understand, the phoenixes who carried the fever die out, never to evolve to an alpha."

Fury squawked and jumped into the air, circling the ship before landing on Queen Hira's metal shoulder plate. Takumi jumped up from his resting place and came over to stand on his hind feet, sniffing in the direction of the phoenix. Tori stared at the bird in wonder. She had never been so close to one before.

Tentatively, she reached out to stroke its glorious feathers. "So, Fury was never sick?"

"None of the phoenixes from our side of the ocean contracted the disease."

Fury bowed its head and stretched out its neck, allowing Tori to touch its feathers. Tori gasped when she felt the soft texture. It tickled her fingertips. She smiled, and Fury let out a coo.

"I didn't know they made that noise."

"He only does it around people he likes." Queen Hira gave Tori a wink. Takumi gekkered, and Tori let out a small laugh, thinking he was jealous.

Over Hira's shoulder, Tori noticed Zhadé approaching with Bram, Aurora, and Princess Wrena in tow. Hira followed her gaze and placed her fists on her hips.

"Much better," Queen Hira said. "I hope the water was warm enough for you, Your Highness."

"It was. Thank you."

"I apologize for not having any of the gowns you are used to."

"I suppose wearing trousers and leather vests will take a little getting used to," the princess said, "but they're a thousand times better than a bloody wedding dress."

"Now that you're washed up, I might just allow you to join us for dinner."

"Why are you being nice to us?" Aurora asked. Bram tried to shush her.

"I can just as easily be cruel to you, Lady Aurora. Would you prefer that?"

"Did I see you petting that phoenix, Lady Tori?" Bram asked, his interjection an apparent attempt to change the conversation.

"You did," Tori said. "His name is Fury. Queen Hira was just explaining how the phoenixes on her side of the ocean never contracted the fever."

"Really?" Princess Wrena asked. "How peculiar."

"Not really," Hira said. "After all, it makes sense if you understand how the disease came about."

"What do you mean?"

The pirate queen narrowed her eyes at the princess. "Do you mean your father never mentioned the origin of the sickness?"

"My father?"

"Yes. Good King Henry." Hira scoffed. "I suppose you were probably too young. There's so much you don't know about him—your own father. Some of the biggest problems the nine realms have seen were his doing."

The princess's demeanor went from complacent to furious. "I beg your pardon, but you don't know what you're talking about."

Queen Hira and Zhadé exchanged a look. "Don't I?"

"Would you care to elaborate?" Bram asked.

She let out a sigh. "Not now. I don't like to be upset while I eat. Perhaps another time. For now, let us depart for the dining chambers."

PARAGON RISING

◦⟋⟍❊⟋⟍◦

Queen Hira did not revisit the subject of Wrena's father. Instead, she drank too much during dinner and retired early. Her crew escorted the captees to a small bunking chamber for the night. Still, it was better than the cold, hard floor they had slept on in the small hired boat.

As they were preparing for bed, Tori slipped out the remainder of her shuriken and hid them under her pillow. Takumi was already asleep at the foot of her bunk.

Bram cleared his throat and approached her. "You weren't searched for more weapons?"

"No. I think the Queen didn't want to further tempt the wrath of the Divine Mother by imposing her power over a holy woman. But it doesn't matter. We are outnumbered. There's no way we're getting out of here. Not by fighting the pirates. Besides, I have a better idea."

"What?"

"Queen Hira hates the Nostidourians. Perhaps they would be willing to fight alongside Gadleigh against their enemy and Avarell."

"You think they would?"

"I think Queen Hira would do anything to destroy Nostidour, yes. If she had the strength of the Gadleigh army behind her, her chances of defeating them would double."

"It's worth a shot," Bram said. "What do you think Queen Hira meant when she brought up King Henry?"

"I'm not sure. I don't remember hearing anything specifically about him when I was growing up in Drothidia. Only that Avarell, as a whole, was a realm that put itself first. They would play no part in helping us in our fight against Khadulan. I was always taught that Avarell was our enemy because of it."

Bram smirked. "You're not the first person to refer to me as an enemy in the last week."

"I never saw you as one."

His eyes flitted over her face. She took a step back.

"But all that talk of the princess's father got me thinking. I should tell her about her mother."

Bram blanched. "Do you really think that's a good idea?"

"The longer we wait to tell her, the worse she'll take it. She needs to know the truth."

Bram regarded her a moment longer. "You're right. You're right."

Tori placed a gentle hand on his arm and squeezed it, and then she walked past him and toward the princess.

"Your Highness," Tori said, her voice small. "I need to speak to you about something important."

"What is it?"

"There's something I've been keeping from you. Something you need to know. I'm just frightened of how you'll take it."

"Lady Tori, you're worrying me. What do you need to tell me?"

"It's about your mother."

"What about her?"

Tori spared Bram a quick glance before she continued. "The night of the birthday banquet, I found myself in the high tower. I made my way to your mother's room, and when I got inside, I found her chained to the bed."

"Chained?" The princess's hands flew to her mouth. "Whatever for?"

"She was being held captive there. My first instinct was to rescue her. But when I released her from the chains, the Queen... tried to attack me."

"What do you mean? Why would she attack you?"

"I hadn't seen it at first, but her skin was gray, and there was no color in her eyes. Wrena, I'm so sorry. Your mother is no longer alive. She is Undead."

"What?" Wrena shook her head. "No. No." She backed away from Tori and pulled at her own hair. She paced, wailing and rubbing at her arms. Aurora reached for her, but she flinched away. "No. It's not true." Wrena's body shook. Then she crouched down on the ground, covered her mouth, and her body jerked, as if she were going to heave up her insides.

Aurora wrapped her arms around herself, her head dropped down in silence. It took a while before Wrena's sobs diminished. She stood as if she wanted to say something. So Tori waited.

"What happened?" Wrena asked. "I want to know."

"I confronted Lady Maescia and asked her how your mother became ill. She told me they had been out together one day and drifted too far into the woods by the castle. They came upon an Undead, and it chased them. Your mother was not as fast as your aunt, and she was bit. Your aunt managed to pull her away, helped her escape the Undead, and they ran. But it wasn't long after that she fell ill."

Wrena let out a shuddered breath. "Why didn't she tell someone?"

"At first it was because your mother asked her not to. But after she was no longer coherent, it was the duke. He had information about your aunt that could have made her look like a traitor. He threatened to use this information against her if she were to tell anyone about your mother's true state."

Wrena cried softly and wrapped her arms tightly around herself. This time when Aurora reached out to her, she didn't move away. Wrena buried her head in Aurora's shoulder and let the sobs come.

CHAPTER TWENTY-NINE

$\mathcal{Z}$hadé threw open the cabin door, allowing the morning sun to bathe them in warmth. Tori shielded her eyes, and Takumi sprinted out of the room.

"Wake up, prisoners," Zhadé called. "It's time to swab the deck."

"What?" Aurora asked, sweeping her hair out of her face.

"It's part of your imprisonment. The pirate queen can't let it get out that all she does to her prisoners is give them food and shelter and let them take baths. What kind of reputation would proceed her?"

They followed them to the middle of the boat, where Zhadé handed them the items they'd need. With a foamy sponge and a bucket of water, Tori went to work on the bow of the boat. Aurora was farther back, moaning and groaning about having to do manual labor. Bram scrubbed hard, but he seemed to be continuously going over the same spot for longer than was necessary. The princess wiped at the wooden planks rather than scrubbing them, checking after each swipe of the hand if the wood looked any cleaner. Takumi sat beside the princess, sniffing the same plank of wood she was cleaning. But Tori let herself fall into the job. It helped her think. It was much like the chores she did back home with her family, and if she closed her eyes, she could imagine her mother was just behind her baking bread in the oven.

"Ah, hard at work, I see," Queen Hira announced as she came above deck. She stretched and flexed her arms and back, adjusting her hat. She then proceeded to scratch at her wrist.

Tori had noticed the Queen doing so now and then. She particularly worried her wrist during dinner the night before.

Tori stood, dropping her sponge in the bucket. "Your Highness, may I have a word?"

"Your Holiness, it is very unlike a woman of the spirit to complain about servitude."

"No, it's not that. I wanted to speak to you about two things. The first is that I noticed your scar is bothering you."

Queen Hira's smile faltered. "It's nothing."

"It's just that I'm well versed in herbal remedies. I happen to have a salve with me—"

"With you?" The Queen crossed her arms over her chest. "I'll have to speak to my crew about performing a more proper search of our prisoners."

"It was easy to miss," Tori explained, slipping the small tin out of the hidden pocket of her skirts. "If you apply this ointment a couple times a day, it should help."

"But you don't even know what caused the wound."

Tori shrugged. "This salve is good for practically anything. You can keep it."

Queen Hira studied her a moment, then took the tin, slapping it against her palm while she thought. "What was the other thing you wanted to talk to me about?"

"Nostidour."

That seemed to get her attention. Hira crossed her arms again. "Continue."

"When we left port, King Stoneheart and his army had just arrived at Avarell."

Hira nodded. "I did hear they were considering a union. Do you know anything about it?"

"I know there were negotiations set to take place. I have no doubt Duke Grunmire plans to use a combined army to attempt to conquer the other realms. I'm just not sure that Avarell can hold its own against Nostidour."

The princess, obviously overhearing their discussion, stood to join them. "My aunt did mention the negotiations. I thought her mad. I never thought negotiations would ever carry through with those savages."

"Stoneheart has a habit of sticking his head in places it doesn't belong. He's also extremely manipulative. Avarell will be crushed under his control."

By this time, Bram and Aurora had come to huddle with them. "I was actually on my way to Gadleigh when you captured us," Bram said. "I'm set to join their army."

Hira's forehead wrinkled. "An Avarell soldier in a Gadleigh army?"

"Gadleigh is actually my homeland. I'm returning to fulfill my destiny. My plan was to suggest a retreat to Avarell to drive Nostidourian forces out."

Hira caught Zhadé's eyes for a moment. "We spotted Nostidourian ships a few days ago, headed in the direction of Avarell. I wasn't sure what to believe, but now it's been confirmed."

"We'd like to propose a deal," Tori said.

"What kind of deal?"

"Master Stormbolt and I will put in a request for Gadleigh to join forces with your army to fight against Nostidour and Avarell."

Queen Hira tapped her finger against her bottom lip. "It's an interesting proposal. But how can you be sure they will agree? Not to mention, if we waltz in there with the very princess who broke off her engagement with Prince Liam, it might strike a heavy chord."

"I know I won't be welcome there," the princess said. "Which is why I will continue to travel north to Creoca to propose the same deal to my uncle. I have no doubt he will do his part to liberate his homeland from those tyrants."

The pirate queen studied them all. Tori held her breath awaiting an answer.

"And the deal is," Queen Hira began, "that if you can get these realms to agree on an alliance, you will be free to go?"

"Yes," Tori said. "That's the general idea. Of course, that freedom can only begin if we beat Nostidour and live to tell about it."

Hira let out a laugh. "That is true. All right, I acquiesce to your proposal." She clapped her hands and shouted to her crew. "Let's get our guests something to drink. They've been working hard."

Crew members scurried about, and eventually a tray landed in Zhadé's hands. They presented the tray of mugs to the group, and they all took a drink. When Tori handed her mug back to Zhadé, their hands brushed up against each other. Zhadé pulled back.

"Your Holiness, your skin burns like the midday sun."

Tori studied her hand, puzzled. "They don't feel hot."

Zhadé pressed the back of their hand against Tori's cheek. "You feel as though you have a fever."

Tori furrowed her brow. "This has happened before. I don't know how to explain it. I have… or I *had* the phoenix fever."

"Oh, Your Holiness!" Wrena remarked.

Tori waved a dismissive hand. "But something happened. I used to take a daily medicine for it that got me by. But the night of the Queen's birthday celebration, my heart gave out. Master Stormbolt actually saved my life, injecting a syringe into my heart to stop the fever from seizing it. I can't really remember anything after that, but when I awoke, all symptoms of the phoenix fever vanished."

"Was it the immunization in the syringe?" Aurora asked.

"I do not know." Tori shrugged. "But, although the symptoms were gone, every once in a while, my skin would grow hot. Not to me, but to anyone who touched me."

Zhadé gazed upon her with a scrutinizing eye. They circled Tori, keeping their eyes on her.

"What is it, Zhadé?" Queen Hira asked.

"It would seem that some transference might have been made when Lady Tori contracted the phoenix fever. When her heart gave out, she most likely *did* die."

"What?" Tori blinked in confusion. "No. I lived. I was simply blacked out."

"I think you died," Zhadé said. "And I think, like the omega phoenix who is taken by the flames, you rose again. But this time as an alpha."

CHAPTER THIRTY

*L*ady Maescia stared into nothingness as her handmaidens tended to powdering her face and fixing her hair. She didn't care about any of it, but she didn't bother dismissing them. Resting in her sitting room, allowing them to dote on her was as good a place as any to be at the time. At least there weren't any Nostidourian soldiers in the room to bother her. This place was off limits to them. Though she doubted

Nostidourians heeded any warnings of places being off limits; they tended to go where they pleased.

Movement behind her handmaids caught her eye. Clearing the small serving cart was a familiar face, and it took Lady Maescia a moment to place her.

"Excuse me," she called to the woman. When the handmaid looked up at her questioningly, she nodded. "Yes, you there. Could I have a word please?"

The handmaid set down the decanter on the cart and smoothed her vest. "Of course, Your Grace."

Lady Maescia waved off her handmaids. "That's enough. Please leave me to hold a private audience with this woman."

Fidgeting with the ruffles at her collar, Lady Maescia waited until the room was cleared before she addressed the handmaid. "I seem to have forgotten your name."

"It's Finja, Your Grace."

"Yes, Finja! You're Lady Tori's handmaid, aren't you?"

Finja seemed to hesitate before answering. "Yes, I am."

Lady Maescia stood and drew nearer. "I know Lady Tori is gone, and though I don't know where it is she went, I know it involves my niece."

"Your Grace, I can honestly say I do not know where Lady Tori or your niece are."

"I believe she may have left in a hurry, yes. But I think she may have trusted you with some important information. Something that might be useful to me."

Finja shook her head. "I'm not sure of what you speak of, Your Grace. I'm sorry I can't help you."

"Please. She mentioned making a poison."

Finja blanched and quickly averted her eyes. "A poison? What would a simple handmaid know about something like that?"

"Please." Lady Maescia grabbed her hands. "I'm desperate."

Finja held her gaze. And her expression slowly changed. Something in Lady Maescia's eyes must have convinced Finja that she wasn't trying to manipulate her into confessing an intended crime. The desperation she felt must have come across, because Finja gave her a curt nod.

Lady Maescia's heart sped up. "This conversation does not leave this room, do you understand? It would mean the end of both of us."

"I understand."

Though they were alone, the queen regent lowered her voice. "Lady Tori promised she would help me get rid of the duke. She said she was close to being able to make the poison. Please tell me you know something about it."

Finja's mouth was set in a straight line, as if she was contemplating revealing what she knew. "I do know something. There is an ingredient missing, something Lady Tori said can only be found in the Rift. I have hired someone to search for it, but he has not yet returned."

"And when he returns with the ingredient?"

"*If* he returns, Your Grace. As I'm sure you are aware, the Rift is filled with terrors."

"Yes, I'm aware." The queen regent pressed her lips together and nodded. "If he returns with the ingredient, do you know how to make the poison?"

"I'm afraid I'm no potion maker, Your Grace. I am not skilled in the ways of botany. But I remember Lady Tori sorting her herbs. I think I might be able to make it. However, I don't know the proper portions. I can't guarantee it will work."

"It's worth a try."

Finja studied her. "But what about after that? If it works on the duke, what will you do about the Nostidour army?"

Lady Maescia held her chin high. "I'm still regent. I can command my guard."

"Do you think they stand a chance against those savages?"

Lady Maescia opened her mouth, about to answer, but her doubts kept her from doing so. She rubbed her temples, the weight of the situation pressing in on her skull.

The door opened, and Finja stepped away, gathering and organizing the objects on the serving cart. Lady Maescia pressed a hand on her chest to keep her heart from leaping out of it.

"Who in their right mind would serve that atrocious tea to a lady of royal blood?" Lady Maescia shouted at Finja, hoping her tone would convince the duke. "And ice cold, at that. Unheard of! Take it away at once. And I would hope that the next time you dare approach me with a tea, it is the one I have asked for. Do you understand me?"

For the smallest of moments, their eyes locked. Lady Maescia hoped Finja caught the true meaning of her words.

"Yes, Your Grace." Finja nodded and wheeled the serving cart out of the room, keeping her eyes down.

Lady Maescia covertly released the deep, panicked breath that had lodged in her throat. She turned away from the duke, casually making her way back to her chaise. She hoped he could not see the sweat that had formed near her hairline.

"What brings you to the lounge, Duke Grunmire? Do you have news?"

The duke straightened the cuffs of his blazer. "Yes, quite prosperous news. Eleazar is faring better. The physician believes he will fully recover. That said, I believe it is time for him to take over as King."

Lady Maescia gaped at him as his words sunk in. "But the princess is not at court."

"Your Grace," the duke said with a laugh. "I assure you, your niece's presence is not necessary during the coronation of the future king. Besides, there should be a man in charge now that the Nostidour army is here. It would adduce Avarell as more adept."

"I would have to disagree. The other realms held Avarell in high regards when my sister was sitting on the throne."

"It amuses me that I am here for your opinion. I do not care for it, and I do not need your approval. I merely came to inform you of my decision so that you could prepare an announcement for the citizens of Avarell to inform them that the Queen is dead."

"What? But how—?"

He marched up to her. She was too alarmed to track his movements. The element of surprise on his side, he reached out and snatched her necklace, breaking the chain. Hanging from it was the key to the locked room in the high tower where he believed the Queen to be secluded. She gasped, attempting to grab back the key.

His smirk chilled her to the bone. "I'm headed there presently to put her out of her misery." Without waiting for a response, he turned on his heel and headed for the door.

"Wait! No!"

Before she could even stand from her chaise, he had reached the corridor. She made haste to catch up to him, her mind swimming with panic and her heart thrumming painfully in her chest.

"Duke Grunmire, you must stop. We need to think this through."

He didn't bother looking behind himself at her. "I've done enough thinking. Now is the time for action."

He turned the corner, heading for the high tower. In her attempts to cut the corner to quickly, she tripped on the hem of her gown. She let out a grunt as she stumbled to her feet. "No, wait. I beg you."

His pace seemed to pick up. Or perhaps her fear was dragging her down. She was sure he thought she was protesting because she didn't want him to kill her sister. Her mind raced with the possible outcomes of what he would do when he found the Queen's bed empty.

When he reached the door to the room in the high tower, she practically pounced on him, trying to free the key from his grasp. The duke clenched his jaw and shoved her away. Her backside landed on the floor, and she was breathless when the key clicked in the lock.

She scrambled to her feet, but he had already trudged into the room.

When she came in after him, she found him wide-eyed and frozen in place. Her hands flew to her mouth, fearing what would happen next.

Slowly, he turned to her, his face reddening more and more by the second. "What is the meaning of this?"

She considered lying. Maybe if she told him the Queen had been moved to a different room, he might believe her. But then he would just demand to be brought to her. She had no choice but to tell him the truth. Not the whole truth, but the gist of it.

"She escaped," Lady Maescia said, her voice barely above a whisper.

His chest heaved, and his hands balled into fists. "Escaped?"

One second, she was nodding, and the next, her cheek had been pummeled with a hard strike. She hit the floor with a thump before she even felt the sting of the slap. It burned so much she couldn't open her eye.

"This is beyond unacceptable!"

He reached down and grabbed her by her top, dragging her up toward him. His hand was raised, ready to strike her again. She braced herself, a sob escaping her throat.

But then he stopped, slowly closing his hand. He pushed her backward, and her shoulders connected with the wall. Her teeth rattled with the impact.

He adjusted his blazer. "Perhaps you've done me a favor. She is gone. No one would recognize her in the state she's in, if she's even survived out there... wherever she is."

Lady Maescia placed a gentle hand against her hot cheek, speechless. She was sure the burn in her chest was because her heart had stopped beating.

"Yes. Very well." The duke stretched out his neck from side to side. "We shall announce the Queen's death tomorrow."

CHAPTER THIRTY-ONE

The morning dawned bright yet windy, carrying a flock of phoenixes that rode like gold shooting stars through the clouds. Tori stood at the bow of the ship, her gaze temporarily fixed on the magnificent birds before the welcome sight of the Gadleigh bay came into view.

When they arrived at the docks, they stood back as Bram spoke with the guards standing sentry at the entry point. As they looked over his papers, he pointed to the group. Tori wasn't sure what he had told the guards, but it was obviously satisfactory enough for them to be allowed to continue toward Kanzan Castle.

"How's your wrist?" Tori asked Queen Hira.

The Queen turned her hand back and forth, inspecting the wound. "It feels much better. Doesn't itch and not as swollen."

"Use the ointment on a daily basis. The scar should diminish somewhat."

Queen Hira nodded. "I will. Thank you."

With no horse-drawn carriage to greet them, Bramwell and Tori led the way. Behind them, Aurora and Wrena held hands, their expressions bleak. Whether they shivered from the cold weather or the uncertainty of their future was indiscernible. Queen Hira and Zhadé followed close behind. Though Zhadé's meager clothing left most of their skin exposed, they didn't seem bothered by the lack of warmth in the air. Hira's face could barely be seen beneath the tricorn pulled low on her head.

They took a winding path toward the castle. Takumi was the only one avoiding the path, choosing instead to dart through the tall grass that ran up the mountain. It felt good to stretch their legs on solid soil after having to endure the turbulent waters of the sea. A fresh breeze pushed back their cloaks and rustled through the trees. Petunias lined the sandy path. Tori remembered learning they were the official realm flower of Gadleigh, able to withstand colder temperatures.

After an arduous uphill journey, Kanzan Castle came into view, its triangular silver banners waving in the wind. The guards patrolling the castle were great in number, giving Tori a moment of concern that they were arriving unannounced. Her palms were sweaty, and she instinctively checked that the remainder of her weapons were properly concealed. She was certain Hira's and Zhadé's weapons would be problematic at best. The royals of Gadleigh were only expecting Bramwell, not a mixed and dubious crew, such as they were.

One of the guards near the front of the castle did a double take upon seeing them approach. Once they got closer, Tori realized the guard was smirking at Bramwell. Bramwell smiled in return, marching directly toward the guard and slapping his hand into his to shake it.

"Bramwell, you churl. I heard you'd be running home with your tail between your legs."

"Emil, old friend. They haven't thrown you out yet?" He clapped him on the back.

"I'm sure they'd love to," Emil said with a laugh.

It made Tori smile to see that Bramwell hadn't left Avarell to return to an unwelcoming community. Instead, he was returning into the open arms of familiar faces.

Emil looked past Bram. "I didn't realize you'd be traveling with a company."

"Special circumstances. We need to speak with the king."

Emil studied Bram and then nodded. "I'll announce you.

Come into the entry hall until they can give you an audience."

"Thank you, my friend."

Bram nodded to Tori, then followed Emil into the castle entrance. Tori looked down to see Takumi watching her for a clue of what he should do. She crouched down and stroked his head.

"Find me later, my friend." She knew he would be able to.

The towering structure seemed to be full of echoes. The metallic, chilly feel of Kanzan Castle was different from the warm, elegant atmosphere of Capehill Castle in Avarell. Tori felt as if everything was pristine, almost too hygienic. She was afraid to touch anything, and it didn't help that she had harsh, salty sea air practically embedded in her hair and on her skin.

The wait was nerve-wracking. Tori almost resorted to feeling as if they had been forgotten. But eventually, the castle seneschal approached them, her hands clasped together in front of her. Her silver-streaked hair was pulled back in a tight bun, and the lace at her collar helped to conceal the wrinkled skin at her neck. Behind her was a small group of handmaidens, ready to heed her instructions.

"Welcome," she said. She then turned to the princess and curtseyed. "Your Highness."

Princess Wrena blinked in surprise, perhaps not expecting such a respectful welcome.

The seneschal then turned to Queen Hira. "Your Highness."

Queen Hira tipped her hat at her.

The seneschal faced Tori and bowed her head. "Your Holiness."

Tori returned her bow.

"Master Stormbolt," the seneschal said. "I don't suppose you remember me?"

"By appearance, I do," Bram said. "But if you'll forgive me, your name has slipped my mind."

The seneschal offered him a kind smile. "Quite understandable." She nodded to the others. "I am Miss Robin. I am here to collect your belongings, Master Stormbolt, and bring them to your chambers." Her gaze seemed to stop momentarily on Queen Hira and Zhadé, and Tori wondered if it was fear she saw in her eyes. "I apologize for not being informed there would be others in your party. Is the Queen aware of how long the rest of your party will be staying?"

"We're not even sure ourselves," Bram said, half under his breath. He slipped his pack off his back. "This is all I have with me."

Miss Robin's brow creased. "You've travelled light."

"It was a bit of a hurried departure."

She nodded, though it was clear to Tori that Miss Robin wasn't sure what he meant. "I see. I'll have Madeleine bring your things to your chambers, and I will personally escort you all to the throne room. I believe the king and queen should be ready to greet you."

Tori's heart thrummed as they followed Miss Robin down a

long corridor lined with oil painted portraits of Gadleigh's royals, past and present. The cold, white lights reflected off the silver frames, emphasizing the sharp angles of the royals' features. At the end of the corridor were large, white double doors intricately decorated in ornate silver.

The doors opened to a room similar to the throne room at Capehill Castle, only the throne room in Gadleigh was slightly more narrow with a ceiling twice as high. King Adam and Queen Layla sat upon their gleaming thrones, which were positioned upon a high platform so that the king and queen looked down upon their visitors. To the right, standing beside a group of Queen's Guards, was Prince Liam. His mouth remained in a straight line as he watched the princess approach behind Bram and Tori. Out of the corner of her eye, Tori caught Aurora's gaze dart between them.

Next to the prince stood a younger version of himself. Tori concluded that the young man must be Prince George, Liam's brother. Lady Gabrielle, High Priestess of Gadleigh, stood directly behind them. She studied Tori with scrutinizing eyes. Tori recalled how nervous she had been meeting her for the first time during the Gadleigh royals' visit to Avarell to secure the union of Prince Liam to Princess Wrena—the deal that had gone sour and ended the alliance between Avarell and Gadleigh. Considering their present situation, Tori wasn't entirely sure she felt any more confident than she did then.

Queen Layla sat with a perfectly straight back, her chin held high despite her towering position. "Master Stormbolt, we are glad to see you have arrived safely. And Lady Tori, we are very pleased to meet with you again. However, I feel I must address what my husband and I are thinking. I do not have the reputation of being a rude host, but I do wonder what business the rest of your party has in Gadleigh."

"If I could be allowed to explain, Your Highness," Tori said, stepping forward. She regretted the step as soon as she took it, as it strained her neck more to look up at the king and queen from this angle. "I'm sure I can clear up any misunderstanding."

"Very well, Lady Tori." Queen Layla gestured at Tori to continue.

Tori looked over her shoulder at Bram. The uncertainty was apparent in his eyes, but he nodded at her, encouraging her to continue.

"I fear the fate of the nine realms is in danger," she began. At the king's surprised reaction, Tori knew he hadn't expected this answer. "Avarell's queen regent has been manipulated by Duke Grunmire, who is blackmailing her into ruling the queendom at his command."

"Blackmailing?" Queen Layla asked, obviously wanting more information.

Tori shook her head. "The important thing is that it has come to the point that an alliance between Avarell and Nostidour has been forged."

There were a few mumbles and whispers from the guards in

the room.

"The Nostidour army is now in Avarell, and word is their plan is to conquer the rest of the realms, and it would not be out of the question to presume that Gadleigh would be their first target."

"Why would they initiate an alliance with such a realm?" King Adam asked. "They turned down the alliance with our army for a bunch of unorganized and ruthless savages?"

"No offence, Queen Hira." Queen Layla quickly added.

Queen Hira gave her a slight bow. "None taken."

"It seems the duke is addicted to power," Tori said. "and he will stop at nothing to attain it, no matter who gets hurt—or worse—along the way. It was he who forced the severance of the union between Prince Liam and Princess Wrena."

"Why would he do that?" It was Prince Liam who spoke up.

Tori turned in his direction. "He needed to secure his hold on the throne. You see, Queen Callista… is dead."

The small crowd erupted in shocked whispers and comments of disbelief.

"This, of course," Tori continued, "means that Princess Wrena is now, by birthright, queen of Avarell. The only way the duke could have control over the new queen, short of marrying her himself, was to have her marry his son, Eleazar."

Queen Layla held a hand flat against her chest. "Princess Wrena, did you agree to this?"

The princess took two steps forward on wobbly knees. "I did

not know of his plan. But he left me no other choice. He threatened to harm someone I love." She glanced over her shoulder at Aurora. Aurora came forward and took her hand. "I couldn't let that happen."

Prince Liam blinked, taking in the sight of them. He then turned to his brother. Prince George gave him a look that Tori couldn't decipher, but then the younger prince turned to one of the guards not too far away from him. The look they exchanged was full of emotion.

Tori faced the king and queen again. "I bring this news to you in hopes that we can take action, Your Highnesses."

"By action," Queen Layla said, "you mean fight. You mean war."

"Together, we can prevail," Tori's voice was a bit louder than she had meant it to be.

"Begging your pardon, Your Holiness." King Adam waved a hand as if implying everyone should be silent as he spoke. "But what does a woman of faith know about war?"

"I also find it peculiar," Gadleigh's High Priestess, Lady Gabrielle, added. "A High Priestess should be promoting peace, not conflict."

"Yes," Tori said, feeling flustered. "But you see…"

Once again, she glanced at Bram. He straightened his shoulders and nodded.

"I am not a High Priestess," Tori said.

She almost closed her eyes to block out the looks of shock,

but that wouldn't stop the sounds of surprise from reaching her ears. Instead, she stood up straight, willing to accept their remarks, however cruel they might be. After all, her reputation was a small price to pay if it meant convincing them to ally together to fight against Nostidour. She kept her eyes on the royals in front of her, not even considering glancing back at Queen Hira or Princess Wrena to gauge their reactions to her confession.

"Lady Tori," Queen Layla said, "you must understand the predicament we are in. You have not only lied to the entire queendom of Avarell, but to Gadleigh as well. I won't even ask what you've led the realm of the Crystal Islands to believe. If you count deceiving our High Priestess as well, then I daresay you've also misrepresented Tokuna. That equates to four realms you have deceived. Knowing this, why should we believe anything you say? Would it be wise for us to follow an imposter into war? Surely you can understand if we refuse your request."

King Adam stood, clearing his throat. "That said, I cannot deny that I have considered the prospects of disputing against Avarell for what they did to us. If I were to go to war against them, I am certain my army could stand on its own." He looked pointedly at Queen Hira. "Forming an alliance with the pirate queendom cannot prove any better than Avarell teaming up with Nostidour. Why stoop to their level by inviting such anarchy?"

Zhadé's jaw was set as they stomped forward. Queen Hira grabbed their arm and held them back, shaking her head. "It's all right. Let him speak."

King Adam's brow rose. "I question the wisdom of your presence here, Queen Hira. Who's to say I couldn't have you captured at this very moment?"

Queen Hira's legs were planted, her fists set on her hips, and there was an edge to her laugh. "With all due respect, King Adam, I'd like to see you try."

Before Tori could wrap her head around what happened, the pirate queen's sword had swung, cutting the rope that secured the hanging Gadleigh banner. The banner faltered and fell sloppily onto the heads of the group of Gadleigh guards stationed to the right of the platform. As the guards struggled to remove the heavy cloth, Queen Hira turned to Tori and the princess.

"It's been a pleasure, Your Holiness, Your Highness, but I don't make it a habit to stick around places I'm not wanted. Perhaps our paths will cross again."

Their exit was swift, and as far as Tori could tell, no one stopped them.

CHAPTER THIRTY-TWO

Bram marched forward and bowed to the royals. "King Adam, Queen Layla, if I may."

King Adam sighed and took his throne. "Yes, of course, Master Stormbolt."

"As a faithful, re-inducted member of your Queen's Guard, I ask you to reconsider. Fighting alone is risky, at best. If we were to join forces with the Crystal Islands—"

"And Creoca," Princess Wrena added, sidling up beside Bram.

Bram nodded at her. "We'd stand a better chance against the enemy."

King Adam tapped his fingers on the arm of his throne. "Though I don't believe I will change my mind about working with pirates, your suggestion of allying with the Creoca empire is intriguing. A successful proposal of an alliance would also help smooth over the unfortunate circumstances of the broken engagement."

"I will convey your wishes to my uncle, Your Highness." Wrena bowed her head. "I thank you for consideration."

"Do you have means of traveling north to Creoca, Princess Wrena?" Queen Layla asked.

"I do not, Your Highness."

"Then we shall provide a carriage for you along with the necessities you will need for the journey."

At the Queen's words, servants scurried from the hall to do her bidding.

"You are welcome to remain here for the night to rest before your journey, as I'm sure your expedition across the sea has left you all exhausted."

"Thank you, Your Highness." Wrena bowed her head again. "You are most generous."

PARAGON RISING

The seneschal took them down a long corridor that was dotted with windows that overlooked the bay to one side and the mountains to the other. Wrena gazed upon what she could see of the snow-covered mountains, wondering how far they would need to travel to reach her uncle in Creoca. After ascending a flight of stairs, they were led to a hall with four large, wooden doors, two on either side, set about fifteen feet apart.

"These are the guest quarters," Miss Robin said. "Your Highness, Your Holiness, My Lady, you may choose whichever rooms best suit you to stay in for the night, compliments of the Queen. Master Stormbolt, if you follow me, I can take you to your permanent quarters."

"Thank you, Miss Robin." Bram gave Tori a look before following the seneschal, a look Wrena had seen before between the two of them.

"Shall we take a look?" Aurora asked.

"Wait," Wrena said. "Before we do, I need to be reassured of something. Lady Tori?"

"Yes?"

"I need to know if it's true. You told the king and queen you aren't truly a High Priestess."

"Your Highness, I am so sorry for misleading you. If you would just let me explain why I needed to lie—"

Before Tori could continue, Wrena threw her arms around her, squeezing her tight. Tears of joy formed in the corners of her eyes, and relief washed over her like a cleansing tide.

"Thank you, Lady Tori. Thank you, with all my heart. This means I'm not truly married to Eleazar."

In the corner of her eye, Wrena saw Aurora clasp her hands over her mouth, obviously only just now coming to realize the impact of Lady Tori's confession.

"No, you are not," Lady Tori said. "The wedding was a falsehood."

"Bless the Divine Mother," Wrena said with a laugh.

She reached for Aurora's hand. The liberation Aurora felt was obvious in her features.

Lady Tori bowed her head to them. "If you'll excuse me, I think I'll retire. Do you mind if I simply take this room?" She pointed to the nearest door.

"Of course. You can take any room you want."

Lady Tori gave them a nod and dismissed herself.

Wrena turned to Aurora, and they joined their hands between them. For a moment, nothing was said. Then they heard footsteps echoing in the hall.

"Someone's coming," Aurora whispered, taking a step back and releasing Wrena's hands.

To Wrena's surprise, Queen Layla approached, her son, Prince George, at her side.

"Your Highness." Wrena curtsied, and Aurora followed suit.

"My dears, I hope you found your rooms to your liking."

"You are very kind to offer us shelter, Your Highness," Wrena said.

"With pleasure, of course. I just wanted to come find you and get something off my chest."

For a moment, Wrena tensed, uncertain of what the Queen might want to say.

"It's just that…" Queen Layla hesitated, as if searching for the right words. "I wish I had known. I never would have expected you to enter a marriage contract with Liam if I had known your heart belonged to another." She reached out and hooked her arm through Prince George's. "I understand how the heart wants what the heart wants. Knowing how much my son George loves his Michael, I would not expect him to marry someone from another land—woman or man—simply for an alliance. Love is more important than politics."

"Yes," Wrena said with a small smile. "I've always believed that."

"I wanted you to know that I forgive you. The whole ordeal was not your fault."

Wrena bowed her head to the Queen. "Your Highness, thank you so much for your kind words and understanding."

"Of course, my dear. In case I do not see you before your departure, I wish you good luck on your journey to Creoca. If you manage to get King Rainer to agree, I will do my part to assure my husband keeps his word on the alliance."

CHAPTER THIRTY-THREE

*L*ady Maescia stared at her wine glass, not really seeing it, but mesmerized nonetheless. Instead of wine, her eyes saw all the blood that had been spilled in recent years. She was dressed in black, as most of the Lords and Ladies of the house were now that Avarell had been informed that Queen Callista had finally succumbed to her illness and was dead. On the one hand, she was saddened by the fact that she had to lie about how her sister had died. On the other hand, she was finally allowed to mourn.

She took dinner in the private dining room of the castle along with Duke Grunmire—who had made it a habit of not letting her out of his sight—and Prince Eleazar. They were joined by King Stoneheart and two of his men. A hired quartet played somber music in honor of the deceased queen, the gentle plucking of the harp striking a chord in Lady Maescia's mood.

The purpose of the gathering was to discuss the plan of action, but somehow Duke Grunmire managed to initiate a conversation about his son's upcoming coronation. It took every ounce of resolve for Lady Maescia to keep from rolling her eyes at him.

"The coronation cannot wait," the duke said, patting Eleazar on the back. "It's important that Avarell—and the other realms—take notice that a man was on the throne when their world was conquered."

King Stoneheart waved him off. "Yes, yes, as you please. But let us discuss our strategy. I'm anxious to get this started. And anyone who knows me can tell you that it doesn't bode well to keep me waiting for something I want."

It appeared as if Prince Eleazar was about to speak. But his father quickly cut him off, placing a firm hand on his shoulder and clearing his throat. "I propose we get Khadulan on our side. They've been working with us for years, importing goods and supplying us with workers. I believe proposing that they ally with us could deliver a prosperous outcome."

"No," King Stoneheart said, his voice all but gruff.

The duke blanched. "No?"

"Nostidour does not ask. We will not *propose* anything. We will demand that they follow us or fall under our boot."

For a second, Duke Grunmire appeared at a loss for a response. The look on his face almost made Lady Maescia laugh. Instead she focused on the quartet as they began a new tune.

"Yes," the duke finally said. "Yes, of course. I simply misspoke."

"In the meantime, we need to secure the borders." Stoneheart took a greedy swig of his ale before continuing. He chomped into a roasted chicken leg, chewing as he spoke. "At the same time—"

His words were slightly buried under a high-pitched tone from the violin in the quartet. Stoneheart winced and slammed his chicken leg down on his plate, creating a splatter of grease and juices. At this, one of his men rose from his chair and strode toward the quartet. They stopped playing. The Nostidourian slipped his dagger from his belt and swiped it across the violinist's throat, not missing a beat as he pivoted on his heel and returned to his chair.

The duke's jaw hung open in shock.

Lady Maescia swallowed hard, hoping the bile that threatened to rise from her stomach would stay down. The violinist crumpled to the ground, his instrument still grasped in his hand. The other musicians gaped in silence, their faces pale. Their eyes went to the queen regent. She blinked in horror, then subtly gestured for them to clear the room. They gathered their things swiftly, abandoning their dead companion in their hasty departure.

"As I was saying," Stoneheart continued, acting as if nothing dire had just taken place, "at the same time that we send soldiers to secure the borders, we send troops to Gadleigh to storm their shores. I believe they are our greatest threat at the moment. And they are not very pleased with you, either." He let out a low laugh, then clamped his teeth around his chicken leg once more.

Lady Maescia pressed a palm to her temple. Her clothes suddenly felt too tight, and she feared that if she kept listening to Stoneheart, she might say something she would regret.

"Your Highness." She kept her muscles taut, hoping his lackey would not feel the need to use his dagger on her. "As enlightening as dinner conversation is with you, I do have to apologize. I seem to be suffering from a migraine and ask you kindly if you would excuse me."

The king smiled, bits of chicken showing between his teeth. "Your Grace," he said. "Of course. It must be boring for a woman to sit around listening to military tactics she could barely understand."

Fighting the tenseness in her jaw, she bowed her head and put on the fakest smile she could muster. "Thank you. Enjoy your evening."

She made a point of not looking at the duke as she left the room, though she was sure he was watching her. Once she closed the doors behind her, her shoulders sagged. If she had any energy left in her, she would have sobbed. Instead, she forced one foot in front of the other and made her way toward her chambers.

Halfway there, however, she witnessed a Nostidourian soldier down the hall roughly grab a handmaiden by the arm. Lady Maescia stopped in her tracks and backed into an alcove.

"I said give me that ale," he shouted at the handmaiden.

"I'm sorry, sire. It's for your king." The woman sounded on the verge of tears.

He shoved her against the wall, grabbing the bottle of ale. "You can fetch more."

As he took a swig, the handmaiden slid against the wall, no doubt trying to escape the brute. Noticing her movement, he reached out and grabbed her by the arm again.

"Where do you think you're going?"

A figure behind him suddenly appeared. "Take your hands off her!"

Lady Maescia recognized the woman soldier. Her name was Azalea, the only female in the Avarell Queen's Guard. Though she stood two heads shorter than the Nostidourian soldier, she held herself tall and aimed her sword at the man.

"Ha!" The man let go of the handmaiden and faced Azalea, his scimitar raised in front of him. "Don't be a fool, sweetheart."

Azalea smirked. "You won't think I'm so sweet once you get

to know me."

The man lunged forward, his scimitar swinging toward Azalea's arm. She blocked it with her broadsword and pushed back. Taken off guard by her strength, the Nostidourian stumbled back. He bared his teeth and growled at her, then shot forward, his scimitar raised above his head. Azalea side-stepped his aim while swinging her sword horizontally. Her blade caught his stomach. Blood began to spill, but it didn't stop the soldier. Their blades clashed as he delivered strike upon strike, but Azalea held him off. Frustrated, he yelled and attempted to jab her with the scimitar straight on. Azalea spun out of his path, her sword coming down hard on his neck as she repositioned herself. The soldier's scimitar clattered to the ground as he slapped a hand onto the side of his neck. Azalea kicked him down and stabbed him below the shoulder blade, keeping her sword there until he no longer moved.

The handmaiden held a hand to her mouth as she backed away. Lady Maescia came out of the alcove and rushed to the girl. "Fetch someone to deal with this blood," she whispered to her. "And hurry."

The handmaiden shook with fear but nodded. "Yes, Your Grace."

Lady Maescia dashed to Azalea's side.

"Oh," Azalea said upon seeing her. She was out of breath and sweat covered her forehead. "Your Grace. I didn't see—"

Lady Maescia waved her hands, signaling for Azalea to stop.

"There's no time. No one must see his body. We'll need to hide it."

"But he attacked that woman."

"It won't matter to Stoneheart. Logic is not his strong suit. Come help me move him."

"But where?"

"There's an entrance to the secret tunnels up ahead. We'll have to hide him there until I can hire someone to deposit him elsewhere."

Azalea did most of the carrying, being the stronger of the two. "Your Grace, there's something I need to tell you."

"Now?" Lady Maescia grunted with the effort of dragging the man toward the secret tunnel entrance.

"I'm afraid it's important."

"All right. What is it?"

"There have been sightings of Undead in Avarell. Within the city walls."

✳

Though she was exhausted, Tori couldn't seem to fall asleep. It didn't matter that the bed was comfortable or that the sheets were soft or that the temperature in the room was perfect; she couldn't shut off the thoughts in her mind. She decided to try a meditation technique her mentor had taught her instead. Just as she was about to drift off, she heard a soft rap at the door.

When she opened the door, she found Bram waiting in the hall. He was in his tunic and trousers, but he looked as if he had been battling with trying to sleep as well.

"I'm sorry," he said sheepishly. "I... I wanted to see you. I wasn't even sure this was your room."

She almost laughed. "Did you get it right on the first try, or did you wake everyone else in the castle first?"

The corner of his mouth inched upward. "First try."

"Impressive." She let out a small laugh.

A gekkering caused Bram to jump. His shoulders relaxed when he spotted Takumi circling Tori's legs. Takumi sniffed at him, then turned and jumped on Tori's bed, curling into a ball and closing his eyes.

"He found you without fail," Bram said. "Now *that's* impressive."

She offered him a small smile. "Was there something troubling you, Master Stormbolt?"

"I'm sorry if you were resting."

"No. No. I actually couldn't sleep."

"Nor could I." His gaze seemed to flit over her face. "It's just that I never got a chance to thank you for helping me. For helping Aurora."

"Oh, of course. It goes without question that I would help."

He leaned against the doorframe. Somehow, without knowing she was doing it, her body followed his and leaned against the opposite side of the frame.

"It feels a bit strange," he said.

"What does?"

"After all the time we've spent together and what we've been through the last few days—the last few weeks, actually—it seems odd to know tomorrow we're going to be apart."

Their eyes locked. Something in his gaze—something that had always been in his gaze every time he looked at her—took her breath away. She wanted to avert her eyes, but she was trapped, prisoner to his intense stare.

"If all goes well," she said, "we will be returning. And I will fight by your side for the salvation of the nine realms."

He pushed himself off the frame and inched closer. "By my side. I like the sound of that."

She watched as he closed the distance between them. She couldn't look away from his lips. Her heart pounded in her chest, which felt warm and tingly from their close proximity. He tipped his head down toward hers, and she lifted her chin and placed a hand upon his chest.

The echo of footsteps sounded in the hall. Tori and Bram studied each other's faces, not moving though they were only an inch apart. As a servant walked by, Bram almost winced, taking a step back. Tori let her hand fall to her side.

"I hope to see you tomorrow before you leave," he said softly.

She nodded. "I hope so too."

"Goodnight, Lady Tori."

"Goodnight."

He nodded and turned. Holding back a sigh, she closed the door. She pressed her forehead against the wood, shutting her eyes and questioning whether or not she should have just gone with her gut and pulled him into her rooms.

CHAPTER THIRTY-FOUR

The carriage was loaded with some supplies for their journey, courtesy of Queen Layla. To Wrena's surprise, Prince Liam came out to see them off. He didn't say more than wishing them a safe journey, but somehow Wrena got the feeling he wasn't angry with her anymore. Perhaps the trait of forgiveness was something he inherited from his mother.

Aurora hugged Bramwell goodbye, thanking him for his help,

and got into the carriage. Wrena handed her things to the coachman and climbed in to sit beside Aurora. A flash of fur passed through the space as Takumi scampered in and jumped onto the seat across from them, lifting his front paws onto the windowsill to watch Lady Tori as she approached.

Bram leaned his head into the carriage, looking like a proper soldier again in his silver and blue Gadleigh uniform. "May the Divine Mother oversee your safe passage." He nodded at Wrena. "And good luck, Your Highness."

"Thank you, Master Stormbolt. Good luck to you, too."

Though she couldn't hear what was being said, Wrena watched as Bramwell turned to Lady Tori. The wind blew her cloak off her head, and he reached over to pull it gently into place. The blush that tainted her cheeks didn't go unnoticed. Wrena turned away, wishing to give them some privacy. Prior to Lady Tori's confession, Wrena had thought their looks of longing were taboo, but now that she knew Lady Tori was not actually a High Priestess, there was no reason for them not to pursue a romance. Except for the impending war that could not only pull them apart but leave one or both of them dead, of course.

Once Lady Tori had settled into her seat, the carriage began its wobbly drive over the cobblestoned streets of Mount Kanzan. For the first few minutes, the three women remained silent, watching the view change from the cold urban town to the sparse fields and snowy mountains. Even Takumi had settled down and curled into a ball, snoring in his sleep.

Wrena couldn't stand the silence anymore. Her stomach felt as if acid were slowly burning a hole through it. She needed to distract herself from the nervousness.

"Lady Tori, do you mind if I ask you something?"

Lady Tori gave her a small smile. "You don't have to call me 'Lady' anymore, Your Highness."

"You saved us," Wrena said, her brows raised. "That calls for a status more prominent than 'Lady,' if you ask me. I insist that your title remain as I've always known it to be."

Lady Tori looked as if she was holding back a laugh. "As you wish, Your Highness. What was your question?"

"I didn't want to eavesdrop on your conversation with Master Stormbolt. Did he perhaps mention his idea for convincing King Adam to agree to our terms?"

"Oh, yes." Lady Tori let her fingers trail the hem of her hood, perhaps remembering how he touched it. "Bramwell's—I mean—Master Stormbolt's father was a well-respected commander in Gadleigh's army. He had been highly regarded by both the king as well as the Captain of the Queen's Guard. Master Stormbolt hopes that because they held him in such good favor, their appreciation of his service might play a part in influencing the king."

"That has to work," Aurora said. "From what my parents used to say about my uncle, all of Gadleigh loved him."

Wrena squeezed her hand. "Then we have to believe it will work."

The carriage slowed as the path grew steeper. The bumps in the road did little to ease Wrena's churning stomach.

After a few hours into their journey, the carriage slowed, and Wrena could hear the heavy grunting and huffing from the horses. Once they came to a full stop, the coachmen jumped down from his seat and bowed his head to the passengers.

"The horses will need to rest and be watered," he said. "It'll be roughly an hour before we continue. If you'd like to stretch your legs, now's the time."

He disappeared out of sight, and Wrena turned to Aurora. "Shall we?"

"Yes," Aurora answered. "I could use the air. Lady Tori?"

"I could do with a good stretch myself. Besides, I think Takumi is getting restless."

The three women and the fox climbed down from the carriage, immediately slapped with the icy air. It felt as if the wind were made up of tiny icicles, stabbing and pricking at their skin. Takumi raced off to explore, and Tori headed toward a bush that contained tiny purple flowers.

Wrena examined the breath-taking view from the mountain ridge, looking over the landscape of Gadleigh. A small town could be seen, not far from the castle. She imagined how peaceful it must be there, away from the turmoil and chaos brought about by the duke and the Nostidour army.

"Are you all right?" Aurora asked her.

"I'm worried about Theo. He's so young and helpless. I'd

hate myself if anything happened to him."

"I'm sorry." Her voice was small and meek.

Wrena faced her and wrinkled her brow, curious about Aurora's tone. "My love?"

Aurora shook her head, as if wanting to dismiss it, but Wrena reached out and lifted her chin with a finger.

Aurora leaned her cheek in to Wrena's hand, but she kept her eyes down. "I feel guilty you had to choose me over your own brother."

"No, Aurora, it's not your fault."

Aurora shook her head. "If it weren't for me, Theo would not be in danger."

"No, if it weren't for the *duke*, Theo would not be in danger. This was none of your doing."

Aurora's gaze remained trained on the snow at her feet. "I never want to come between you and your family."

Wrena felt a fluttery sensation in her chest. She took Aurora's hand and squeezed. "Aurora, you are my family."

Aurora raised her head to look into Wrena's eyes. There was a look of uncertainty there that Wrena wished she could erase. Wrena offered her a small smile, then leaned in to place a gentle kiss on her lips.

"We will make things right," Aurora said.

"I just hope that my aunt has figured out a way to keep Theo safe. It's the only hope I can cling to."

An hour later, the horses were refreshed and rested. The

group found themselves continuing up the snowy mountain, though their progress was slow. They were given woven blankets to keep warm as the temperature decreased. Aurora would continuously fog the window with her breath and wipe the residue away, over and over in a loop that eventually made Wrena fall asleep.

It wasn't until the carriage came to a jolted stop that Wrena was roused awake. She opened her eyes to a flurry of white beating the windows.

"What's happened?" she asked, sitting upright.

Lady Tori had already opened the carriage door and stepped outside before anyone could answer. Takumi jumped out to follow her, but immediately disappeared beneath the heavy snowdrift on the path.

"There's a storm," Aurora explained. "I think we might be stuck."

Lady Tori appeared in the doorway, clutching at her windblown cloak. "There's too much snow and ice. The horses can't pull the carriage through anymore. And judging by the blueish pallor of our coachman, I'd say he's not fit to continue either."

"What do we do?" Wrena asked.

Tori peered over her shoulder for a second. "There's a slope to the mountains here, jutting outward. Perhaps it can provide shelter for us until the storm passes."

Wrena took Aurora's hand and helped her out of the carriage.

The three of them slung canvas bags of supplies over their shoulders, and the coachman untied the horses. The snow was so high it covered their knees. With grunts of exertion, Wrena pushed her legs through the resistance of the snow, her fingers laced with Aurora's.

Takumi jumped through the snow toward them. He practically jumped into Lady Tori's arms, gekkering, before he frantically jumped down and bound off again.

Lady Tori shielded her eyes against the icy downpour. "There's a cave up ahead."

"Big enough for the horses?" the coachman asked.

"I can't tell, but it's worth a shot."

Wrena and Aurora followed them, hand-in-hand, their feet soaking and their muscles weary from the struggle. Wrena wasn't sure how Lady Tori could see the cave through the pelting snow. All she could see was white. Still, she continued forward, determined to stay alive another day.

Finally, the entrance to the cave came into view. There was relief in the coachman's eyes as he saw the entrance was big enough for the two horses to fit. The darkness beyond the entrance held the promise that the rest of them would survive the storm. The coachmen tied the horses together, and then he slumped against the wall for a respite. Takumi scampered around, even venturing into the darker parts of the cave Wrena could not see.

They barely made it five steps into the cave before Aurora had to stop and place her hand against the icy wall. Wrena was quick to catch her around the waist so she wouldn't fall.

"Are you all right?"

She nodded slowly. "Yes, perhaps I'm just weak from hunger."

"Look, there's room here for us to sit," Wrena said, dropping the bag of supplies on her shoulder. "And some branches and twigs here. Perhaps we can start a fire to keep warm. Queen Layla provided us with some pastries, rolls, and fruit. They should help."

She put on a relaxed face, forcing herself to seem full of hope. She knew Aurora must have been frightened, but Wrena was determined not to show her how scared she was. With all that was going wrong, she refused to let in any negativity.

Tori surveilled the cave as Wrena helped Aurora find a place to sit. There were some branches at the back of the cave, perhaps brought there by an animal. Tori wondered for a moment if that animal might still be in the cave. Hopefully the group hadn't just sealed their fate in being attacked by a territorial animal defending their home. But the fact that Takumi was sniffing around without alarm somewhat put Tori's mind at ease. Besides, there was still the freezing temperature to worry about.

She knew she should have felt cold. It was apparent from the shivering of the others that the chill was unbearable, but Tori felt warm. She felt comfortable. And it occurred to her that ever since she woke up from her episode with the syringe, she hadn't been in any circumstances where temperature affected her. Though questions burned in the back of her mind, she concentrated instead on making their temporary enclosure more tolerable.

With Takumi's help, she gathered all the branches and twigs she could find and added them to the pile Princess Wrena had started. The coachman came over and attempted to start a fire by rubbing two of the sticks together, but after several minutes had gone by with not so much as a spark, he threw the sticks down and let out a sigh, hanging his head in defeat.

Tori picked up the sticks, determined to give it a try. She had started fires this way before, back home in Sukoshi Village, but they usually had dry wood to work with and kindling to help things along.

After several efforts, the most she could get out of the sticks was a puff of smoke that quickly disappeared. She huffed out a frustrated grunt, closing her eyes and holding her fists to her head. Along with Takumi's gekker, she heard Princess Wrena gasp.

She opened her eyes, not knowing what to expect. "What is it?"

The princess's eyes were wide, while Aurora's were narrowed. "Your hands," Princess Wrena whispered.

Tori moved her hands away from her temples, realizing she was still holding the sticks. Where her skin met the wood, there was a faint blue glow. But in the darkness of the cave, the light seemed bright. Tori dropped the sticks. They landed on the pile of kindling, and the blue glow began to fade. Tori checked her hands, and the blue glow faded from them as well.

For a moment, everyone was silent, but Tori could feel the stares of the others. She couldn't blame them for staring. She was still in awe of this strange power she didn't even understand. When she heard movement, Tori turned to see the princess stand.

"Lady Tori, do you mind if I check something?" Princess Wrena asked, slowly approaching her.

Tori couldn't answer. Instead, when the princess reached out to her, she let her take her hands.

"They're hot," the princess said. She locked eyes with Tori, and she had the expression of someone who was trying to work out a puzzle. "I have a theory that they were even hotter when you made them glow."

"*Made* them glow?" Tori almost scoffed. "You think I did that on purpose? I can't even imagine how I did that at all."

Aurora shivered. "Perhaps you can warm us up with your blue glow. That would be a big help."

Tori stared at her hands again. She remembered how Bram, Finja, and Zhadé all mentioned how hot her skin got. But they'd always retracted away from her, as if she had burned them. Zhadé had said something about blue phoenix fire and being an alpha.

Could any of that be true? Could she create a heat strong enough to keep them warm until the storm passed?

She shook her head, feeling ridiculous. Surely Aurora was joking. Wasn't she? Still, what if it did work? Tori let out a sigh, resolving to give it a try in any case. Having them all gather around her, she sat in the middle of them and closed her eyes. She wasn't even sure what to concentrate on, but when she heard Takumi gekker, she opened her eyes to see the blue glow on the surface of her skin.

Aurora inched closer. "It's warm," she said, her lips curving into a smile.

"Yes," Princess Wrena said. "Whatever you're doing, keep it up. It's perfect."

The coachman stared at her in disbelief but kept close nonetheless.

Tori pushed out her blue fire, warming the cave. But in the back of her mind, she wondered how long she would be able to do it.

CHAPTER THIRTY-FIVE

*U*pon the duke's instructions, the banquet was bursting with food, more than ever before. The feast to celebrate the following morning's coronation of Prince Eleazar to King consort of Avarell was in full swing. Extra tables were brought in to hold all the food and wine the kitchen was instructed to prepare. There were heaps of selected meats, from duck to buffalo, and towers of side dishes practically overflowing onto each other. The desserts were infused with so much sugar, it could be tasted in the air. Lady Maescia found the mixture of scents almost overwhelming.

She found herself sitting between Duke Grunmire and one of Stoneheart's men. Stoneheart sat on the other end of the table, indulging in more than his share of turkey and roasted potatoes. The duke ate very little, the constant smile on his face only vanishing when he took a sip of wine. Lady Maescia doubted he would get any sleep, as anxious as he seemed to have his son wear the crown.

All the better, Lady Maescia thought. With no food in his body to fight against the poison she'd slipped into his wine decanter, the effects should take place quickly. The only dilemma was getting him to drink the right amount—a factor neither she nor Finja were quite sure about.

With his bride missing, Prince Eleazar was surrounded by Ladies of the court. Lady Maescia had no doubt in her mind that they sought to secure a position of importance beside the future king. Judging by their body language, at least two of them had their eyes on the prize of being his mistress.

"What will be your first undertaking as king, Your Highness?" one of the Ladies asked, her wide smile the only distraction from the obvious way she pushed her bosom into his line of view.

"I hear there have been sightings of Undead at the borders of Avarell," another Lady put in. "Will you be fighting them off yourself?"

Eleazar waved them off, looking unbothered. "My father has it under control. We've sent out some of our best men to patrol the area. The Undead have no chance against them."

Stoneheart let out a husky laugh. "Perhaps I should send out some of *my* best men. At least they would be sure to return."

"I assure you," the duke said, leaning over so Stoneheart could hear him, "our men have had sufficient training. I have no doubt they will succeed in their quest."

"No doubt," Stoneheart said, almost laughing. "Then again, I can't offer my *very best* men, seeing as how I've already sent them on a ship to Gadleigh."

The duke almost spit out his wine. "You did what?"

"Consider it a gift. They're merely laying down the groundwork until I can join them and truly conquer."

Eleazar was speechless, clearly in shock.

As the duke wiped the sputtered wine from his chin, Lady Maescia took it upon herself to fill his goblet. She had the advantage that no one else was close enough to the decanter to use it. She made sure to throw off suspicion by filling her own goblet, though she only pretended to drink from it.

"I was under the impression we would agree on any course of action," the duke said to Stoneheart, "together."

"Aw, have I hurt your little girl feelings?" Stoneheart laughed again, smacking the man next to him on the shoulder. "No, Duke Grunmire. I do not see the need to conspire with you before I send out my own army. I will do what I please with my men, send them where I want them to go, and conquer where I want them to conquer, without consulting with you."

Duke Grunmire pulled at the collar of his tunic and grabbed his goblet. He took a long swig, and Lady Maescia held back from wringing her hands.

"I am not insisting that you couldn't, King Stoneheart," the duke said, a red tint spreading upon his skin. He took another long swig of his wine. "I was merely suggesting I be notified sooner rather than later."

Stoneheart stared at him for a moment before letting out another rough laugh.

"A proper plan requires a steady—" The duke choked out a barrage of coughs, unable to finish his words.

"Father?" Eleazar stood, patting his father's back.

Lady Maescia's heart pounded in her chest as she feigned confusion. "Duke Grunmire, are you all right?"

King Stoneheart leaned back in his chair, watching the duke with a crinkle in his forehead. He didn't seem alarmed, only curious.

His face completely red now, the duke struggled for air. He clutched at his throat with one hand and raised his goblet to his lips with the other. But the sip he attempted to take made him gag. He threw down his goblet, wide eyes staring at the spilled wine.

Eleazar grabbed a glass of water and handed it to his father.

The duke wrapped his hands around the glass and chugged it. He gasped for air as he slammed the glass onto the table.

The crowd had grown quiet, watching the entire ordeal with bated breath.

Lady Maescia stared at the duke, horror embedded in her stomach as the red in the duke's face diminished. The water had diluted the poison—which she now realized must not have been proportioned properly. It hadn't worked.

Duke Grunmire shot her a glare, his chest heaving.

She wanted to run. But she was trapped, surrounded by the duke's guards as well as Stoneheart's men. When her eyes darted to Stoneheart, he narrowed his eyes at her.

"She's attempted to kill me," he shouted, clutching at his throat. He coughed and sputtered, the natural color slowly returning to his face. "Lady Maescia poisoned my wine."

"I... I..." She shook her head, unable to get the words out.

"An attempt of murder has been made on me, the Captain of the Queen's Guard. This is treason!" He shook with fury as he turned to his men. "Guards, arrest her!"

The drone of the shocked crowd elevated, all eyes on Lady Maescia. She stood, backing away from the table but was quickly surrounded. She let out a yelp as his soldiers seized her arms. Despite her flailing, she was no match for their strength. With the duke leading their way, they dragged her out of the room.

Her eyes widened once they moved down two corridors. She realized they were not headed for the dungeon.

"Where are you taking me?"

"I think you know all too well." The duke cast her a smirk over his shoulder as he continued to walk.

All at once, it came to her. He was going to lock her in the high tower, just like her sister. "You'll never get away with this."

His laugh was eerie. "My dear, it seems I already have."

Every step they took made her heart thrash faster in her chest. Her arms were sore from the tight grip of the Queen's Guard soldiers. When they reached the room—the very room her sister had been kept—the duke whipped out the key and shoved the door open.

The guards hurled her inside, where she tripped onto the floor.

She stood, wiping her fallen hair out of her face, gaping at the duke as he neared.

"Foolish woman. You've given up everything for nothing,"

"You can't do this to me. I'm the queen regent. Someone out there will rescue me."

The duke sneered at her. "You can protest all you wish. The fact remains that my son now holds reign over the queendom. With myself at the helm, of course."

She ground her teeth. "How is that any different than the last few years?"

"Because now I finally have you out of the way to do what I please. Maybe now we can finally get this queendom to push some boundaries and excel above the other realms."

He marched toward the door.

"Why lock me up?" she asked, not holding back the bitterness that laced her voice. "Why not just kill me?"

"Because I need leverage. I'll find a way to get word to your niece about your captivity. I'm sure young Wrena would rush back to save her aunt if the threat of a beheading were present. I will even sweeten the pot by allowing you to live if she returns and obediently stands by Eleazar's side." He toyed with the key in his hand. "I suppose it remains to be seen if you'll still have a breath left in you before she returns."

The door slammed shut. Lady Maescia's bones shook as the sound of the key turning in the lock met her ears. Her legs gave out, and she let her weight fall to the floor. She sat, sobbing, watching how her teardrops dampened her dress. There was a strange buzz in her head, as if her brain was resisting the reality of what had just happened. She had nothing left. Yet, in a strange way, she finally felt free.

As her sobs quieted, she wiped her tears away. She pressed her hands together so hard the skin on her knuckles turned white. She had never been a woman of extremely devout faith, but in that moment, in the isolation of the quiet room, she prayed to the Divine Mother that her niece and nephew remained out of the duke's grasp.

CHAPTER THIRTY-SIX

*W*rena could feel actual relief flood through her as her uncle's gleaming castle came into view. The horses pushed hard through the ice and snow as if seeing their objective, as if knowing of the rewards of water and food and rest that awaited them there. Aurora pressed her nose against the window, her eyes moist with happy tears at the sight of the Creoca flags waving in the wind. The pale gray castle stood tall, halfway up the mountain, but accessible by a stone road. They were almost there.

Every minute that ticked by was a moment closer to home, to family. When Wrena finally emerged from the carriage, her feet touching the ground was like a welcome from an old friend. She used to play here once a year when her family visited her Uncle Rainer and his wife, Queen Emiliana. She remembered how she and her cousin, Princess Dahlia, would sneak into Queen Emiliana's closets and secretly try on her clothes.

A massive stone staircase led to the grand front entrance of the castle. Guards stood watch, their uniforms shining in the sun, their long spears held in absolute straight positions. Her Uncle, King Rainer, and her aunt Emiliana, stood at the top of the stairs. At first, they smiled at her, happy to see her. But as they gazed upon Wrena and noticed the tears streaming down her cheeks, their faces fell.

"Wrena," her Uncle Rainer said, rushing to meet her and placing his hands on her arms. "Is everything all right?"

She stared into his eyes as she shook her head. "Not entirely, no. I'm afraid I come bearing bad news. Mother is dead."

"I'll kill him myself." King Rainer pounded his fist into the table, his face red and strained. His voice had echoed off the walls of the private dining room. "And that despicable father of his as well."

Queen Emiliana set a hand on his arm to calm him. At the same time, her eyes filled with sorrow as she gazed upon Wrena.

"It seems there are many volunteers to see he meets death," Wrena said. "Myself included."

Seated at the table with her aunt and uncle, Wrena looked over at Aurora, who had kept her eyes down the entire time Wrena had recounted the story of her attack and the events that led to that moment. Lady Tori had also sat quietly as Wrena told her tale. Feeling vulnerable and exposed, Wrena was grateful no one else had been in the room to hear it.

"And now look what the duke has done to Avarell," Rainer said, his voice gruff. He shook his head and leaned back in his chair. "Consorting with savages! Your mother would have never stood for this."

"What of the other realms?" Queen Emiliana asked. "Has anyone challenged them?"

"The duke no doubt believes there are few queendoms brave enough to stand up against them, especially now with Nostidour as their allies."

"Khadulan will fight against Avarell," Tori put in. "If only I could contact the captain in charge, I could confirm. Alas, he is missing."

"But that is why we have come to you," Wrena said. "We need to join with Gadleigh and anyone else who accepts our alliance to fight them."

"Drothidia has a small army," Rainer said, tapping his chin with his fingers, "but they've lived humbly and in peace for a decade. I doubt their army would be up to the battle."

"We can still send word," Tori said. "The general does not know me personally, but we could mention that my grandfather served in his army. Perhaps that would help."

"Tokuna has no army," Emiliana added. "And the Coldlands are a place of isolation."

Rainer leaned forward. "And Gadleigh is ready to fight? Have they made it official?"

"I believe they are considering it, depending on your position." Wrena glanced at Lady Tori. "In the meantime, we've got a well-respected soldier there doing his part to convince them to join."

"The Crystal Islands may be with us, if we can settle the animosity between them and Gadleigh," Tori explained.

Rainer nodded, his eyes far away. "The numbers are impressive. If those realms join us, we stand a chance."

"So, you'll consider it?" Wrena asked.

He reached over and took her hand. "I'm not a man who goes into war lightly, but if there was ever a time to make a move, it's now. Yes, we'll fight."

Wrena stood and hugged her uncle. "Thank you."

"Of course, my dear. It's only right."

She took a step back, wringing her hands. "There's something else I wanted to talk to you about. It's about my father."

A crease appeared in Rainer's brow. "What is it?"

"I was told something recently, something that has left me confused. I thought, if anyone would be able to clarify things, it would be you."

"All right. What did you hear?"

Wrena glanced at Aurora and Lady Tori before continuing. "That father was the reason for most of the bad things that have happened to the nine realms."

Rainer simply stared at her for a moment. Then he let out a sigh and nodded to his wife. She looked nervous, and Wrena's stomach began to churn.

"Would the rest of you kindly let my niece and me have a moment alone?" he asked.

"Yes, of course," Emiliana said. "Come Lady Tori, Lady Aurora. I'll show you to the grand tea room. It's got the most breathtaking view of the mountains."

Wrena kept her eyes on her uncle as the room cleared. She wasn't even sure she wanted to hear what he had to say, but she knew she would always wonder if she never found out the truth.

Her uncle stood and paced, his hands laced behind his back. If someone were to enter the room at that moment, they might think he was simply appreciating the damask wallpaper and the crystal light fixtures. But Wrena knew he must have been searching for the right words to say.

"Your father," he began, "was a man who admired power.

Much like his cousin, the duke."

Wrena crossed her arms, uncomfortable with the comparison. She didn't want to imagine her father being anything like the duke.

"His reputation was great, and many realms adored and respected him—even at the young age at which he married your mother. But it wasn't enough. He didn't only want their respect. He wanted to be revered, feared even. He wanted to weaken the other realms, so he began coming up with outlandish strategies. There was a woman who helped him. In town she was known as a healer, but others considered her a witch. She knew things about potions and tinctures no one else had the faintest idea about.

"Together they came up with a plan to weaken the minds of his enemies. The witch claimed to be able to concoct a potion that would bend people to his will without question. She made the potion, and he tested it out on the prisoners in the dungeon. It seemed to work, and he was pleased. So, he decided to test it on a small Avarellian village in the south, relatively close to the border of the Rift.

"Of course, at the time, the Rift was simply a jungle. There were species of animals and plant life, all thriving. There used to be wooden bridges that crossed over the valleys of the Rift so that journeyers could cross into Drothidia or Khadulan. Anyway, the village he had experimented on became a place of abiding citizens. Your father was thrilled. He was so pleased, he and the witch celebrated... privately, in a certain manner that proved to be a favorite of your father's. No one knew about any this, of course, aside from them. But your father tended to go heavy on the drink, and sometimes he would tell me of his conquests. I didn't believe all his tales, but in time, I would learn that they were true.

"Things seemed to be going according to plan. But that's when those test subject of his began turning."

"Turning?" Wrena's hand gently covered her throat, afraid of how he would answer.

"Their brains were not only tainted to do the King's bidding. They were rotted. But their bodies remained alive, and they walked the land as Undead."

Wrena's breath caught in her throat.

"Of course, by the time he found out, they had infected more people. It took a secret band of the King's men to round up the Undead and drop them in the Rift. Then they burned all the bridges so the Undead couldn't get out. But they kept it a secret. And any hunters or hikers that might have ventured into the Rift at that time were not warned of the dangers that lurked there."

"They were attacked," Wrena said, guessing what must have happened. "Turned as well."

"Your father never took credit for it. Instead, he needed a way to get rid of the Undead before anyone found out he was responsible. So, his witch concocted a poison, something strong enough to kill the Undead. She made the poison—it was a powdery substance that clung to the plants—and the King hired men to spread the poison in the Rift. Only it didn't kill the Undead.

"Instead, it killed most of the animals—those that weren't already being killed by the Undead. It did something different to the smaller creatures: the mice, the squirrels, and other rodents. It made them sick. But before they could die, the phoenixes—who did not eat the plants—contracted a disease."

"The phoenix fever," Wrena guessed.

"Yes. Of course, no one knew anything about why this was happening. When your father would tell me in his drunken stupor, I only then started to understand what was happening. And then he came up with the clever idea of selling the cure—the antidote his witch had made, of course—to the other realms. He hired Khadulian chemists to replicate the witch's formula and turned a profit. The other realms paid unquestionably, of course, for fear of contracting the disease."

Wrena shook her head in disbelief. "Why didn't you tell anyone?"

Her uncle averted his eyes. Letting out a deep breath, he shook his head. "Because of your mother. I couldn't do that to her. Now I know that I should have confronted her and told her everything, but I just couldn't break her heart like that. And I feared the queendom would turn against her for supporting him."

Wrena wrapped her arms tighter around herself, shocked by the story. How did she never know? This must have all happened before she was born. For as long as she could remember, the

Undead and the phoenix fever had existed. To think that it was all her father's doing was inconceivable. Her father. Her blood.

A shiver ran through her. Both her father and the duke seemed to be men whose blood ran with greed and corruption. What if she was like them?

"Why didn't you stop him?"

There was apparent shame in his eyes. "When I confronted him about it, he threatened Emiliana. I couldn't let anything happen to her, so I left Avarell. That's when I came here, and we were wed."

"So you kept it a secret? All this time?"

He nodded. "Yes. Up until now."

CHAPTER THIRTY-SEVEN

*L*ady Maescia pressed her face against the bars of the window, attempting to catch sight of something—anything—that might give her a clue as to what was happening in the queendom. But all she could see was vacant windows across the courtyard and the roof of the chapel. With a huff of frustration, she backed away from the window, futilely wiping at her face.

On the first night locked in the room, she refused to sleep in the bed, resolving to sleeping on the floor. She was frightened to fall asleep in the same place her sister had slept as an Undead for years. But after waking with a sore back, Maescia gave in and spent her nights on the musty sheets of the canopy bed.

Twice a day, a servant came by with food and a bowl of soapy water to wash up with. She wasn't sure if this was on the duke's orders or if someone in the staff was being generous with her. Whatever the circumstances were, she was not allowed to leave. She supposed she should be grateful she wasn't locked up in the dungeon. But it wouldn't matter anyway. If Wrena returned to save her, she was sure they would both die at the hands of the duke.

Hearing the key turning in the door, Maescia backed against the wall, bracing herself for anything. To her surprise, it was Lady Raven who entered the chambers.

"Raven, thank the Divine Mother."

"Your Grace," Lady Raven studied the queen regent, shock apparent in her eyes. "I can't believe he's done this."

"How did you find me?"

"One of the servants told me. She has a habit of gossiping. And I managed to get the key." She waved the subject away. "How are you faring?"

They sat on the end of the bed, and Maescia did her best to hold back a sob.

"As well as can be expected. At least I'm still alive."

"Do you know anything about where the princess might have run away to? Or the High Priestess and Bramwell, for that matter?"

Maescia rubbed at her neck. "I'm afraid I don't know where they are. I can only gather that they are together. And safe, away from the chaos this place is suffering. Please tell me, what's happening out there?"

Raven patted down the hair on the sides of her head. "Well, Nostidour is practically running Avarell, duke or no duke. They're turning it into an uncivilized place, taking what they want, hurting people. Trashing businesses. Overturning vendor carts and taking food without paying, and then shoving the people away when they complain. They even broke a chair over the local bar keep's head because he didn't pour their ale fast enough. He's in bad shape, hasn't woken up yet. His wife is both scared and furious. And the Queen's Guard seem to have no power over them. Nostidour soldiers crush anyone who gets in their way. The citizens are in an uproar, demanding answers from the duke. But he doesn't care."

Lady Maescia closed her eyes and pursed her lips. "I wish there was something I could do."

Raven took her hands. "It's worse. Witnesses have reported spotting Undead in Avarell. At first it was just one or two, but now they've been seen in groups."

Lady Maescia held a trembling hand to her mouth. "I can't believe it."

It crossed her mind that her sister—even as an Undead—might have something to do with the recent sightings. Could Callista really be leading them in for an attack? She was having a hard time wrapping her head around the fact that it could actually be happening.

"Lady Raven, you have to promise me something."

"Yes, of course. What is it?"

She swallowed hard before continuing. "If anything should happen to me, you must get word to Princess Wrena that Theo has been sent to Tokuna for sanctuary. Don't tell anyone else where he is. You must keep it secret, for the prince's safety."

"Yes. Yes, all right." Raven nodded. "I promise."

CHAPTER THIRTY-EIGHT

*R*eceiving word that the carriages had arrived, Bram couldn't get down the stairs and into the foyer fast enough. The servants were already unloading the carriages when he reached the castle entrance. As soon as he saw Lady Tori, he felt both relief and excitement at the same time.

"Bram," Aurora said, running to him.

He gave her a hug and tugged on the ends of her hair. "Glad

to see you made it back in one piece, cousin."

"Thank you. Have you made any progress?"

"With the Queen's Guard, yes. As for the King, I believe the Queen has been quite effective."

"That's excellent news."

"I believe he was simply waiting to see if the princess came through on her task before making a final decision."

"Well, she came through," Aurora said with a smile. "So, it looks like we're going to war."

"We shouldn't be smiling," he said. "This is dangerous. Many lives will suffer."

Her smile faded. "I know. I just somehow feel uplifted. Like we might have a chance."

Spotting Lady Tori over his cousin's shoulder, he excused himself. He forced himself not to run to her, though every step it took to reach her was torture. When he reached her, he couldn't help himself; he closed the distance between them and embraced her.

At the sound of her gasp, he took a step back.

"Lady Tori," he bowed his head. "I'm glad you've returned."

She didn't look upset about the embrace, he noted.

"As am I," she said, gazing upon him as if she had missed him.

For a moment, they simply stood there, their eyes locked.

"I trust you had a safe journey," he said.

"Actually, we did get caught in the storm."

"How awful. But you're here, so I assume you managed to get through it."

She let out a strange laugh. "The oddest thing happened, actually." She checked over their shoulders and then pulled him closer to an alcove, lowering her voice. "We found a cave to take shelter in, and we tried to start a fire, but it wouldn't light."

"That sounds frightful."

"Yes, it was. But I was able to do something… Here, let me just show you. But promise not to be alarmed."

He narrowed his eyes. "All right."

She let out a breath and took his hands in hers. He noted that they were warm, but the longer she looked at him, the hotter her hands became.

"How are you doing that?" he whispered.

"I'm not exactly sure. It's as if I told the fire in my body to come alive, so it did."

He stared at her hands. "Can you control it, though? I mean, would you burn someone without meaning to?"

"I don't know." She shrugged, almost giddy. "I don't think so. I haven't really tested it out."

His mouth slowly changed into a smirk. "Perhaps I can hold your hand for a while, and I'll tell you if you burn me. May I?"

She bit back a smile. "Yes, let's consider it an experiment."

Wrena walked into the throne room, flanked by her uncle and aunt. Behind them marched some of King Rainer's top soldiers.

"Rainer," King Adam said with a nod. He stood and stepped down from his platform, closing the distance between them to shake King Rainer's hand. "It's been ages."

"Yes," King Rainer responded. "Too long, indeed."

"I understand you're on board for the revolt against Nostidour and Avarell."

"I am."

"I have to tell you: I'm a bit surprised. Avarell was once your home."

"It still is," King Rainer said. "That is why I need to defend it."

A smile crept upon King Adam's face. "Then we should begin planning out strategy. Shall we adjourn to my war room and iron out the details?"

King Rainer gestured for King Adam to lead the way. "After you." He turned to Wrena. "Dear niece, I understand your heart is set on revenge, but perhaps it would be wise for you to stay in Gadleigh until the attack is over."

"No." The princess held her chin high. "No, I want to go back and face the duke. I won't be able to sleep until I see the life drain out of his eyes."

Her uncle bowed his head to her. "Understandable. Then we shall do as you wish."

CHAPTER THIRTY-NINE

$\mathcal{A}$urora and the princess set down their swords. They had been practicing the moves Bram showed them for about half an hour and were ready to take a break. Tori watched them from the bow of the ship, taking note that their enthusiasm was helping their footwork.

They rode a Gadleigh ship. Behind them, a fleet from Gadleigh and a fleet from Creoca followed, riding hard on the sea. Despite King Adam's reluctance, word was sent out to both Khadulan and the Crystal Islands to inform them of their alliance, along with an invitation to join in the fight. Time had come to choose sides.

Tori turned to face the sea. The rolling fog made it impossible to see very far, and the choppy waves kept her on her toes to remain balanced.

"They're coming along," Bram said, suddenly beside her.

"They're eager," Tori agreed. "But they wouldn't stand a chance in battle. Not yet, anyway."

He nodded. "True. I remember being a cocky kid and thinking I could take on Logan. He'd knocked the sword from my hands before I even took my second breath."

She smiled at him. "The armies will do most of the fighting. And you and I. But we can't stop them from joining us, I suppose. We'll have to make sure they remain safe."

"I don't suppose I need to worry about you?" he asked, his smile crooked.

"I know a thing or two about how to beat an opponent."

His smile faded. Suddenly his eyes widened as his gaze focused over her shoulder.

"Get the princess and Aurora below deck!"

She turned to see that he had spotted a ship. "Nostidour," she whispered, her heart beginning to hammer.

Because of the fog, they had been unable to spot it in time, and now it was fast upon them. Bram continued to shout to his fellow soldiers. Hard footsteps pummeled the deck as guards scurried to defend the ship.

Tori checked her weapons. She turned and headed for the fore mast, grabbing a long length of thick rope before she climbed. With a sudden surge of energy, she used her tree-climbing skills to hoist herself high enough and tied one end of the rope to the mast. She wasn't about to wait for the enemy to jump on board their ship. She needed to take the offense. She just hoped they didn't use their cannons.

Their only advantage was their numbers. With the thick fog hiding the presence of the Gadleigh and Creocan fleets, they had the element of surprise on their side.

The ship neared. A barrage of Nostidourians stood on the railing of the ship, ready to jump them. Arrows flew, and axes were held at the ready.

"Have at us, you filthy savages!" one of the Gadleigh soldiers shouted.

"For the queendom!" shouted another.

Tori couldn't wait any longer. The jump would be risky, but she had to take a chance.

Grabbing the other end of the rope with all her might, Tori sprung and swung toward the enemy ship. Mid-air, she heard a cannon fired. She caught sight of it striking the Gadleigh ship as her rope came to the end of its arc.

Just as she landed on the deck, she was grabbed around the waist. Her feet skidded across wood as the Nostidourian soldier dragged her back. She tried to bend, her hand reaching for her thigh, where her kunai was sheathed. If she could only reach it through the layers of her skirts, she could even the playing field. With a grunt, she threw her leg back, kicking him in the shin and causing his grip to loosen. She seized the opportunity and whipped out the kunai. She shifted away from him and took aim, watching the shock in his eyes as her blade came down hard and stabbed him in the chest.

But as soon as he was down, another came at her. This one landed a blow to her shoulder before she could react, the impact throwing her down and sending her kunai flying out of her reach.

"Filthy savage, eh?" His yellowed teeth bared as he hovered over her, he lifted a fist and swung across her face.

Her blood pounded so hard against her temples she thought her skull would explode. Biting back the ache, her knee came up to catch him in the crotch, but he knocked it away with his metal hammer. Shockwaves of pain ricocheted through her at the impact, and tears of anguish pooled at the sides of her eyes.

She meant to scream, but no sound could make its way through her throat. She clawed at him with vigor while trying to kick him away.

One second, he was drooling above her, his metal hammer held high above his head ready to thunder down on her, and the next second his head was gone. She gaped at the hammer that had landed with a *thunk* beside her. It wasn't until she felt the warm splash of blood on her neck and face that she realized Bramwell had slashed the savage's head off. The foul man's body slumped down, and it took everything that Tori had to push it off her.

No sooner had Bram helped her up than they were ambushed from both sides. Tori's heart pumped furiously, priming herself for the fight. Withdrawing a handful of shuriken, she took her aim, her back up against Bram's as he took on the attackers on the opposite side. A spear came at her. She ducked, hoping it wouldn't hit Bram, and threw the first shuriken, the flashing metal zipped through the air and hit her attacker between the eyes. The second shuriken caught the next savage in the neck, slicing into his carotid and gushing blood everywhere. His bow dropped to the ground beside him, its arrow still nocked.

Bram's arm suddenly wrapped around her and pulled her down. She barely caught sight of the spear missing their heads as they rolled to the side. She got her footing at the exact moment Bramwell's sword plunged upward into their attacker's ribcage.

It wasn't until she saw his form grow still that she could finally take a breath.

CHAPTER FORTY

Wrena crouched down, asking her uncle for the hundredth time if he was all right, as Tori wrapped his calf. The bleeding had stopped, and he insisted he could walk, though Tori noted that he did so with a slight limp. But limp or not, he had taken down his attacker and helped them win the battle. They'd lost one ship to the Nostidourians, but in the end, they'd defeated them all and taken no prisoners.

"Uncle, the duke has Aunt Maescia. She's being held prisoner."

"Who told you this?"

"One of the Nostidour soldiers. He said he had a message for me. The duke promised to release her if I come back and give myself up."

Rainer narrowed his eyes. "It's a trap, for sure."

Wrena nodded. "Yes, I believe so too. He doesn't exactly have the greatest track record for being honest." She pushed her hair back from her face. "What do we do?"

"We look for her and save her."

Wrena nodded again.

Tori turned away from them, unable to wrap her head around everything that had occurred in the last week. This is what it came to. This was how peace was obliterated. She hoped they stood a chance against Nostidour and the duke. If Bram's plan worked out, he would be able to convince at least some of the Avarell soldiers to fight on their side.

Despite the cool breeze wafting off the ocean waves, a trickle of sweat made its way down Tori's spine. The bay was in view, and every jostle of waves brought them closer to dock. There were no Avarellian Queen's Guard to be seen on the dock—and thankfully no Nostidourian soldiers either—but a familiar ship was moored in its usual spot.

Goran.

She shifted her gaze to the south. In the distance, Khadulian ships headed their way. Tori's heart filled with hope as they pulled into port. Their odds had just improved.

If felt like ages before they docked. Though she felt slightly bad for running off the ship and abandoning her companions, she had to see if Goran was truly on his ship. She had to be sure he was even alive.

Her heart fluttered. He stood on the dock, instructing his crew to unload crates.

"Goran," she called, coming closer. Takumi kept in step behind her.

He turned to her, surprise apparent on his face. But before he could say anything, she threw her arms around him.

"Thank the Divine Mother you're alive," she said into his shoulder. "I thought I'd never see you again."

"You underestimate me, child," he replied. He took a step back and gave her an inquisitive look. "Did you just get off that Gadleigh vessel?"

"Yes," she said. "I brought reinforcements."

Goran looked past her, spotting the Creocan and Gadleigh fleets in the bay. He smirked at her and nodded his head toward his ship. "So did I."

Stepping off the gangplank was Queen Hira, Zhadé and a few of her crew close behind her. Fury let out a squawk, perched on Hira's shoulder.

"Lady Tori." Queen Hira bowed her head.

"You came," Tori said, more to convince herself that it was

true.

"You can thank Goran for that. He's quite a convincing man—for a Khadulian."

Goran laughed, and Hira smacked his back good-naturedly.

"I suggested they come on my ships to throw off the soldiers—Avarellian and Nostidourian alike." Goran gave Tori a wink. "Less likely to cause alarm if they think this is simply a delivery for the duke."

"But it doesn't look like anyone is checking," Tori said, glancing over her shoulder.

She did a double take when she saw Finja approaching, her cloak pulled low over her brow. Takumi rose on his hind legs and gekkered at her.

At the same time, Hira tossed a look over Tori's other shoulder. Tori followed her gaze to see the princess approaching from the ship. Bram and Aurora were behind her, the kings of Creoca and Gadleigh following close behind. Hira looked as if she anticipated words of protest at her presence, but the kings simply bowed their heads to her. Hira tilted her head in surprise and bowed her head in return.

Since not all the ships could moor at the dock, the ships were sending rowboats full of their soldiers to the shore. Their reinforcements would be coming in at a steady pace, but their numbers were impressive.

Finja walked up to Goran, giving him a nod. "Goran, I should have known you wouldn't be so stupid as to let anyone kill you. I trust you found your wife."

He gave her a small smile. "Yes. My family is safe. And not too thrilled about me joining this fight, I might add. But I knew this was coming. I need to be here and see this through."

Tori placed a hand upon his arm. "I'm glad you did, Goran."

Tori's companions came nearer, listening as Finja spoke.

"Things are bleaker than we expected," Finja said. "The duke has lost control, the queen regent is locked in the high tower, the Nostidourians are ruining Avarell, and the Undead have invaded the city."

"The Undead?" Princess Wrena asked. "But how?"

Bram and Tori exchanged a look. Tori silently warned him not to mention Queen Callista. Some things were better left unsaid.

"What's the plan then?" Queen Hira asked.

"We have the numbers to fight off the Nostidourians," King Rainer interjected, nodding to King Adam in agreement. "Especially with help from the Crystal Islands and Khadulan. As for the Undead—"

"I have an idea about how to deal with them," Queen Hira said.

With a click of her tongue, Fury spread his wings and took flight, his phoenix squawk sounding like a war cry.

They kept a quick pace as they headed into Avarell. Their numbers were so great, when Tori looked back over her shoulder, she couldn't tell where the throng of troops ended and the ocean began. In front of them, a slow rise of smoke clouded the city. Shrieks of fear and sorrowful sobs could be heard, drifting toward them from the city center. As they breached the town walls, she couldn't believe her eyes. Her breath came out in a gasp and her stomach twisted in knots. This was not the Avarell she had left. All of the vendor carts in the market were abandoned, many of them overturned. A couple even appeared as though they had been set on fire.

Peering past the market and into the town square, shop windows were broken. Doors hung off hinges, and barrels of ale and wheat lay upturned and broken on the street. Up ahead, fighting could be seen, the clashing of swords causing a din to sound in the air. She could just make out the soldiers in Avarell uniforms being slaughtered by Nostidourian brutes, despite their efforts to ward them off. Innocent citizens cowered behind barrels, mothers covering the eyes of their small children to keep them from witnessing the brutality.

And then she saw them. The Undead wandered freely. Both Nostidourian and Avarellian soldiers fought back as the gray-skinned monsters relentlessly pushed forward with their attacks. The Undead reached for the living with their yellowed nails, their slacked jaws hanging open as they growled with hunger. Tori felt a shudder thunder through her, removing her kunai and keeping it at the ready. She wasn't sure how many shuriken she had left, so she decided to keep them until she absolutely needed them.

Beside her, Princess Wrena's face paled. "There are so many."

Lady Aurora shook with fear.

Suddenly, there was a piercing cacophony of phoenix cries filling the air.

The group turned their heads toward where the road led to the Rift. Flying above them and heading toward the city center was a flock of phoenixes so great in number it darkened the sky. The flapping of their wings was deafening. The group couldn't help but duck their heads as the flock swooped down past them into the heart of the city. Judging by the blue fire shooting from the spearhead's beak, Tori knew Fury must have been in the lead. He was an alpha, and he had gathered the phoenixes from the Rift to join him in the fight. They followed him unquestioningly, just as Queen Hira had said.

The flock swiftly dove down over the town and let loose a barrage of fire. Blue and orange flames rained upon the Undead. The monsters groaned in shock and flailed their arms as the fire burned through them. They beat their burning arms against the buildings, against each other, trying to put the fires out, but their efforts were futile. A group of the phoenixes swept back over the town square, fire beating down on the Undead. The creatures were defenseless. With cries that could only come from creatures of hell, they began to fall. A putrid stench of burning flesh and ash filled the air. Some of the fire hit the fighting soldiers, and those who did not act quickly enough to roll on the ground to put the fire out burned to their deaths.

They had their defense from the sky, and now it was time for them to do the groundwork. Bram and Tori exchanged a look. Inside, she was shaking, acid roiling in her stomach from the fear that pulsed through her. But she didn't want anyone to see it. She nodded, and Bram was the first to draw his sword and storm forward. He let out a loud war cry, a call to action. The rest followed, swords, kunai, flying arrows, spears, and battle axes at the ready, charging into battle through fire and adversaries to take back the queendom of Avarell.

CHAPTER FORTY-ONE

*B*ram barely recognized the castle. Evidence of Stoneheart's presence was everywhere he looked. It was as if the very evil the Nostidourians brought into Capehill Castle was scorched deep into every stone and tile and crevice of the place Bram once called home.

Where were all the soldiers?

He'd seen a mass of them in the city, fighting back the

Undead, but he knew they were much greater in number. Had Stoneheart's men slayed them all? The thought of it made Bram's heart drop into his roiling stomach. He had to get to the barracks. He needed the Avarell army on his side if they were to stand a chance.

"Bramwell?"

The sound of Logan's voice sparked a ray of hope in Bram's chest, and upon seeing Logan hurry toward him, the spark grew into a flame of resilience.

"Logan!" The men clapped each other on their backs as they embraced, and Bram breathed in aching relief that his friend was still alive.

"I see you've returned to witness the chaos," Logan said.

"I've brought armies from the other realms. We're going to fight back."

"Against the Undead? Or the savages of Nostidour?"

"Both." Bram marched toward the barracks with Logan fast at his side.

"It's not going to be easy to sway the duke's faithful men."

"What kind of a soldier would I be if I didn't at least give it a try?"

As Bram made his way into the crowded barracks, the thrum of the soldiers in the crowd grew quiet, all eyes focused on him. Logan helped him stand upon a chair so that more of the soldiers could see him. There were whispers in the crowd. Some of them were glaring at him with hatred in their eyes, yet some of them were curious about what he had to say.

"My good men," Bram began, keeping authority in his voice. "The duke has misled you. The negotiation with Nostidour was an obvious failure. This allegiance was simply the duke's way of manipulating power and control. It was never what Lady Maescia intended, and it certainly would have been frowned upon by Queen Callista. Your rightful ruler, Queen Wrena, implores you to join her in the fight for peace. Not against Gadleigh. Not against Creoca or the Crystal Islands, but against Nostidour."

"Stormbolt brought a bunch of pirates to Avarell," someone shouted. "We can't trust him.

Bram held his hand up. "The pirates are a thousand times more well-mannered than the Nostidourian savages. Look at what Stoneheart's men have done to our home."

"This isn't your home anymore," Nils yelled.

Some of the crowd responded in agreement. There were mumbles and more dirty looks.

Logan stepped onto a chair next to Bram. "Avarell is in Bram's heart, and so it will always be part of him, always be his home."

Nils scowled, his eyes narrowed. "Look who our next traitor is. Taking the side of a Gadleigh soldier."

A number of the guards shouted in concurrence. Logan and Bram exchanged looks. Logan nodded for Bram to continue. Bram clenched his fists and forced himself to continue.

"We will lose Avarell if we allow the Nostidour army to take control. Do not be fooled by the duke's empty promises."

"Look at the loss we've suffered already," Logan added.

"He's right," someone shouted.

"It's gotten out of control," another added.

His face reddening with rage, Nils grabbed Logan's arm and yanked him down off the chair. "I have the right mind to deliver your head to the duke myself, Rathmore."

"You and what army?"

With that, Nils raised his axe. Bram barely had time to think. He jumped down from his chair to catch Nils's arm mid-swing, colliding with the flat end of the axe before knocking it to the ground. Nils let out a shout of fury, his eyes wild with anger. The room erupted in pandemonium, soldiers taking sides, pushing each other and throwing punches.

Coming in from outside, Azalea charged in with wide eyes. She pushed herself through the calamity and climbed atop a table, raising her sword. "Brothers! Brothers! The Undead have breached the bridge! We're under attack!"

Nils sneered at her. He had found his axe and clambered onto the table, glaring at her as if she were his mortal enemy. "Another traitor. I should have known we couldn't trust a woman to be loyal."

She held her sword in front of her, clenching her teeth. "Don't do it, Nils."

With a brash shout, Nils swung the axe sideways. Azalea was quick to dodge it, lunging forward after clearing the axe, and plunging her sword into Nils's side. His cry of pain was ear-splitting.

The fighting in the room ceased as Nils clutched his side and fell to the ground. Azalea panted, staring at his dying form and swallowing hard before turning to Logan.

"We need to get out there and save Avarell," she said. "Our city is perishing."

Logan and Bram climbed up onto the table next to her.

"It's us or them," Bram yelled, his voice booming. "Who's with us?"

The room responded in shouts and cries. Guards unsheathed their swords and charged out of the barracks, roaring with vehemence. Bram couldn't be sure they were all on his side against Nostidour, but he was certain the Queen's Guard would defend Avarell against the Undead.

Logan pulled Azalea into his arms. They panted for breath, eyes wide in disbelief.

"I can only hope I convinced some of them," Bram said.

"There are four realms fighting on our side," Azalea said. "We stand a chance."

"Stay strong, my friend. Those who are not with you will fall."

Bram slapped Logan on the back, nodded to Azalea, and then jumped off the table to find Grunmire.

CHAPTER FORTY-TWO

o one was in the chapel. It surprised Tori, because
people often sought refuge with the Divine Mother
when lives were at stake. Though, evidence of a struggle could be
seen, judging by the upturned pews and scattered books and
candles on the chapel floor. Hira sprinted to the door of the
sacristy and threw it open, her dagger held in front of her. The
way she turned away and pursed her lips told Tori the room was

empty.

"Let's keep looking," Tori said. Though her heart thrummed in her chest, she told herself to restrain her emotions. It was all she could do to keep herself from snapping.

Hira gave her one curt nod.

They turned to charge out of the chapel, but a monstrous figure suddenly blocked the entrance. Tori recognized his bulk and his long braid.

"Stoneheart," Hira said through clenched teeth.

"Kaliskan." Stoneheart flexed his back, his muscles bulging. He needed to duck to get through the archway entrance. "I thought you were dead."

"Sorry to disappoint you."

"I'm sure it won't happen again, Your Highness." Stoneheart cracked his knuckles, then retrieved the Dao sword from the leather strap tied to his thigh.

His feet pounded onto the floor as he neared, each step making the furniture in the room shake.

It's two against one, Tori told herself. The odds should have been in their favor, but taking in Stoneheart's colossal form, she felt as if they were outnumbered. She tensed her muscles, and she couldn't tell if the rise in her body temperature was the rage surging inside her... or something else.

Before he could get too close, she whipped the shuriken that was in her hand, aiming for his nose. But with one swift swoop of his arm, he deflected it. Tori gasped. She was sure one of the sharp edges had cut him, but it didn't seem to faze him. He raised the Dao sword, a malicious smirk stretching his mouth. He was built like a giant, seeming to snuff out the sun as his shadow fell over them.

With a grunt, Hira lunged low, attempting to aim for his legs with her dagger. The second her blade struck his skin, he wrenched it out and hurled it at the altar. No sooner had she dodged it, did Hira pull out another dagger, but Stoneheart was quicker to move. He grabbed her by an arm and a thigh and lifted her as easily as if she were a bushel of wheat. She shrieked as he tossed her over the pews. When she landed, air shot from Hira's lungs like a cannon being fired.

With her kunai drawn, Tori hurriedly climbed atop the back rest of one of the pews and leaped at Stoneheart. She aimed for his throat, but he shifted, the blade landing in the muscle of his shoulder. He swung his enormous arm around and knocked her quickly onto the floor. Before she could catch her breath to stand, he snatched her up, raising her above his head and throwing her hard against the chapel wall. It knocked the wind out of her, and her ears rung as pain shot through her body. Black spots clouded her vision as she tried to get up.

She winced as a massive hand clutched her throat. Stoneheart lifted her off the ground, leaving her legs flailing. She fought to breathe, her vision swimming from the lack of oxygen. Then there was an explosion of pain as her back was slammed against the wall.

She tried to gasp for air, but nothing came. She hit his arms with tight fists, but he was relentless. She grabbed his hands, trying to pry his fingers from her throat. She kicked, but her legs wouldn't reach him. As tears of agony formed in her eyes, the ringing in her ears transformed into a phoenix cry. She thought she might have imagined it, but regardless, it snapped her to attention.

Heat boiled within her. Mustering all the energy she could summon, she forced the heat into her fingertips, digging them into Stoneheart's wrists. Her fingers suddenly glowed, the bright blue light reflecting in Stoneheart's widened eyes. She pushed harder. An intense flood of blue light blasted across Tori's vision. Her pain began to lessen until all she felt was the will to destroy her enemy. Stoneheart's snarl disappeared. His skin sizzled and blistered, the flesh tearing as smoke rose from it. He gaped at her hands on his wrists, then let out an ear-piercing scream. But she didn't let go.

He released her neck and attempted to throw his arms out to the sides to free himself from her grasp. The velocity sent her swinging. She lost her grip with one hand, but she hung on with the other, unwilling to lose focus. He thrashed, yelling as he tried to escape her hold. Smacking her into a row of pews, he broke free, and she fell to the floor. Pain rippled through her again. Stoneheart turned slightly away from her, clutching at his still-smoking wrists.

Though the pain was intolerable, she forced herself to get up.

Her stores of strength were low, but still she propelled herself forward and jumped on his back. A scream left her mouth as she wrapped her glowing hands around his neck, her fingers scorching his throat. She could feel his skin melting, turning to a thick liquid like the honey her mother used to put in her tea. Her fingers dug deeper into the flesh, her will to abolish him returning. She held on tight as he flailed, dodging his aim as he turned and swung and reached behind himself to get to her.

Blood began to flow from the depressions she created in his skin, and then his whole head was enveloped in smoke. She felt his neck bone as his voice disappeared.

He slumped toward the ground, first crashing to his knees, and then landing hard on his chest with Tori clinging to his back.

Her breath came out in shudders as she slowly pulled her hands away from him, her fingers wet with his blood. She waited, but there was no rise and fall of breath.

She rolled off him, dropping to the floor. Her aching body shook as sobs escaped from her lungs.

She lifted her head. She had to find Hira.

Unable to stand, she crawled across the floor toward Hira's body. She could hear the strained gasp for air.

"Queen Hira," Tori whispered, her voice weak.

With a moan, Hira shifted, her eyes red. She had landed on her dagger, its blade embedded in her stomach. Blood stained her clothes and puddled the chapel floor. "Lady Tori."

"I'll get help."

As Tori was about to get to her feet, Hira's eyes widened. She pulled Tori down swiftly. In a quick move Tori almost couldn't track, Hira snatched up the kunai beside her and jumped to her feet. Tori rolled to the side just in time to see the pirate queen jump onto Stoneheart, who hovered above them—still alive. Hira swung the kunai while she was still in the air, and it slashed across what was left of his throat. His head snapped backward, and he crumpled to the ground.

Hira landed hard on the floor beside him, clutching her stomach.

Tori hurried to them, her eyes focused first on Stoneheart to make sure he was dead this time. Once she was convinced he was no longer among the living, she put her hands on Hira.

She tried to speak, wanting to say something full of hope, but there was way too much blood.

"It's over," Hira said. Though she squinted in pain, she nodded as if satisfied. "It is done."

"Queen Hira. No!"

"I'm afraid our time together has come to an end, Lady Tori."

"Don't say that."

"I know you're not really a High Priestess, but perhaps you can say a prayer to the Divine Mother anyway. I'm sure you'd agree that even a ruthless pirate deserves a final blessing."

Tori put pressure on the wound, careful not to touch the dagger, but the blood wouldn't stop. "Maybe… maybe I can help. Somehow."

"No. It's too late. Let me go."

"I can't."

"I've accomplished what I needed to," Hira said. "It's time for me to see my mother."

Tori cradled her, tears streaming down her cheeks.

She looked up when someone charged into the chapel. Seeing Zhadé, she sobbed some more.

Zhadé rushed to Hira's side, and Tori backed away, clutching her knees.

"My love," Hira said, taking their hand. Tori was surprised to see a smile on Hira's face.

"No. No. My love. Don't leave me." Zhadé held Hira against their chest and rocked her.

"It's all right," Hira said, her voice getting weaker. "I'll always be with you."

Zhadé's cheeks were stained with tears. They pressed their lips against Hira's head. "I'm sorry. I'm sorry. I should have been by your side."

"Promise me you'll take my place," Hira said, squeezing her hand. "Take care of our people. Lead them to peace."

"Of course. Of course, I promise. I love you, my queen."

Hira's mouth opened as if to answer, but the light faded from her eyes, and she spoke no more.

CHAPTER FORTY-THREE

*T*he key turned in the lock, and Lady Maescia held her breath. Her senses sent into high alert, she readied herself. If it was the duke at her door, she was prepared to fight. She wouldn't give in so easily. Not to the duke.

As Lady Raven entered the room, Lady Maescia let out her breath, her body almost shaking in relief. Raven appeared harried, fidgeting with the key and looking over her shoulder.

"Come on," Raven said.

"What?"

"I'm setting you free. Avarell is in chaos. You don't deserve to be locked up in here. Run while you have a chance."

At first, all she could do was stare. But then Lady Maescia took Raven's hands in hers. "Thank you, Lady Raven. Thank the Divine Mother she sent you."

Raven squeezed her hands. "Go, Your Grace."

Maescia swallowed back her anxiousness and ran into the hall. Her pulse hammered in her ears. She wasn't sure where she could go that was safe, but she thought perhaps the secret passageways might be her best bet. If nothing else, she could hide there until the massacre was over.

She slipped behind the tapestry and pressed on the secret spot that triggered the door to pop open. With jittery fingers, she gathered her skirts and pushed her way into the secret passageway. Her eyes slowly adjusted to the darkness, and she cursed herself for not thinking to find a candle to bring with her. The narrow passage was cold, and her heavy breathing echoed off the stone walls. She found the stairs, taking great care not to trip on them. She hoped her memory served her right to get to the secret door that led to her chambers.

Another set of stairs and a few turns later, she ended up at the door to her rooms. For a moment, elation rushed through her. She could make it. With the Divine Mother's blessing, she might actually survive. She pressed on the secret release panel and cracked the door open a bit, but her room was not empty. Holding her hand over her mouth so as not to make a sound, she took a step back and pressed the door closed. She wasn't sure who the couple on her bed was, but she was certain they would see her if she entered the room from behind her tapestry. She decided, instead, to find another exit. Perhaps the ramparts would serve her better.

She pivoted and headed in the direction of the ramparts at the back end of the castle. This passageway was not as familiar to her. In fact, she couldn't remember using it before. But she knew it existed. Forcing herself not to give up hope, she pressed forward. She felt the walls and prayed there weren't too many stairs or turns that would get her lost.

Her fingers came across a separation in the wall, and she felt around for the release lever. When she heard the click of the release, she let out a sigh of relief.

She pushed on the door, but it swung too quickly away from her. She leapt forward to grab the door, but it was out of her reach, and she fell forward. Landing on her stomach, she looked around and realized she hadn't reached the platform of the ramparts but the walkway underneath them.

An unearthly groan sounded, and she turned her head to see two Undead pacing toward her. Their empty eyes were locked on her, and they reached for her with long, crooked fingers. Her heart felt as if it were in her throat, cutting off her air supply. She scrabbled to her feet and ran forward, only to spot a handful more

Undead coming toward her from that direction. When she pivoted around to run toward the courtyard, her jaw dropped. Her sister, the Undead Queen Callista, glared at her, her yellow teeth bared as she snarled.

Lady Maescia's body sagged at the sight of her. When she had been chained up in the darkness of her room in the high tower, it was easy to ignore the danger her sister might encompass. But now, looking at her coming at her with bared teeth and reaching fingers, she found herself wavering on her legs. Her lips trembled as she backed away.

"Callista. Please."

Callista tilted her head, her lips curled into a sinister smile. There would be no getting through to her. How could she have let it get this far? Had she failed her sister as well as the queendom?

Backing into one of the wooden beams that held up the ramparts, Maescia's head shot up. She would have to climb. Lifting her skirt to get her leg high enough, she began scaling the wooden struts that connected the beams to the ramparts. She wouldn't look behind her, but she knew the Undead were not far.

Sweat dripped from her brow, and she prayed that the moisture on her hands wouldn't cause her to slip. It was a twenty-foot climb, but she had to keep going. Though she felt her energy depleting, she pushed herself to climb until she reached the top of the ramparts. When her hand found the railing of the rampart, she pulled herself up. But to her horror, the Undead Queen

Callista was directly behind her, duplicating her movements and climbing up to the ramparts. She stared at her sister in shock, unable to fathom that an Undead could climb.

The other Undead did not ascend the beams, but they banged against the wood with their fists, growling and groaning, and watching Lady Maescia with empty eyes. With each blow they delivered onto the wood, the ramparts shook.

Lady Maescia turned to run, but her foot caught the length of her gown, and she fell to her knees. By the time she could stand up again, her sister grabbed her by the arm.

"Callista, I'm sorry." She pulled back, trying to escape her sister's grasp. "I never meant—"

Her words turned into a scream as Callista's rotten nails dug into Maescia's arm.

Maescia pushed against her sister, trying to throw her off balance, but Callista reached for her hair and pulled her toward her, her mouth coming close to her cheek. Maescia lashed out and scratched Callista in the face, gagging when the skin of her face came away under her nails.

The structure shook more, as the number of Undead below multiplied. Maescia lost her footing, but so did Callista. Callista's hands held fast to Maescia's clothes. They fell together sideways and rolled to the edge of the ramparts.

Maescia let out a scream as Callista was knocked off the edge. Her arm reached out and clutched Callista's hand before she could drop to the ground below. With her other hand, she grasped the railing. She held on, not wanting to let her sister go, Undead or not.

The Undead below continued to pound on the wood, and the damage was beginning to take effect. The wood cracked in several places, and the structure was no longer sound.

Maescia yanked on Callista's hand trying to pull her up. If she could pull her up, maybe they could run to the end of the ramparts and find safety. She yanked her higher, then stared in disbelief as her sister opened her mouth and dug her teeth into Maescia's hand. Maescia's scream filled the air. Pain shot through her, and she lost her grip on the railing. And then there was nothing holding her up. The earth below grew closer in her vision as they both toppled to their deaths.

CHAPTER FORTY-FOUR

Outside of the training room, the city was burning, the smoke rushing toward the sky in plumes. Phoenix fire had decreased the number of Undead, their burning corpses leaving a lurking stench. The Nostidourians persisted in fighting off the armies of Gadleigh, Creoca, Khadulan, and the Crystal Islands. Swords and axes swung. Spears pitched through the air. Throats were sliced, and bones were broken. But the

Nostidourian soldiers were no match for their adversaries, their numbers beginning to fall.

Bram charged ahead, cutting his way through the chaos of growls and shouts and blood, taking down a few of the Undead as well as a couple Nostidourian soldiers before breaching the training room doors. Blood pumped through him like a raging river. He needed to find the duke.

Behind him, a group of Undead followed. But the voices of Princess Wrena and the duke beckoned him to continue forward. He didn't turn to fight the monsters. Instead, he ran to the main training room, then slammed the doors shut to lock out the Undead.

Bram turned in time to see Grunmire's palm landing hard against Wrena's face. The impact had sent both her and her sword to the ground. Bram, taken by surprise, stared in shock.

Anger flashed across Grunmire's face. "You disrespectful bitch. The nerve of you showing your face here after you tried to kill my son."

Wrena held her cheek, sneering at the duke. "Too bad I couldn't finish the job."

He took two swift steps toward her, but Bram dashed between them, clenching his sword.

"Leave her alone, Grunmire!"

The duke tightened his fists and held his chin high. "This is no concern of yours, lad."

"The safety of the princess is my concern. You've done

nothing but destroy the welfare of this land. Your politics are worthless. It was unwise to bring Nostidour to Avarell; they've ruined it. It was senseless to try to negotiate with them. Face it; you've failed as a ruler."

"Stormbolt." The duke shook his head, glaring at Bram. "Always the hero. Always trying to prove yourself. You're pathetic. Just like your father."

Bram blanched, almost faltering. "Don't speak of my father. You didn't know him."

The duke smirked. "Oh, but I did. He was arrogant and egotistical and always had to show off the fact that he was better than everyone else. But he didn't look so pleased with himself when the enemy ambushed him on the field."

Bram clenched his teeth. "You were there? Did you not have the decency to try to save him?"

"Save him?" The duke let out a cynical laugh. "Who do you think led the enemies to him?"

Bram's skin grew hot. "You bastard!"

Bram crossed the distance between them in three precise strides, sword at the ready, meeting Duke Grunmire head-on. He drew in a great breath as he swung, wincing at the sound of his blade striking the duke's.

A cold grin spread across the duke's face. "You won't come out of this victorious, boy. You know I always win."

"Haven't you heard?" Bram retorted. "I've stopped listening to your lies."

The duke withdrew and lunged, his sword clattering against Bram's. The room filled with the scrapes of their shoes and the grunts of their efforts, the loud clang of their clashing swords growing at a faster pace. At the duke's next swing, Bram was expecting the blow, and followed the force of the hit, spinning to his knee and rolling to a stance, swinging at the duke from his new standpoint. The duke shifted, but a second too late. The impact to his sword had the duke stumbling backward. He sneered as he snapped back into a readied stance, his sword held out with both hands.

Something thrummed inside of Bram. Not just his rapid heartbeat, but a call to destiny. Perhaps it was the sound of the Undead groaning and clawing at the door, making him aware that he couldn't give up. He could win this. He adjusted his grip, his muscles feeling flexed and ready.

The duke lunged forward, but Bram sidestepped. But on the duke's next swing, his blade slashed into Bram's arm. The sting of pain exploded in his arm as he raised his sword to block the duke's next blow. Sparks flew as their swords struck. Bram moved into the duke's path, his sword blocking the next upswing. He then whirled his blade and swung at Grunmire's midsection, catching him off guard.

A slash of dark red began to pool at the duke's side. Grunmire's eyes widened in shock, his hand covering the wound as if to stop the bleeding.

Bram's labored breathing was the only thing to be heard

above the throng of the Undead. He ignored the numbness in his arm.

The duke's gaze came back to Bram, his brows lowering slowly.

"Well, boy, aren't you going to finish me off?"

Only Bram was aware that the princess had managed to get to her feet. Though she limped, she reached the door, and cast Bram a look as her hand reached for the latch. The nod he gave her was short but confirmed that he agreed to her plan.

"I've got a better idea," Bram said to the duke.

In that instant, he again nodded to the princess. She pulled the door open, yanking it toward her so that she stood behind it and out of harm's way. The duke turned swiftly, jarred from what Wrena had done, as the snarling Undead marched into the room. With strained muscles, Bram lifted his foot and gave the duke a hefty kick, sending him stumbling into the path of the Undead. The duke swung with his sword, but the Undead were not easily put off course from losing a limb. His screams filled the room, growing more desperate with each second.

"Bram, this way," Wrena shouted, climbing the weapons case.

Bram's gaze went upward, to where windows lined the high walls of the training room. Above the weapons case, there were enough notches in the wall for them to be able to reach the windows.

The duke's screaming had stopped, and Bram had to assume

he was dead.

Bram swung his sword to clear a path through the Undead, scrape by scrape, making his way to Wrena despite the agony in his arm. She was already on top of the weapons case, her fingers digging into the wall notches. He had to sheath his sword or drop it in order to climb, but, knowing there were bound to be more Undead beyond the training room, he decided to sheath it. His deliberation cost him precious seconds, however, as an Undead grabbed at his leg on his way up the case. Bram kicked, and though he caught the Undead in the jaw, its grip was still on him. Another swift kick finally got him released, but the movement shook the weapons case. Bram's heart thundered in his chest as the case righted itself, and he continued his climb.

Above him, Wrena was halfway through one of the windows. Below him, the duke was lost in the grabbing hands and teeth of the attacking Undead. Bram bit back his terror and ascended the case, praying to the Divine Mother that it would not topple. Every pull of his injured arm sent fireworks of pain through him.

Scrambling after the princess, Bram squeezed through the window and onto the portico.

"Come around the side," Princess Wrena called to him.

The move took them to a section of the roof that overlooked a storage yard. It was separated from the entrance of the training room—and the Undead—by a high wall. Looking down below, Bram spotted bales of hay.

"Think we can make the jump?" the princess asked.

"I don't think we have a choice."

The princess let out a shuddered breath and nodded.

"I'll go first," Bram said. "Perhaps I'll be able to help you when you land."

"All right."

Bram scooted to the edge of the portico. He said a silent prayer, then jumped. On his landing, something hard and metallic hit him in the head. His vision went black, and pain shot through his neck as the world faded around him.

CHAPTER FORTY-FIVE

hen Tori and Zhadé reached the throne room, Aurora had the tip of her sword pointed at Eleazar's throat. They slowed their pace, taken aback. Aurora did not dare to spare them a glance. Her eyes were trained on Eleazar, and they were filled with rage.

"You can't kill me." Eleazar scowled at her. "I'm the king. You'd be committing treason and would be beheaded."

Aurora scoffed. "You're not the king. Your wedding was a fallacy. Lady Tori is no High Priestess. You are nothing but greedy, disgusting scum."

"Nice try." Eleazar sneered, but there was doubt in his eyes. "It doesn't matter. I was crowned. I am King."

"No, she's right," Lady Tori said from the entrance of the room. "You are not truly married to the princess. You have no claim to the throne."

"I don't believe you," he shouted, nostrils flaring. "I don't believe any of you."

"It doesn't matter." Aurora took a closer step. "It ends here. All the lies, all your disgusting ways—it's all over."

Eleazar's growl turned into a scream of rage. Before anyone could stop him, he charged over to one of the standing candelabras on the side wall of the throne room and hurled it to the floor. In a flash, fire sparked onto the carpet, sending it ablaze.

Gasping, Tori reached for Aurora, but Eleazar already had her around the waist, her sword wedged in front of her by his arm. Aurora's eyes were wide and filled with fear as she screamed in protest, trying to wrench free from his hold. Zhadé and Tori exchanged shocked looks, unsure of what to do.

The flames grew higher. The brightness of the fire cast their shadows on the walls.

"Eleazar, you'll burn to death," Tori yelled.

"Then I'll take her with me. Wrena may not want me, but I'll be damned if she's happy with this whore."

Clenching her teeth, Aurora lifted her leg and slammed her foot down on his. Eleazar shouted in pain. The second he released her, Aurora swung around and stabbed him through the side with her sword. Blood spurted out onto Aurora's clothes, but still, she pushed the sword in farther. As Eleazar's jaw hung open and his eyes filled with tears, Aurora wrenched the sword out of his side.

Eleazar dropped to the ground, clutching his stomach, the flames creeping closer to him. He moved a blood-soaked hand to reach out for her, but she stepped out of reach.

"You'll never hurt her or anyone ever again, you worthless prick."

Aurora dropped the sword and turned her head. Her breath came out in harsh puffs as smoke surrounded her. She squinted against the heat that pushed in on her. She may have been free from Eleazar, but she was trapped behind the wall of fire.

There was no time to lose. Without thinking, Tori rushed forward, concentrating on her power as she walked through the flames. She was faintly aware of the blue glow that surrounded her entire body, protecting her like a shield. Once she was through the wall of fire, she wrapped her arms around Aurora, guarding her from the flames. Aurora ducked her head and pressed it against Tori's shoulder as she led her out of the throne room.

⟨✻⟩

Tori, Zhadé, and Aurora reached Goran as he stood, panting, above Chod. The Nostidourian's spiked club was impaled in Chod's head, blood pooling around him. Chod's body shook, his raised hand giving a final shudder before it dropped to the ground. As Chod's form grew still, Goran bent forward and rested his hands on his knees, letting out a grunt of relief.

Takumi, who was close by Goran, bounded over to meet Tori, gekkering and running in circles.

"Well done, Sir Goran." Zhadé nodded at him in approval, clearly impressed that Goran could have taken down a man of Chod's size.

"I had a little help," Goran said, gesturing with his head at Takumi.

"How do we stand?" Tori asked, searching their surroundings. Her mind whirled, unable to properly assess the situation.

"The phoenixes took care of most of the Undead," Goran said. "Fury is still making his rounds, so I'm sure he and his flock will get the last of them."

Aurora glanced around, her expression one of sadness. "Looks like they burned most of Avarell with them."

Goran nodded, still catching his breath. "Avarell can be rebuilt. But the Undead will remain gone."

Aurora nodded but cast her gaze to the ground.

"What of the rest of Nostidour?" Tori asked. Her muscles were still taut. She was still on high alert and unable to let her guard down.

"Outnumbered. A few fled, but not enough to worry about. The rest perished at the hands of the armies of the combined realms."

Tori felt herself nodding, but her mind wouldn't let her accept it. She felt as if the prospect of war had built for so long that it seemed an impossibility that it would ever end.

"Is it truly over?" Aurora asked, her hands on her cheeks.

"We can hope," Tori replied.

Out of the corner of her eye, Tori spotted Princess Wrena racing toward them. Aurora gasped when she saw her and closed the distance between them with open arms. They embraced, holding each other so tight Tori thought they would meld into one person. But the sorrow etched on their faces didn't go unnoticed.

Tori gave them a moment to embrace, but then had to ask, "Your Highness, where's Bram?"

Princess Wrena stepped back from Aurora but kept a hold on her hand. She turned to Tori with a furrowed brow.

"I'm sorry, Lady Tori." The princess shook her head. "It doesn't look good."

Tori's chest seized up and she forced away the dizziness that threatened to make her vision swim. She fought to control her breathing. "Show me."

CHAPTER FORTY-SIX

His arm itched. No. It wasn't an itch; it was an ache. He attempted to shift positions so he could scratch it, but even the slightest movement sent his body into a seizure of pain. His head felt as if something heavy sat upon it. He opened his eyes, blinking as he took in his surroundings. He was in the infirmary, his head and arm wrapped in bandages.

Making a valiant effort to sit up, he let out a loud groan of agony.

"Master Stormbolt, you're awake!" The nurse rushed over, relief apparent in her expression. "Please don't try to get up yet. Master Rathmore insisted I fetch him when you were conscious again."

"Conscious?" Bram shifted, grabbing his ribs as if able to stop the pain there. "How long have I been unconscious?"

"Almost a week," she replied "Please, stay still. I'll get Master Rathmore right away."

As she scampered out of the room, he looked around at the other patients in the infirmary. The beds were filled with blood and bandages and badly bruised bodies. None of them were Nostidourians. He hoped they were gone for good. He tried to look around some more, but the movement made him nauseous. He squeezed his eyes shut and waited for his head to stop spinning.

It had taken the nurse a good fifteen minutes, but she had finally succeeded. Bram opened his eyes to see his good friend charging into the infirmary. Logan raced to Bram's side, his look of concern slowly dissolving into an expression of relief.

"Good man," Logan said, leaning over him. He smiled and gave Bram a slap on his good arm. "You've awoken just in time for the wedding."

"Who's wedding? Yours?"

Logan let out a laugh. "Just come. If you can manage it."

It took some help from Logan and the nurse, but eventually

Bram was steady on his feet. He wasn't able to walk as fast as he normally did, but he was getting used to the ache associated with each step and able to keep pace with his friend.

"The nurse said I was out for nearly a week," Bram said as they made it halfway to the throne room.

"Well, the blow to your head is to blame for that. To tell you the truth, I was worried you might not be yourself when you woke. But you seem to remember who you are, and your words make sense, so I guess your skull is stronger than I thought."

Bram shook his head, still fazed by the fact he'd slept through multiple days. "The last thing I remember is jumping from the training room roof." He stiffened, panic gripping his heart. He suddenly found it hard to breathe. "Wait. Did everyone survive? Tell me, is Lady Tori all right? And Aurora? The princess?" He couldn't believe he hadn't thought of them right away. It was as if his brain was taking longer to wake up than his physical self.

"They are all fine. We did lose a few, however. Lady Maescia. The duke and his son. The pirate queen from the Crystal Islands. A few of our good men from the Queen's Guard."

"Oh, stars. That's horrible." He didn't say out loud that it wasn't horrible that the duke had perished. He was sure Logan already knew how he felt about him. "And the Nostidourians?"

"Most of them defeated, amazingly enough. The rest of them fled when they realized their leaders had perished. I don't think they'll be returning any time soon, but the guard is setting new training strategies, just in case."

"What of the Undead?"

"Burned. The phoenixes took care of them all. It was an unfathomable sight to behold."

Bram nodded, in wonder at how much had happened. "Okay. So, who's wedding is taking place? I'm not exactly dressed for it."

"Don't worry about that. Let's just say that the princess insisted the attire, the decorations—everything really—remain casual."

When they entered the throne room, Bram was met with a barrage of familiar faces. Their expressions told him they were glad to see that he was faring better. Or perhaps they were surprised he was alive at all.

He was suddenly confronted with a tight hug.

"So glad to see you, Bram," Azalea said.

He winced, his voice coming out strained. "Thank you."

"Oh," she grimaced and took a step back. "Sorry about that."

Logan smirked at him, seemingly holding back a laugh, and wrapped his arm around her.

Bram's gaze found its way to the altar. His jaw hung open when he saw Aurora standing there. Her hair was combed back into a perfect braid, and a small wreath of tiny white flowers sat upon her head. Her dress was white satin, and her cheeks were rosy. She placed a hand on her heart and smiled at him, nodding her head once in greeting.

He gave her an awkward wave, still not able to wrap his head around what was taking place.

The music started, and he turned his attention to the opposite side of the aisle.

"Oh, she looks lovely," Azalea said.

Bram watched with reverence as Princess Wrena came down the aisle on the arm of her uncle. King Rainer sported a black eye and had a slight limp to his gait, but Bram was glad to see he had survived the battle. Though the princess's dress was simple, she wore a queen's crown upon her head.

"She's Queen now," Bram whispered. It was more of a statement to himself than a question.

"It was a bit of a speedy coronation," Logan told him. "She thought it best to mark the establishment of a new reign before anyone might refute it. They were still clearing out the dead Nostidourians when they placed the crown on her head."

As she got closer, Bram bowed his head to her, wincing at the dizziness that ensued by doing so. Her eyes widened when she spotted Bram, and she smiled at him with a nod as she passed him.

Bram gazed upon the happy couple as Queen Wrena reached the altar, then blinked in surprise when Zhadé stepped in front of them with the book of Marriage Divinities.

"Since when is a pirate allowed to conduct a holy ceremony?" Bram asked.

"Zhadé was trained in Tokuna and has holy domain," Azalea answered, keeping her voice low. "They've also accepted the position of Royal Sovereign of the Crystal Islands, due to the passing of Hira Kaliskan."

"They agreed to stay to marry them before they head back to begin their reign," Logan added.

As Zhadé read from the Marriage Divinities, Wrena gazed upon Aurora and reached out to stroke her cheek. The Lords and Ladies of the court, along with as many citizens that could fit into the throne room, watched with anticipation as the happy couple received the sacred wedding sash, which was placed over their joined hands. Bram smiled, happy for his cousin as she and Wrena drank from the golden goblet and Zhadé pronounced them wed.

After the wedding, everyone was invited out to the front steps of the castle, where more citizens waited for them to appear. There were cheers and applause, and Bram had to steady himself as the noise threatened to bring an ache to his head.

The crowd quieted as their new queen lifted her head to speak. Behind the newlyweds stood Zhadé, standing tall with Hira's phoenix, Fury, on their shoulder. Though they offered a quick smile to the couple, their expression remained somber, their mourning for their lost love apparent.

"My dear citizens of Avarell," Queen Wrena said, holding Aurora's hand, "my bride and I thank you for your support in these trying times. My uncle, King Rainer, has promised to help us in our efforts to rebuild and restore Avarell into the place it was before my parents died. We also have the support of the queendom of Gadleigh, our alliance now stronger than it was before. And we have a new alliance in the queendom of the Crystal Islands. Most of Nostidour has fallen, but we are aware that an upset of peace can occur at any time, for any reason. My new bride and I promise to use everything within our power to keep the nine realms a place of peace. For you, and for all future generations."

The citizens applauded, the mood of the city obviously lifted. Hope blossomed in the air. Prince Theo then appeared, running up to wrap his arm around his sister's waist. She ruffled his hair, and he joined them in waving at the crowd.

Bram stretched his neck, trying to see past and above the faces in the crowd as they began to depart. He'd looked everywhere, but he could not find Lady Tori. Logan and Azalea had wandered off together, perhaps to celebrate their own love in the spirit of the wedding. Bram decided the one person who would have an answer for him would be Finja.

He found her in Lady Tori's rooms, the door wide open. Finja stood before an open trunk, packing her belongings. She had a bandage on her neck and a healing scar on her cheek.

"It appears as though you are leaving," Bram said, entering the room.

She didn't look up at him. "Is the habit of stating the blatantly obvious one of the requirements necessary to join Gadleigh's Queen's Guard?"

He pressed his lips together, not knowing whether to be

insulted or to laugh.

She closed the trunk and turned to him. "She went home to her family in Drothidia. I thought you would have gotten to know me well enough to come straight out and ask me the question that's most pressing, instead of dawdling around."

He pursed his lips and let out a heavy sigh, nodding solemnly. "I thought, perhaps, she might wait to see if I would recover."

"Don't blame the girl," Finja said. "I told her to go. She had waited as long as she could to see her family. There was no sense in the poor girl waiting any longer."

Bram gave her one curt nod. If Tori was truly gone, he wondered if he would ever see her again.

He lifted his head as she shut the balcony door. "And where will you go?"

"Back home as well." She touched her scar gently. "I have served this realm longer than desired, and now it is time for me to rest. I shall enjoy my retirement in the peace of my hometown, with no one telling me what to do. Perhaps I will get a pet to keep me company. I've heard foxes can be quite loyal."

He laughed, then fell into a bow. "I wish you well, dear Finja."

The smallest of smiles appeared on her face. She bowed her head in return. "And I you, Master Stormbolt."

CHAPTER FORTY-SEVEN

The quaint village of Sukoshi sat at the edge of the Drothidian border. Bram stared in wonder at the abundance of trees and plants, many of them varieties he had never seen before. The green scenery in front of him was a welcome change from the desolate hollows of the Rift. The Rift had been quiet and empty, but he had still jumped when he heard a sound, fearing that an Undead would jump out and attack him.

There was no way to know for sure if they had all perished in the phoenix fire, but he hadn't spotted any on his travels to Drothidia.

The small houses within Sukoshi were connected by simple stone paths. Some of the houses were marked with red painted symbols on the doors, a sign that the phoenix fever had affected the area not too long ago.

Bram continued walking the stone path, receiving curious looks from men and women going about their chores. Most of them seemed particularly interested in the fact that his arm was in a sling. He didn't stop and ask anyone about Tori, not until he came across an old man sitting on his porch in a rocking chair, smoking a pipe.

He approached the man with a friendly nod, and the man removed his pipe to inspect him. Leaning forward in his chair, the man narrowed his eyes.

"Begging your pardon, dear sir. I was wondering if you could tell where Lady Tori—I mean Tori might live."

"Yes, I could. Her home is down that way. The house with the white birdhouse hanging from a tree." The old man pointed him in the right direction, then lowered his arm and tilted his head. "I hope you're not here to lead her away; she's just returned home from being absent for a long while. I'm afraid you'll break her family's hearts if she was required to leave again."

Bram bowed his head to the man. "No, sir. I would never dream of separating her from her family. Thank you for your help."

Bram forced himself not to run toward Tori's house. He'd traveled this far without getting anxious and doing something rash; he could very well make it the rest of the trip with a practical head on his shoulders.

Finding the white birdhouse the old man spoke of, he walked up to the door of the house and gave it a solid knock.

A moment later, a little girl—a miniature version of Tori— opened the door and eyed him suspiciously. She pursed her lips when she noted his sling, then she lifted her chin and looked into his eyes.

"Are you a soldier?"

He laughed, because he wasn't in uniform. "Yes."

"Are you here to arrest someone?"

He raised a brow. "Is there someone here who needs to be arrested?"

She screwed up her lips. "No, but if you need someone, maybe you can take my brother."

"Taeyeon, stop being sassy." The woman who approached them from behind the girl studied Bram. She adjusted her shawl and cleared her throat. "Hello, may I help you?"

"Yes, ma'am," Bram said with a slight bow. "My name is Bramwell Stormbolt. I'm a friend of Tori's. I'm guessing you are her mother?"

"Yes, I am." Tori's mother nodded slowly, but her eyes were still scrutinizing Bram. "I suspect you are the reason she gets quiet every now and then. That far-away look in her eyes was a sure sign she had met someone… special during her journey."

"Oh," Taeyeon said with a sing-song lilt, her smile widening.

Bram felt his cheeks warm. "I, uh, can't say for sure, ma'am. Is Tori home?"

"Actually, she is out in the Rift."

"The Rift? Why?"

"If you know Tori, then you know she won't rest until she knows that that place is absolutely clear of the Undead."

He smiled and nodded. "Yes. That sounds like her."

"She should be back soon," Taeyeon said. "Maybe you should stay for dinner."

"I don't want to impose."

"You're not imposing," Taeyeon said. "Come, let me show you my shuriken. I'm carving them myself."

He let out a laugh. "All right."

"I'll set an extra plate at the table," Tori's mother said. "Tori will be delighted you've come to visit."

"Thank you, ma'am."

"Come on!" Taeyeon pulled on his available hand.

He followed her into the house's backyard, where there was a lovely garden separated from the grass by an assortment of stones. There was a wooden bench that sat under a cherry blossom tree, and close to the house was a work table, where an assortment of wooden shuriken was piled in a heap.

"I made all of these myself." She placed her hands on her hips.

"Tori said I'm the fastest carver she's ever seen. I don't think they look as good as Tori's. But if you ask me, they fly much faster."

"Taeyeon, are you talking to yourself again?"

Bram straightened his shoulders at hearing Tori's voice. First, a flash of orange fur caught his eye. As Takumi entered the backyard, he suddenly stopped running and sniffed the air, then ran in a circle around Bram before pawing him gently on the leg. Tori then came around the back of the house, but she was busy unloading supplies from her canvas bag and not looking at them. Bram breathed in deeply, happy to see her, watching her not as a High Priestess or even a renegade warrior, but as a lovely young woman from Drothidia, playing her part to take care of her family.

In that moment, Tori looked up. She froze when she spotted Bram, her jaw hanging slightly open. Her eyes widened, and her hand rested on her heart.

"Hello, Tori."

Tori cleared her throat, her heart suddenly pounding in her chest. She was at a loss for words.

He stood there, staring at her, and seeing him in person was a thousand times better than any memory her mind had conjured up in the last week. His arm was in a sling, and his hair was windblown, but she couldn't remember him looking any more handsome than he did in that moment.

"I was showing him my shuriken," Taeyeon said.

Tori smiled at her sister. "That's nice, Tae. Um, would you mind giving us a moment alone?"

Taeyeon rolled her eyes at Tori but did what she asked and ran into the house, Takumi in tow.

"Bram, what—uh—What are you doing here?"

She wiped the grime from her hands and attempted to clear her cheeks, but she was sure she still looked a mess. She couldn't know from his expression if she *was* a mess, however, because all she could see was adoration in his eyes.

"It's good to see you, Lady Tori."

She nodded once. "It's just Tori. And it's good to see you, too."

For a moment, they stood there in silence, simply gazing at each other.

"I see your family is well again," he finally said, breaking the silence.

"Yes." Tori nodded, feeling foolish, as if her movements were too exaggerated. She stopped nodding and pushed a strand of hair back behind her ear. "They are immunized. They're going to be fine."

"That's wonderful."

"It really is. It feels like we've been given a gift. A new beginning. My brother, Masumi—who swore he'd never settle down—has even gotten engaged to be married."

The corner of Bram's mouth lifted. "Love has a way of finding even those who are resistant."

She smiled at him and dropped her gaze to her hands.

"They invited me for dinner."

"Oh?" She turned her head, spotting her mother through the window, cooking with her sister.

"If you'd rather I not—"

"No, no. I mean, yes, of course." She rested a hand on his good arm. "Please. Stay."

The corner of his mouth inched upward, and Tori's heart swelled.

"Come with me," she said.

"Where?"

She let out a small laugh. "You don't trust me anymore?"

He stuttered, then laughed in return. "Of course I do."

She grabbed a handful of flowers that she'd set by her equipment and motioned for him to follow as she walked farther into her backyard. They continued on toward the woods into the cleared-out field laid out with large white stones. Tori could see the realization on Bram's face as he discovered it was a cemetery. She led him to a nearby stone, marked with her sister's name.

"Miki," Bram read quietly.

"I think my sister would have wanted to meet you."

He gazed upon Miki's gravestone for a short while before looking back up at Tori. He had a content look on his face that warmed Tori's heart.

"It's really beautiful here," he said. "If I had known how lovely Drothidia was, I would have come sooner."

"Speaking of coming here—and not to sound unwelcoming, but—shouldn't you be in Gadleigh?"

"Did you want me to leave?"

She opened her mouth to protest, but he let out a small laugh.

He lifted his sling a bit. "I have a little time off to heal."

"Let me see."

They headed back to her backyard, and he sat on the bench in the garden. She took a seat beside him, a small thrill trembling through her.

He slipped off the sling from his shoulder and carefully peeled back the bandage. She gently touched the skin around the wound, grimacing when he winced in pain.

"It doesn't look infected," she said, still studying it.

"That's good."

As she backed away, he redressed the wound and pulled the sash of the sling back over his shoulder. She reached inside her satchel, searching, and then took out a tin. "Here. Take this. Put it on the wound twice a day."

"What is it?"

"It'll help speed up the healing."

"Hopefully not too fast." With one hand, he took the tin, his fingers brushing hers. With the other, he reached out slowly and lifted her chin, gazing deeply into her eyes. His voice was soft when he spoke again. "I'm not exactly in a hurry to return."

She struggled to catch her breath. His gaze was so intense, it sent a shiver down her spine. This time, she didn't back away. The burn of temptation overrode her senses, and she let herself close the distance between them. She didn't want to be apart from him anymore. She had once told him that she would stay by his side, and that was a promise she intended to keep.

As their lips met, soft yet firm, a welcoming warmth spread through her, a heat like she'd never experienced before. A heat that sent her senses into a frenzy. A heat she hoped would never be extinguished. The phoenix fever had nothing on this.

ACKNOWLEDGEMENTS

It takes a community to bring a book to life. Not only am I overwhelmingly aware of this fact, but I'm eternally grateful to the people in my community—both book people and personal friends and family—who have helped me bring this series to fruition.

As always, I am honored to have such a wonderful human being as my agent, Italia Gandolfo. Thank you, Italia, for all you do for me and all the support you give me.

I wouldn't get anywhere without the help of my first line of defense, Sarah Howell. Sarah, I am forever indebted to you for your selfless help and encouragement and your willingness to read anything I throw your way.

A big thanks to Lyssa and everyone at Snowy Wings Publishing. I'm so glad to have found such a supportive and uplifting family.

Heartfelt gratitude goes out to my editor, Cheree Castellanos, who not only beat this series into shape, but showed me an outpouring of love and excitement for the books.

Thanks to my fellow authors, Jessica Gunn, Melanie McFarlane, Jenna Lee, Jennifer Grey, Pat Esden, and so many more, for their continuous support.

A shout out goes to my friends and colleagues—especially the Monkey team!— who always have great things to say. Deepest and warmest thanks of course to my home base team: Bonnie, Sasha, Carol, Rose, Cassie, Holly, Kyra, Renee, April, Nikki, and my loving Aunt Barb and Uncle Vic, Uncle Ron and Aunt Joan. Thanks also to my TM friends, who celebrate me at every turn.

A special nod of gratitude goes out to the winners of the Name-a-Character contest who came up with the name of our antagonist, Grigori Stoneheart. This name is a combination of two fabulous entries from Athena Brown and Laura Stockman. Thank you, ladies, for giving the king of Nostidour the perfect name.

Thanks again to the Sora Sanders translation team for their wonderful work on the German versions of the duology.

And of course, I wouldn't be where I am today without the help of my family. Thanks to my mom Rebecca, my dad Dave, my awesome-sauce brother David, and my extended family Hilde, Charlie, and Darlene.

Last but not least, I have everlasting appreciation of my husband Stephan, my super talented daughter Kirsten, and my son Zachary. Thank you so much for letting me do this author thing and forgiving my shortcomings around the house. I love you all so much, and I would be nothing without you.

ABOUT THE AUTHOR

Dorothy Dreyer is a Philippine-born American living in Germany with her husband, her two college kids, and two Siberian Huskies. She is an award-winning, *USA Today* Bestselling Author of young adult and new adult books that usually have some element of magic or the supernatural in them. Her repertoire also includes adult romance and adult thriller novels. Aside from reading, she enjoys movies, chocolate, take-out, traveling, and having fun with friends and family. She tends to sing sometimes, too, so keep her away from your Karaoke bars.

Visit www.dorothydreyer.com to learn more.

Delve into the world of
THE EMPIRE OF THE LOTUS SERIES
A seven-book New Adult Urban Fantasy series

Upon the one hundredth reincarnation of the Lotus empress, the dark god Kashmeru would send out his shadow army — Pishacha — to destroy the reborn empress, which in turn would bring about the collapse of the universe.

The world changed at the time of the Eradication. The New Asian Administration outlawed mages, forbidding any use of their powers. To protect her imprisoned family, Mayhara Guatama made a deal to surrender her mage status and pledge her life to the New Order.

Years have passed, the chaos from the upheaval long since settled. Or so Mayhara believed... until she receives a mysterious message from the past.

Mayhara is stunned to learn the empress—also known as the Lotus—has been reincarnated. She'd been kept in hiding to conceal her identity, and now her brother Jae pleads Mayhara for her help.

Jae and Mayhara must seek out the other elite mages to stop the enemy and rescue the empress. But the enemy—and the government—is already on to their plan, as many of the elite mages are found murdered. With mage powers deemed illegal and a powerful shadow army out to destroy them, the elite mages must band together and carry out their mission under the radar.

CPSIA information can be obtained
at www.ICGtesting.com
Printed in the USA
BVHW031036220921
617258BV00009B/187/J